CHEREE ALSOP

Girl from the Stars Book 1

Daybreak

By Cheree L. Alsop

CHEREE ALSOP

DAYBREAK

BOOKS BY CHEREE ALSOP

The Silver Series-
Silver
Black
Crimson
Violet
Azure
Hunter
Silver Moon

The Werewolf Academy Series-
Book One: Strays
Book Two: Hunted
Book Three: Instinct
Book Four: Taken
Book Five: Lost
Book Six: Vengeance
Book Seven: Chosen

The Haunted High Series-
The Wolf Within Me
The Ghost Files
City of Demons
Cage the Beast
Ashes of Night

Heart of the Wolf Part One
Heart of the Wolf Part Two

The Galdoni Series-
Galdoni

Galdoni 2: Into the Storm
Galdoni 3: Out of Darkness

The Small Town Superheroes Series-
Small Town Superhero
Small Town Superhero II
Small Town Superhero III

Keeper of the Wolves
Stolen
The Million Dollar Gift
Thief Prince
When Death Loved an Angel

The Shadows Series
Shadows- Book One in the World of Shadows
Mist- Book Two in the World of Shadows

The Monster Asylum Series
Book One- The Fangs of Bloodhaven

Girl from the Stars
Book 1- Daybreak
Book 2- Daylight
Book 3- Day's End
Book 4- Day's Journey
Book 5- Day's Hunt

The Pirate from the Stars

The Dr. Wolf Series
Book 1- Shockwave

Book 2- Demon Spiral
Book 3- The Four Horsemen
Book 4- Dragon's Bayne

The Wolfborne Saga
Book 1- Defiance
Book 2- Ricochet
Book 3- Dark Coven
Book 4- Ghost Moon
Book 5- Demon Crew
Book 6- Hunter's War

The Prince of Ash and Blood

Game Breaker

Orion's Fall

The Rise of the Gladiator Series
Book 1- Forgotten Planet
Book 2- Dark Universe
Book 3- The Godking Conspiracy

The Demon Guard Series
Book 1- Prophecy
Book 2- Underground
Book 3- Phantoms
Book 4-

To the best family a mother could ever hope for-
To my husband, Michael, my soul mate,
For bringing a new meaning to love.

And to my children, Myree, Ashton, and Aiden-
For adding so much joy, love, and adventure
To each and every day.
Never stop dreaming, and maybe someday
You'll have your own space adventures.

Don't eat the banarang.

Equality of race,
Exploration of the Macrocosm,
And advancement of knowledge for the
Growth and understanding of mortalkind.

DAYBREAK

Chapter 1

A bright light pierced the darkness. Tiny motes of dust danced within the beam. Liora's muscles tightened. The urge to run filled her despite the pressure of the bars against her back. She had tested them a thousand times, yet the need to do so again was difficult to suppress.

"Can you believe this?" a male voice asked. "I've never seen such a collection."

"Yeah, and to think they were just left to rot. This has to be worth thousands," a second voice mused.

Liora listened to their footsteps. Occupants in the other cages snarled, yipped, hissed, or ignored the men's presence.

"What a freak show," the first said. "Whoever ditched this carrier must have been collecting for quite some time." He paused, then said, "I think this one's from the Ursa Minor Galaxy."

"Careful," the other man warned. "Its venom can burn through your suit."

"I don't think it's- ahh!" the man yelled.

The crashing sound of cages being knocked over followed.

The second man chuckled. "Told you."

Liora's heartbeat sped up when they rounded the last aisle. Their heavy boots thudded along the floor and the beams of their flashlights swept to the left and right. She wanted to duck, to hide, to fight, anything but be caught like the spectacles around her, yet she had no escape.

The light crossed her face and the man on the left paused. He brought the flashlight back and she blinked at the brightness.

"Look at that," the man whispered.

His companion's light followed. Liora stared back. It had been a very long time since she had seen a true human. Now, two of them stood in full form-fit Coalition atmosphere suits in the belly of the Iridium Osprey Kirkos. Their lights reflected on the glass of their close-fitting face shields, highlighting cheekbones and startled gazes.

"Tariq, is she human?" the first man asked.

The second shook his head. "Look at the tattoos on her neck and arms. She's Damaclan." The hate Liora expected showed in his gaze and the tightening of his jaw. As much as she resented the expression, she knew it was very well deserved.

Liora glanced at the other man, expecting to see the same revulsion. Instead, he took a step closer. "Shouldn't we let her out?"

Liora stared at him. The man's dark eyes showed curiosity and a hint of something that resembled pity. Hope, an emotion Liora hadn't felt in so long she barely recognized it, sparked in her chest.

"No," Tariq said; his tone left no room for argument. "Leave her, Devren. We'll report it and see what the captain decides."

"I see you've found my ship."

A chill ran down Liora's spine at the sound of Malivian's voice. She had hoped he was killed in the dispute, but apparently she had no such luck.

Both men drew their guns.

Malivian stepped into view and raised his hands. A half-smirk, half-smile touched his reptilian lips.

"Now, gentlemen, let's be reasonable. According to the Coalition Laws of Ownership, you are trespassing on my ship. Pointing weapons at me only makes it that much more of an offense. I'd recommend lowering those guns before you harm my own precious being or any of my private collection." Malivian's voice dropped and his lizard-like eyes blinked sideways once. "And by private, I mean I've paid a pretty copper for them. You wouldn't want to reimburse me for any damage you might cause, would you?"

The men glanced at each other, then slid their guns back into the sheaths on their atmosphere suits.

Malivian gave a nod of approval. "Good choice. I've already spoken with your captain. He has agreed to taxi my ship to the closest Gaulded so that I can see about repairing the damages done by the Revolutionaries." His eyes glittered greedily in a look Liora knew too well. "The sooner I get my show back on the road, so to speak, the better."

"Your show?" Devren asked.

Malivian gave a sweeping gesture with both arms,

encompassing the contents of the huge room.

"My circus," he said. His forked tongue slid out on the last syllable.

Both men winced visibly.

"Why is she in here?" Devren pressed.

Malivian glanced back and his eyes locked on Liora. The reptilian smile returned.

"Ah, I see. Liora's captured your thoughts, has she? She has a way of doing that, you know." Malivian tapped his forehead with a clawed finger. "She stays in your mind, that one does."

"I don't know what he's talking about," Devren whispered to Tariq.

Tariq shook his head with suspicion in his gaze. "We need to get out of here."

"But," Malivian said in the earsplitting tone that he used to capture the attention of crowds and draw spectators to his tent, "Don't be fooled by Liora's beauty, for once a Damaclan, always a Damaclan."

He leaned closer and the men took a step back.

Malivian lowered his voice dramatically. "What's worse than a trained killer, gentlemen?" He gave a knowing smile and said, "A trained killer with the beauty of a goddess. I've always felt it unfair that the Damaclan race was gifted with such an attractive outward appearance, yet they remain so lethal to the touch."

Tariq grabbed Devren's arm. "Let's get out of here."

"Good choice," Malivian said. He turned with a shake of his head as though bored of them and muttered just loud enough for Liora to overhear, "The sooner we can get underway, the faster I can be clear of this Coalition scum."

Devren glanced at Liora once more before following his friend. Liora saw her chance to escape fading quickly. She didn't have a choice. She had to at least try.

Don't leave me here.

Devren stopped in his tracks.

"Did you hear that?" he asked Tariq.

His companion looked around. "I hear enough screeching and hooting to last a lifetime. The sooner we get clear of this ship, the better."

Devren met Liora's eyes. She didn't dare speak again. If Malivian knew, he would punish her. He already thought she had been pushing; a shiver ran down her spine at the knowledge of what her disobedience would bring. She dropped her gaze.

When Liora looked up again, Devren and Tariq were gone. The glimmer of hope fled, leaving Liora feeling empty and numb. She slid down the cold metal bars and rested her head on her knees. The pressure of the steel on her back reminded her of the punishment she would soon receive. Her hands balled into fists and a tear slid down the side of her nose. Liora gritted her teeth and wiped the drop away. Malivian would never see her cry.

***

"Liora?"

The voice was muffled.

Liora jerked awake. The fight or flight surge of adrenaline that rushed through her body tightened her muscles and caused her back to ache. Liora grimaced and the form in front of her drew back.

Her eyes focused in the darkness. The beasts in the cages around her either slept or appeared entirely unalarmed at the presence of the human who watched her from the other side of the bars.

"I'm getting you out," Devren said.

He put a pair of bolt cutters up to the lock on her door. With one push, the lock snapped and the door swung free.

Liora stared. It felt too easy. Part of her wondered if Malivian had come up with another cruel trick while the other part toyed with the hope that had been dashed hours ago.

"Come on," Devren urged. "If we don't leave now, we'll be caught for sure."

He reached a hand inside the cage as if to help her. Liora met his searching gaze. He withdrew his hand and waited.

Liora shoved down the trepidation that made it hard to breathe and stepped out.

The tiled floor felt cool. The slight swishing sound her bare feet made as she followed Devren's clipped strides barely reached her ears. The creatures around them stirred. A three-headed bird with only two beaks gave a small squawk and ruffled its feathers. A scaled beast with six legs turned in a circle and whined. Two creatures with flippers and fangs barked when they paused near the door.

Devren held up a hand and peered out.

"It's clear," he whispered. He opened the door and motioned for her to pass.

Liora shook her head and motioned for him to go first. Devren did so with only a hint of concern showing on his face.

She followed Devren down a long, clean hallway. The ship appeared older but tidy, its white tiles washed and ceiling panels whole unlike several places in Malivian's ship that were in dire need of repair.

At the first hallway junction, Liora's attention was captured by the paintings that garnished each corner. At first, she thought they were posters like those of past circus gatherings that littered the halls of the Kirkos Malivian continued to plaster over because he was too lazy to take any of them down, but a closer look showed paintbrush strokes. Each painting had been done by a careful hand as though the flowers and sunsets she viewed were memories preserved by a loving artist.

"You can stay in my quarters until we break free of this wreck," Devren whispered as he led her down the hall. "I just hope we'll have enough time to—"

Voices caught Liora's keen ears and she grabbed his arm. Devren stared at her with a mixture of trepidation and fear as though he had just realized that freeing a Damaclan may not have been the best idea.

Liora motioned over his shoulder. The voices grew louder. Devren touched his palm to a reader and a closet door slid open. He waited until Liora crouched beside him, then hit the button for the door to shut. They listened with bated breaths as the footsteps drew near and then passed them without pausing.

Devren didn't talk during the rest of the winding journey through the ship. From what Liora could tell, it looked like an Iron Falcon, a Coalition starship crewed by trained military personnel. Liora knew it was the last place she should be. The irony that she had left one cage to possibly be trapped in another wasn't lost on her.

"Here it is," Devren said. He put his palm on the print reader and the door slid open. He lifted a hand as though to motion for her to enter, then dropped it and walked in first.

Liora glanced down each side of the hall. Her ears strained for signs of pursuit; hearing none, she followed the officer inside.

When the door slid shut, Devren put his hands on either side of his helmet, pressing the release buttons and lifting at the same time. The airlock shield slid free. He pulled the helmet off and took a breath of the clean air.

Dark brown hair fell around Devren's face. Liora was surprised to realize that they were roughly the same age. He had looked older with the helmet on. Early twenties was young for someone with a lieutenant's stripes. His handsome face was balanced by the knowledge in his gaze as if he had seen far more of the Macrocosm than his years let on.

Devren walked the few short steps to the bed and turned on his heel as though he had followed the same path thousands of times.

"We have to hide you," he said. "If they find you here, we could both get quartered." His gaze traveled over the tattered robe that was the only clothing Malivian had allowed her to wear. A brush of red touched his cheeks. "Let me find you something a bit more concealing," he offered.

Devren slid the door of a small closet open and rummaged inside. A few seconds later, he withdrew a faded uniform top and a pair of black pants with patched knees.

"I'm not sure on the sizes," he said apologetically.

The thought of wearing anything other than the tattered robe that was barely more than rags by that point meant more than Liora could express.

19

"They'll be fine," she said, her throat tight.

Devren turned away. She had just finished buttoning the shirt when the door to Devren's quarters slid open.

"Communications are down and I need—" The man with salt and pepper hair and captain's stripes on his uniform stared from Devren to Liora.

"Captain Metis, I can explain," Devren began.

The captain's jaw clenched and he straightened his shoulders. "Officer Straham, take these two to the brig."

"Yes, Captain," a skinny man behind him answered.

"But Captain Metis," Devren replied, "You need me on the bridge."

The captain shook his head. "I'll deal with both of you later." He disappeared back up the hallway.

Chapter 2

Liora fought down a rise of panic. They were in a tiny room handcuffed to rings in the wall. It sent chills across her skin at the thought that she had just traded one prison for another.

"Why didn't you fight him?" she asked quietly.

Devren glanced at her. "Officer Straham was just doing his job."

"You could have beaten him."

She should have beaten him, she reminded herself. Her jaw clenched. When Captain Metis turned them over, it was only Devren's minute shake of the head that kept her from ending any hope Officer Straham had of ever shooting a gun again. As it was, she had obeyed and could only blame herself for the position she was in.

"Beating him would have only made things worse. I committed treason by bringing you on board. An action like that risks the life of every member of this ship. It wasn't my decision to make."

Liora made herself ask the question that burned inside her. "So why did you?"

Devren let out a quiet breath and averted his gaze. It was a few minutes before he said, "Tell me I risked my career for a good reason."

Liora owed him at least that much. Even though she had traded one cage for another, so far the brig was far better than the situation from which he had freed her.

"I'll show you," she said quietly.

The image was rough at first. Liora hadn't used the ability since Malivian became her captor. She concentrated, pushing the memory forward so that it reached Devren's mind.

The image was from the third person. It was a memory of earlier that day after the two officers had left. Despite Malivian's nonchalant attitude about Liora, he had returned with fire in his eyes just like she knew he would. The cords hung from his clawed hand and the twinkle of glee glimmered in his reptilian gaze as it did every time.

"Talking to strangers without my command, are we?" he asked.

Liora shook her head.

"Come now," Malivian cooed. "I saw the way he looked at you. You called them here, didn't you?"

Liora shook her head again.

Malivian's eyes narrowed. "Speak to me, Liora."

"I-I didn't," Liora said, her voice raspy from lack of use.

Malivian's tongue flicked out between his lips. "You know what I

22

mean," he said. "Send your voice inside my head." The tongue ran the length of his lips as though he relished the idea.

Liora turned away.

"Fine," Malivian spat. "Then you deserve your punishment."

Liora grabbed the bars. She heard the flick of Malivian's wrist and felt the answering pain when the two small half-circle blades embedded in her back. Blood trickled from the wounds that would later look like small piranth bites. If that was all Malivian did, Liora could handle it; but she knew the worst was yet to come.

"Speak to me, Liora."

Liora ground her teeth together so tight they felt like they would break. She gripped the bars in both hands.

"Now, Liora!" Malivian demanded.

At her lack of obedience, the dreaded click sounded. The creatures from across the hull of the Iridium Osprey Kirkos fell silent and a moment of fearful anticipation filled the air. Liora's back arched at the surge of electricity that flooded her body. The scent of burning flesh touched her nose. She bit back a scream and tasted blood.

I'm sorry! She finally pleaded, pushing her words into his mind.

Malivian let the device run for another full minute. When he finally left, Liora lay immobilized on the floor.

She shut off the image in time to see Devren stumble. His handcuffs kept him from falling. He caught himself against the wall and leaned there for a moment.

"I forgot pushing can be hard on a person if you're not used to it," she said quietly.

She watched him, certain when he met her gaze that she would read loathing and disgust on his face. She was Malivian's possession, his pet. Maybe Devren would send her back.

"Liora," he said.

"Don't—"

Her words were cut off by a huge bang and a shudder that

shook the Iron Falcon. Sirens sounded and the lights in the brig flashed white and red. Explosions caught Liora's ears and another shock hit them so hard it threw Liora and Devren against the wall. Liora's handcuffs bit painfully into her wrists as she fought to steady herself.

"What's happening?" she asked.

"The ship's under attack," Devren said, his words tight.

They both listened to gunfire and explosions that rocked the massive starship. Liora could only imagine the destruction that was happening beyond the door. She glanced at Devren. The Lieutenant's hands were clenched into fists so tight his knuckles were white. Red marks around his wrists showed the impact of the handcuffs, but he no longer fought them. Devren stared intently at the door; only the shallow rise and fall of his chest made him more than a statue as he listened to the battle they couldn't see.

Footsteps caught Liora's ears.

"Someone's coming," she told him.

Awareness of what would happen if an armed assailant entered the room tightened her muscles. She wouldn't have much of a chance bound to the wall, but Liora refused to go down without a fight.

The door burst open. Officer Straham appeared through a haze of smoke. A gash colored the side of his face in red and powder burns soiled his pressed uniform.

"Lieutenant Devren, you're needed on the bridge," the officer said, gasping for air.

"What's going on?" Devren demanded.

Officer Straham fumbled with the cards he held. It took him a moment to slip the right keycard into the handcuff on Devren's right wrist. His gaze was distant as if he was seeing something other than the scene in front of him.

"Officer Straham," Devren repeated, "What's happening?"

The man paused at Devren's question.

"C-Captain Metis is dead," the officer stuttered.

Emotions flashed through Devren's gaze. Officer Straham released one handcuff and turned to the other. Devren stood there as if stunned.

"What…who…" He shook his head and forced out, "Who is attacking?"

"Revolutionaries, though they're a mixed clan," Officer Straham replied. He slipped the keycard into the hole in the metal and the second handcuff slipped off.

Devren rubbed his wrists mechanically.

"You're the officer in charge," Officer Straham told him. "You're the captain now."

Devren looked at the officer as if he truly heard him for the first time since Straham's news.

"What did you say?" he asked.

"You're the captain," Straham repeated. "The ship needs you, sir. We're in serious trouble."

Devren gave a sharp nod. "Let's go." He glanced at Liora and paused.

Another explosion rocked the ship. Both men leaned into the crash to keep from falling over.

When Devren met Liora's eyes, the intensity of his gaze startled her.

"I need to know if you're telling the truth," he said.

"Shouldn't we leave her here?" Straham protested.

The ship shuddered as though it was about to fall apart.

"Everyone deserves a chance to fight for their life," Devren replied. "But I need to know for sure." He grabbed Liora's shirt. Before she could react, he lifted the back.

A dozen emotions ran through Liora. Anger, humiliation, and embarrassment came first. The need to protect herself filled her limbs with strength. Liora tensed, ready to take them both down whether her hands were cuffed to the wall or not.

The want to fight fled at a glimpse of Devren's expression. The shock of seeing the hundreds of scarred burn marks across her flesh from Malivian's favorite torture device along with the other scars of being raised Damaclan showed in Devren's gaze. Even Officer Straham appeared less adamant at the sight.

"Uncuff her," Devren said in a tone Liora couldn't read.

His dark eyes studied her face. Liora turned away on the pretense of bracing herself against another shudder.

As soon as her handcuffs were free, Devren was out the door. The sounds of yelling, beeping monitors, and gunshots echoed down the hall as Devren and Liora ran behind Officer Straham. Acrid smoke filled the air and the flashing lights and detonations turned the starship into a battlefield of chaos.

They rounded the corner and a volley of gunfire met their charge.

"Look out!" Devren yelled.

They fell back into an alcove.

"There're guns down hallway thirteen," Devren said.

Liora glanced over her shoulder. The brief sprint would expose them to the trigger-happy Revolutionaries.

"Run for it," she shouted over the uproar. "I'll distract them."

"What are you— Liora!" Devren called.

Liora took off up the hall. The gunfire paused as if the Revolutionaries hadn't expected an unarmed attacker to charge straight at them. She saw the lead human's eyes narrow.

"Damaclan!" he yelled. "Shoot her down!"

Guns aimed and fingers tightened on triggers. Liora was almost to them. She wasn't afraid of pain, but the impending threat of a dozen bullets sent adrenaline surging through her frame.

Liora leaped at the wall without slowing her run. Bullets whizzed past her with the sound of angry swarthans cutting through the air. As soon as her right foot met the wall, she pushed off and soared to the left, arching over the shocked Revolutionaries. The slight squeaks of shoes on the waxed floor met her ears with a bizarre hint of hilarious normalcy amid the chaos.

Liora's feet hit the ground. She turned to meet her attackers and her body fell into the grace of her Damaclan ancestry. A sweep of her forearm knocked three guns to the right. She slammed her left palm into the first human's throat and brought her elbow back to drop a gray-furred Ventican. His gun clattered to the ground. Liora dove for it and rolled back to her feet. She used the gun to batter three others to the left and slammed the barrel into another human's head.

Liora shot an orange-scaled Belanite and a gilled female Salamandon, then ducked in time to miss a thrown Zamarian star. She dove at her attacker, barreling the human to the ground. A quick roll of the shoulders and a push off of the tiled floor had her behind the human with the Revolutionaries' guns aimed at the rebel's body. The caliber of the bullets in the barrels she stared down would tear through them both. Liora gritted her teeth, determined to take as many Revolutionaries with her as she could.

Gunshots rang out from down the hall. Liora's attackers fell right and left until only Liora stood with the last human still caught in her headlock. She lifted his jaw to the left, straining his neck to full tension. Using a microburst of strength, Liora jerked left again. A pop sounded and the human's limbs relaxed. She let him fall to the ground.

"What was that?" Devren demanded when he caught up to

her.

"A diversion," Liora replied. She looked from one rebel to the next, checking to make sure they were down for good.

"That wasn't a diversion," Devren argued. "That was idiotic!"

The calm that always filled Liora after a fight must have shown in her gaze when she looked at Devren. Whatever argument he was about to say next left. His eyes narrowed and he gave a shake of his head. "Let's go."

Liora grabbed a gun from a fallen rebel and followed Officer Straham and Devren up the hall. They led the way as if it was second-nature to them. Both officers met the skirmishes they ran into without hesitation. Liora respected their determination and matched their aggression. By the time they reached the bridge, a trail of bodies showed in their wake.

The doors slid open to reveal a battered-looking crew. Fallen Revolutionaries littered the ground. Weary but defiant gazes and raised guns met their entrance from the crew ready to defend against further attack. The relief that filled their expressions when they realized they weren't under fire again told of how hard the battle had been.

Devren didn't waste time. "Officer Hyrin, what is our status?" he asked as he made his way to the chair in the center of the bridge.

"The shields are down completely," Hyrin reported. The skinny Talastan's fingers shook as he ran a hand through his yellow hair. "The warp drive is down and we've lost half our cannons. We're sitting ducks."

"Where's the Osprey Kirkos?" Devren asked. "We can use the ship's firepower."

Liora kept her face carefully expressionless at the mention of the ship in which she had been kept a prisoner. Inside, her stomach clenched.

"The ship fled at the first sign of attack. Apparently, the owner had exaggerated a few of its damages." Officer Hyrin's tone left no doubt how he felt about the deception.

"Tell me about our attackers," Devren said.

"The Revolutionaries have a Copper Crow," a humanoid with purple hair answered. She glanced back at Devren from her computer near the main screen and her purple eyes showed her worry. "They've put extra shielding over the hull. Our concentrated firepower has yet to put a dent in her."

A resounding explosion rocked the ship. Those crew members not seated grabbed onto the walls and computer panels for support.

"Here," an older man with dark skin and bands woven through his ears directed Liora. "Take a seat."

He pulled a chair from a panel on the wall and motioned for Liora to sit down. She did so just before another explosion hit them. She grabbed the Earthling's hand before he fell and helped him to the seat beside her own.

"How did they transport aboard?" Devren demanded. Frustration that his ship was being torn to pieces showed in his angry gaze. His hands gripped the armrests of his captain's chair.

"They must've gotten someone aboard the Kratos from the last Gaulded," a girl with slicked-back green hair and matching green skin said. "We have reports of encounters all over the ship."

"Seal the doors," Devren commanded.

Everyone stared at him.

"But Captain," Hyrin protested. "The crew will be at their mercy until we can overhaul the Kratos."

Devren met the Talastan's wide eyes with a look that gave no room for argument. "If the Revolutionaries attack the bridge in force, we lose the ship for good. Let's hope that our crew can remember their training and return lead for lead until we are able to get far enough from their ship that they'll stop transporting over. Otherwise, the Kratos will be our coffin."

Hyrin's Talastan eyelids blinked sideways and he touched the screen of the computer in front of him. The door next to Liora slid shut, blocking out the sounds of multiple gunfights. A moment later, a pop sounded followed by a dull hum. The scent of acrid smoke filled the air.

"The doors are sealed," Hyrin said in a flat voice.

The ship rocked.

"But we're still being decimated," the purple-haired humanoid reported. "Captain, if we don't disable that Crow, the Kratos will have enough holes to meet the black regardless of our internal firepower."

Devren stared at the screens in front of him as if searching for an answer. On one panel, the blueprint of the SS Kratos showed several locations on the hull that blinked red. Another monitor revealed spiking engine temperatures. A shockwave sounded and two more panels lit up. The ship was indeed being shot to pieces.

"Captain?" Hyrin asked nervously.

"What do we do?" the green-skinned girl queried when Devren didn't answer.

Liora's muscles tightened with each percussion. The fact that Malivian had fled instead of assisting the Coalition ship stayed in the back of her mind. There was no doubt the Revolutionaries had stopped to loot the Kirkos that had only barely survived another pillaging attempt. Malivian had probably hoped the presence of a Coalition starship would protect him until he got his ship to a repair station. When that plan failed, he had run like the coward she knew he was.

The SS Kratos jarred sideways.

"Captain!" Hyrin shouted.

Devren stood, his expression sharp. "Officer Shathryn, dump the cargo holds and the trash bay."

"Yes, Captain," the girl with the purple hair answered.

"Officer O'Tule, dump the secondary water cache and the holding room."

"The Coalition won't be thrilled about us abandoning the salvage," Hyrin pointed out.

"We need to make this ship as light as we can if we're going to force the thrusters with damaged shields," Devren replied.

The crew stared at him as if he was insane. Devren grabbed onto the arm of his chair as if another explosion had rocked the ship.

Liora hadn't felt anything. She watched the captain closely.

"Officer Hyrin, put all power into the thrusters. On my go, dump missiles from box four, five, and six. When we run, we'll use their explosions to hide our course."

"Yes, Captain," Hyrin replied.

Liora watched the yellow-haired Talastan push several buttons. Sweat had broken out across his skin.

"Salvage and secondary water are dumped," Officer O'Tule announced in quick, clipped words as if she couldn't get them out fast enough. "We've created quite the mess out there. I hope the Coalition doesn't mind us littering. Last time, their fines were quite heavy and I'd hate to take a cut of pay just to—"

"Cargo holds and trash are clear," Officer Shathryn cut in.

"Ready, Hyrin?" Devren asked.

At the man's quick nod, Devren turned his attention to the monitor.

"Two more blows and we lose our shields completely,"

Officer Straham called.

"We only need one," Devren said. "Wait for them to fire. As soon as the aftershocks are gone, drop the missiles and perform the jump. Officer Duncan, prepare the crew."

The man next to Liora touched his earpiece and his voice came over the speakers. "Attention crew of the SS Kratos, brace yourselves for a run."

"I hope they're ready," Shathryn whispered worriedly to O'Tule.

"If not, they'll be flying across hallways and quarters like a ball caught in a Gaul's horns," O'Tule replied.

Liora had no idea what the tiny woman meant, but she braced herself as O'Tule took Shathryn's hand. Their fingers intertwined and they watched the monitors in front of them with matching anxious expressions.

A warning siren sounded.

"Hold," Devren called.

A moment later, the ship was knocked sideways. Devren caught himself against the chair. Liora saw blood slick the metal where it impacted his side. Devren straightened.

After quick glance at the screens in front of them, Devren shouted, "Now, Hyrin!"

A sound of sliding metal followed. Two percussions sounded, and Liora was knocked backwards in her seat.

Chapter 3

"Status update," Devren called out.

Liora blinked in the darkness that filled the bridge. Emergency lighting flickered on overhead and cut dimly through the smoky haze.

"The hull is intact," Officer Shathryn said. Her purple hair was mussed and her fingers were still linked with the green-skinned officer's next to her as if neither could believe they had made it.

"Pursuit?" Devren asked.

A moment later, Hyrin replied, "No sign of them,

Captain."

A cheer went up from the crew.

"Officer Duncan, tell our troops to hold their ground and radio if they need backup."

The man beside Liora pushed the button on his headset. His calm, deep voice reverberated through the cabin and down the halls.

"Crew of the SS Kratos, we have successfully jumped away from the Revolutionaries' ship. Take down any hostiles in your area with extreme prejudice. They have no retreat left and should surrender if they know what's smart." A small smile creased the man's lips. "And if you are in need of assistance, feel free to radio and a hundred officers will be there immediately."

Hyrin chuckled and Devren gave Officer Duncan a smile.

"Was that necessary?"

"Yes, Captain," Officer Duncan replied in the same calm tones. "Instill fear in the enemy, then smash them dead. Officer training one-oh-one."

Devren sank into the captain's chair with a shake of his head and another wry smile. "If we had a hundred men, we wouldn't be in this mess." His smile fell. "Where is Captain Metis' body?"

"In the med wing," Officer Straham said. Any enthusiasm at surviving the encounter fled his face at the words. "Officer Tariq pronounced him dead on arrival."

Devren nodded. He sat up straighter and Liora saw him wince. A glance around the room showed that none of the other crew members had noticed.

"What is our destination?" Hyrin asked.

"Set her down on the closest asteroid you can find. We'll make stationary repairs and limp our way to Titus to resupply," Devren answered.

"Yes, Captain."

Devren rose and stumbled.

Liora was ready. Before the closest officers could react, Liora caught the captain and lowered him carefully to the ground. She pulled back his jacket. Blood soaked the black material from a wound in Devren's side.

Officer O'Tule gasped at the sight of mangled flesh. "Oh no! The captain's been hit!"

"I need a med kit," Liora said.

"I'll get it," Duncan answered.

Liora gave Devren a dry look. "You weren't planning to tell anyone you got shot?"

"Lieut— I mean Captain, when did that happen?" Officer Shathryn asked, her face pale.

"We startled some rebels when we left the brig," Devren replied, his voice tight.

His gritted teeth and the tight muscles in his neck told Liora how much pain he was in. The thought that the human had gone so long with such a wound amazed her.

"It looks like the bullet went shallow, tearing you open instead of lodging inside," she assessed.

Officer Duncan dropped to his knees next to them and opened the box he carried. Liora riffled through the contents and withdrew the tools she needed. Duncan set them efficiently on a cloth he spread across the floor.

Blood flowed from the wound. It caked Devren's pants where it had bled during the attack. By his pale skin, Liora knew she didn't have time to waste.

She met Devren's gaze. "This is going to hurt."

He nodded and looked away. Liora could hear the shallow breaths of the other crew members. Everyone was anxious about their new captain. Liora didn't know if he had hidden his wound to give them a strong front to believe in during the attack, or if he was just stubborn and had a death wish; either way, she vowed to do everything she could to help him.

Devren gasped when Liora flushed the wound with antiseptic.

Liora could have sworn she had lost all ability to be empathetic. After growing up half-Damaclan and the trials that brought, her chaotic childhood, and captivity in Malivian's ship of circus horrors, Liora had wondered if she had any ability left to care for others at all.

But when the captain winced and bit back a cry of pain at her persistent cleaning, Liora's heart turned. She couldn't take the agony in his dark eyes. The pool of blood around her knees and the way he held himself perfectly still so as to make her job easier filled Liora with the emotions she had long thought banished by utter cruelty.

She cleared her thoughts and pushed.

Relax, Devren," she thought toward him.

The captain's eyes widened and he stared at her.

Let me cover it for a moment.

He hesitated, then nodded.

Liora let her push expand to the pain that overshadowed everything else in his mind. It pulsed at the edges of her touch, bright red, throbbing, aching. Liora pulled back, drawing the pain with her like taking a breath.

The pain flooded through her side with red-hot agony. Devren's tight muscles relaxed, allowing her to work more efficiently. Liora's hands shook slightly when she finished cleaning the wound. The stinging, burning sensation in her side made her nauseous.

Using the needle was worse. The prick of the curved metal and the slide of waxed thread through the wound gave the feeling of pulling her skin as if she performed the stitches on herself. Sweat made her borrowed shirt stick to her skin, and it took all of her concentration to keep the needle from slipping through her fingers. As soon as she finished, she quickly packed gauze against the bullet hole and wrapped bandages around Devren's waist.

Liora gently eased away from Devren's mind, allowing the pain to return to him a little at a time so as to not overwhelm his system. When she released her hold completely, she met his gaze.

Devren's dark eyes were clear and filled with surprise as he watched her. Satisfied he wasn't going into shock, she rocked back on her heels and would have fallen if not for Duncan's quick hold.

"Easy, girl," the older officer told her. "Come sit. I'll take care of the captain." His expression said he guessed more of what had happened than he let on.

When Liora was seated by the door once more, Devren let Officer Duncan help him back into his chair.

"Captain, I found an asteroid about two clicks away," Hyrin reported. He glanced over his shoulder at Devren.

Liora could read the crew member's worry for his captain. It touched her how much the crew cared. It felt more like she was seeing a family interact than the barking of orders and military-like mentality she had expected from a starship under the Coalition's command.

"Good job. Find us a landing spot that hopefully won't tear the rest of our hull to pieces," Devren replied.

"Will do."

Devren turned gingerly in his seat. "Officer Duncan, Officer O'Tule, open the door. The threat should be over by now."

Liora watched Duncan and O'Tule work to cut through the door seal. The handheld blow torches they used did the job, but slowly.

"Can I help?" Liora offered when the feeling of being stuck in the bridge forever became more than she could stand.

"Yes, thank you," Officer O'Tule replied. "It takes a lifetime to get through a sealed door, and I can't imagine the state of what we're going to find on the other side." The green-skinned woman spoke so quickly Liora could barely keep up with what she said. "It's one of those tasks that goes on forever as though we're never actually going to make it through, but yet the more we cut, the more we've melted, and eventually, hopefully, we're going to break the welding down and make it to the other side. It just takes so much longer than I have patience for!"

She handed Liora her small torch and left to retrieve another from the supply cabinet set into the far wall. Liora stared after her.

"Keep the flame small and concentrate on one area at a time," Officer Duncan instructed, bringing Liora's attention back with a warm smile as if he knew how overwhelming the tiny green woman could be. He pulled the tool he held down slowly, cutting a smooth line through the sealed door.

Liora followed his instructions.

As they worked, the monitor beeped. "Captain?"

Devren pressed the intercom button. "Go ahead."

"We've cleared the ship of hostiles. Bodies are being piled in the cargo hold to be jettisoned."

"Good job, Lieutenant," Devren said with a relieved smile. "Tell the men I'm proud of them. Captain Metis would be, too."

"Is the captain not there?"

"He was a victim of the attack."

"I'm sorry to hear that," the lieutenant replied. "I'll let the others know."

"Thank you." Devren released the button and eased back.

Liora and Duncan cut through the final seal and the door slid open with a sigh.

"Finally," a voice called out.

Tariq, the human officer Liora recognized from the Osprey Kirkos, entered in a huff. He shoved his black hair back from his eyes and his light blue gaze sparked with annoyance.

"Two dozen injured, our captain and two officers dead, and Officer Caston barely hanging on," Tariq said. "Then you seal me out so the Chief Medical Officer can't ensure the health and wellbeing of the bridge crew? Ridiculous."

"I didn't want the bridge to be overrun with rebels," Devren told him with the patient tone of one who didn't need to explain himself, but chose to anyway.

Tariq rolled his eyes. "Good thing you weren't shot."

"He was," Officer Duncan replied.

Devren gave the older man a weary look.

Duncan lifted his shoulder. "She took care of it." He gestured to the patch of blood still on the floor.

Tariq turned slowly as if afraid of who he would find. When his gaze met Liora's, outrage took over his expression. The impartial side of her noted that he would be handsome if it wasn't for the look of hatred in his eyes.

"You let a Damaclan patch a bullet wound?" he demanded. "You're lucky she didn't kill you!"

"She saved my life," Devren replied, his voice level.

"And mine," Straham said. Tariq glared at him and Straham spun back around to face his monitor.

The medic gave Liora a flat look. "And you just happen to know how to fix bullet holes? That seems a little ironic, don't you think?"

"Leave her alone, Tariq," Devren warned.

"No, seriously."

Tariq stepped closer to Liora.

Her muscles tensed. After all they had been through, her nerves felt fried; she had no qualms about sending the officer to the floor if he dared to attack her.

"From what I see, you're the reason we're in this mess in the first place. What was the Osprey Kirkos doing limping around in space? Your captain might as well have been waving a flag and screaming, 'Attack us!'."

"Malivian isn't known for his common sense," Liora replied levelly. "I wouldn't be surprised if that's why we were attacked in the first place."

Tariq's eyes narrowed. He glanced at Devren. "You're risking us all by keeping her here."

"What do you want me to do, jettison her?" Devren asked.

Tariq's lifted eyebrows were agreement enough.

The command in Devren's voice left no room for argument when he said, "Go back to the med wing. If I need your assistance, I'll ask. For now, we both have work to do."

Tariq opened his mouth, then shut it again and spun on his heels. He stormed past Liora and paused in the doorway.

"Fine, but as soon as we touch down, I expect you in medical for an evaluation." Liora could feel his burning gaze. "Don't trust *her* as far as you can throw a haffot." With that, he disappeared down the hall.

Devren turned his attention back to the monitors.

"Duncan, notify the crew of touchdown."

A few minutes later, Hyrin said, "I'm setting her down in five, four, three...."

The huge rock loomed past the window. It looked like a misshapen tarlon egg left to crack within the endless reach of space. The crevices and craters grew the closer they drew to the surface.

"Two, one."

A last-minute exhale of exhaust gentled the Kratos' landing.

"We're secure," Hyrin announced.

"Duncan, summon the repair crew. Tell Lieutenant Argyle to concentrate on the hull. We need our shields back in full before we leave this rock. Hyrin, send a report to the Coalition and let them know of our losses." Devren glanced at Liora. "I'd better make my way to medical before Tariq tears this ship apart from the inside."

He rose without showing any sign of the pain Liora knew he felt. He paused beside her chair.

"Will you walk with me? We have some things to discuss."

Liora stood without speaking and followed him into the hallway.

As soon as the door slid shut, Devren's expression changed from carefully commanded calm to fierce anger.

"What were you thinking back there?" he demanded.

Put on the defensive, Liora snapped, "I thought I would save your life." His hostility threw her off. Her senses were threadbare from the push and she wasn't prepared for a verbal attack. Her thoughts were sluggish despite the need to defend herself. "You're the one who would rather pass out than tell your crew you need help!"

"Their captain had just died," Devren replied, his chest rising and falling with his outrage. "They didn't need another wounded officer at the helm. What good would that have done them?" He shook his head. "That's beside the point. You threw yourself at a group of armed Revolutionaries. You're just lucky they didn't try to shoot until you were on the other side! It was reckless and completely unnecessary."

"Unnecessary?" Liora stared at him, shocked that was the reason he was upset. "If I didn't do something, you and

Officer Straham wouldn't have made it as far as medical. They'd be jettisoning your bodies into space with the rebels. I did what I had to."

Devren shook his head. When Liora turned away, he grabbed her arm. The tightness of his grip surprised her. Instead of breaking free, she spun back around. "What is your problem?"

"The problem is that I just saved your life, and I don't need you throwing it away like it's a piece of garbage," Devren nearly shouted.

"My life isn't worth a captain and crew getting decimated over," Liora replied.

Devren blinked and let go of her arm. He glanced back at the closed door to the bridge, then at Liora again.

"How can you say that?" he asked.

"How can you not?" Liora replied. She gestured to the body of a fallen rebel near the door. "Thanks to Malivian, your crew got attacked and your ship was nearly destroyed."

"They'll attack any ship," Devren pointed out.

"Only if they have something to gain," Liora replied. "They might not have attacked an Iron Falcon out of the blue, but they couldn't pass up the Osprey Kirkos' hull of treasures. The entire Macrocosm knows of Malivian's horde. It's his own fault he ran into a Crow after a transport. He couldn't get his shields up in time. I just don't know why they came back after a Coalition starship reached us."

"It's their own fault they got greedy, although we barely made it out alive." Devren motioned for her to continue with him down the hall. "You need to value your life. I've never seen anyone throw themselves at an attack like that." He glanced sideways at her. "I don't know if it's your training that's made you brash, but we work as a team here."

"Must be nice," Liora said quietly.

42

DAYBREAK

Chapter 4

Devren led the way through the sliding doors into the medical wing. They entered a white-tiled wide room with a low ceiling partitioned by clean white curtains. The sterile scent of sanitization agents touched Liora's nose. She glanced around at the cloth-spread tables and trays that pulled from sections in the walls. She had never been to a medical ward that was so tidy.

Tariq gave Liora a look of annoyance, then ignored her presence entirely. He motioned for Devren to sit on a table while he and several other medics worked on a man with several nasty burns across his body.

"The explosions caught the tertiary fuel pump line," the man was explaining. "We had to do everything we could to get the fire put out before the others caught."

At Liora's searching look, Tariq slid a curtain across and blocked the man from view.

Shielded from the sight of the others, Devren let out a small breath and eased onto his back. Liora took a seat in the chair reserved for the medic. It meant something to her that Devren held up such a strong front around his crew, yet he didn't mind letting down his walls when it was only her. She didn't know what that meant. She stored the thought in the back of her mind to examine later.

"How did you do it?" he asked after a few minutes had passed.

"Which part?" Liora replied. "The fighting or getting on Tariq's bad side so quickly?"

That brought a chuckle from Devren. He winced and put a hand against his bandaged side. "Tariq has his own issues. Don't bother trying to figure them out; it'll take a lifetime."

"I heard that," Tariq called from the other side of the curtain.

Devren closed his eyes and asked in a softer voice, "How did you get rid of the pain? My control was slipping. I thought I was going to pass out and then suddenly it lessened enough that I could stand it until you finished."

Liora didn't know how to answer. The question was dangerous for both of them. If Malivian had ever guessed her abilities went beyond pushing, she would never be away from him. As it was, she knew it was only a matter of time before the Hennonite came back for her. Taking her would be an entirely different story.

The curtain slid open before Liora was ready to form a

reply.

"Let's see what damage she's done," Tariq grumbled as he slipped on new gloves. He didn't bother to look at Liora. "Maybe next time you'll remember that your best friend is a medic and stop asking the first *creature* you meet for help."

"Is that really necessary?" Devren asked.

Tariq gave him a bland look. "Yes. It is. Do you even need to ask?"

He picked up scissors from the tray a gray-uniformed medic brought him and proceeded to snip through the bandages Liora had carefully wrapped.

She couldn't help herself. "Don't make the bleeding start again."

Tariq speared her with a look. "What did you say?" he asked in clipped tones.

"Tariq, really," Devren began.

Liora met Tariq's glare. "I said, don't make the bleeding start again. If you're such a good physician, you'll know that once a wound has started to clot, it's best to leave it alone to ensure its ability to heal properly."

"You're asking me to assume that you did the job correctly," Tariq replied. "I don't base the lives of my friends on the word of some Damaclan." He pulled hard on a particularly stubborn piece of bandaging when he said the last word.

"Tariq!" Devren protested.

"Sorry," Tariq replied. He gave Liora a look that said he blamed her for Devren's pain.

Liora gave up arguing and let him work. While it upset her pride that the human felt the need to second-guess her bandaging, she couldn't blame him for being concerned about his friend. They were strangers, she reminded herself. Less than a day ago, she hadn't known either of them. It was hard to remember that when she saw Devren in pain.

"Hmm," Tariq said from the other side of the table.

Devren glanced at him. "What does that mean?"

Tariq sniffed, then answered, "It means she did a fairly good job."

Liora's eyes narrowed when she met his gaze across the table.

"Alright," Tariq gave in. "The stitches are perfectly spaced, the wound was cleaned well, and I'm assuming the bullet was removed in one piece?"

She nodded at his question.

Tariq dropped his gaze back to the wound. "She did a good job."

Devren stifled a chuckle. "Was that so hard to admit?" he asked.

"Her work is adequate." Tariq's voice lowered. "But you still can't forget we're talking about a Damaclan."

"No, you can't forget. You're the one who insists on talking about her like she isn't here." Devren sucked in a breath when Tariq pressed new bandages against the wound. He continued in a stifled voice, "Liora's heritage has no meaning to me other than I'm grateful she's handy in a tight situation."

"She could decapitate you in a closet," Tariq pointed out.

"So could a cleaver," Devren replied. "Should I avoid cleavers, too?"

Liora fought back the impulse to laugh at the ridiculous conversation. It amazed her. She hadn't laughed at anything in a very long time.

"It would probably be good for your health," Tariq said.

"You're mistaking my meaning on purpose," Devren replied. He sat up gingerly so Tariq could wrap the wound easier. "The cleaver is only dangerous if the one handling it has the intent to kill. I'd hate to think that Jarston is deadly just because he chops our rations with a sharpened blade."

"Yes, but you're talking about inanimate objects, not—"

The speaker sounded above them.

"Captain Devren, you're needed on the bridge."

"I'll be right there," Devren answered.

"You can't go," Tariq said.

"I've got to," Devren replied.

"You've lost too much blood. Look at you. You can barely sit up straight. What are you going to be able to do up there?" Tariq reached for a needle on the tray his assistant had left. "I should give you a sedative so you'll take the time to rest and get over this. It isn't a minor wound."

Devren caught his hand despite the pain the abrupt action must have caused. "Tariq, this ship needs a captain and I'm all we have. The Kratos has nearly fallen apart, half our crew is injured, and we had to dump our cargo to escape the rebels. The crew needs a strong captain and I'm the only one who can give it to them." He lowered his voice. "Don't second-guess me again."

Tariq dropped his gaze. "Yes, Captain," he said quietly.

Devren waited for Tariq to tie off the bandage, then slid his damaged shirt back on. Liora rose from her seat.

Tariq watched them go. Just before Devren passed through the door, he called out, "You'll be back here for a transfusion if you keep this up."

"Get the blood ready," Devren replied.

He and Liora left the medical wing just as a yell and a loud crash sounded behind them.

"I'm guessing that was Tariq's supply tray," Devren noted.

Liora glanced at him. "Doesn't that bother you?"

Devren's lips twitched as though he fought back a smile. "Tariq will always be my best friend first and my medical officer second. We've survived some pretty bad situations together; I've learned to take his bad moods in stride."

They reached the bridge and the door slid open. The remaining few bodies of the fallen rebels had been removed and the floors scrubbed while Liora and Devren were in the medical wing. The antiseptic scent of cleaners remained pungent in the air.

"Captain on the deck," Hyrin called.

Everybody rose. Liora felt all eyes on them.

"What's going on?" Devren asked.

Hyrin pushed a button on his control panel. The wall screen flickered and revealed the face of a gray-haired man with short-buzzed hair and two stars on the shoulders of his uniform.

Devren put his hand to his brow in a sharp salute.

"Colonel Lefkin, it's an honor," Devren said.

Though he maintained an outward expression of calm, Liora could read the surprise in Devren's gaze. She wondered how often a colonel contacted a lone ship in the Coalition forces.

"Thank you," the colonel replied. He glanced at a paper on the desk in front of him. "I have been informed that Captain Metis lost his life in a skirmish with the Revolutionaries."

Devren nodded. "The loss has greatly impacted the crew, Colonel. Our ship has also taken heavy damages."

"Understood," the colonel replied. His bushy eyebrows drew together. "Lieutenant, the SS Kratos was on a mission to the Cetus Dwarf Galaxy when it intercepted the distress signal from the Osprey Kirkos."

"Yes, Colonel," Devren confirmed.

"At this time, Lieutenant, the SS Kratos is ordered to continue its mission. Arrangements will be made for repairs on Gaulded Zero Twenty-one, and you will be fitted with fresh supplies and weaponry for the mission. Also, I understand that with the loss of Captain Metis, you are the highest ranking officer aboard your ship."

"Yes, Colonel," Devren answered, his voice level.

"Call your crew to the bridge, Lieutenant. You are to be promoted to the rank of Captain of the Starship Kratos."

All eyes turned to Devren.

Devren's hands, which he had been holding loosely behind his back, tightened so that the knuckles showed white.

"Yes, Colonel," he said.

"Signal me when your crew is assembled," Colonel Lefkin told him. The screen went dark.

Devren nodded at Officer Duncan.

The man pressed the button on his earpiece. "Attention all able crew members of the SS Kratos, your immediate presence is required on the bridge for the promotion of our new captain."

Officer Hyrin gave an appreciative whistle. "Sworn in by the Colonel himself. That's an honor."

"Yeah," Shathryn echoed. "That silver fox could swear me in anytime."

Officer O'Tule elbowed her. "His com might still be on. What if he heard you?"

Officer Shathryn winked. "Then maybe he'll come pay us a visit."

O'Tule's mouth dropped open. "Do you know what being married to a colonel would be like? You could spend all your time dilly dallying in the marriage dome of Isonoe. I hear colonels' wives get to shop on the Jupiter channel and…"

Liora turned her attention to the other crew members pouring onto the bridge. Many had injuries that had been bandaged, and all looked the worse for the wear.

Tariq was the last to enter. He stopped near where Liora

stood by the back wall. He gave her a narrow-eyed look before he folded his arms and turned to meet Devren's gaze.

"Aside from a few I won't let leave their beds, all crew members still alive are present and accounted for."

Devren gave his friend a self-suffering look. "All crew members still alive?"

"Well, you wouldn't want me to bring the dead ones from the hold. It's a mess down there and—"

Devren cut him off with a wave of his hand. "Save it. Let's have a little respect for the fallen, shall we?"

"I always do," Tariq replied. He glanced at Liora and said, "It's the living ones I have a problem with."

Devren shook his head and said to Hyrin, "Officer, please signal the Colonel."

"The Colonel?" Tariq repeated. "Whose butt did you kiss to get that honor?"

Colonel Lefkin's face appeared on the screen. "Nobody's, I hope," the man said without a hint of a smile. "I just happened to be available, and the late Captain Metis was a friend of mine."

Tariq had the sense to look repentant. "I apologize, Colonel. No offense meant."

Colonel Lefkin turned his attention to Devren. "Crew of the SS Kratos, due to the unfortunate loss of Captain Metis, and in light of the necessity for continuation of the Kratos' mission without further delay, it is my honor to promote your lieutenant to the rank of captain." He glanced at the paper in front of him. "Devren Ristic Metis, I promote you to the rank of Captain of the Starship Kratos, Iron Falcon of the Coalition of Planets. Should you accept this promotion, you swear to uphold the Coalition's oath of equality of race, exploration of the Macrocosm, and advancement of knowledge for the growth and understanding of mortalkind."

Devren solemnly answered, "I accept."

"Captain Devren Ristic Metis, the Starship Kratos is now yours," Colonel Lefkin concluded.

"Thank you, Colonel," Devren replied.

"The appropriate documents and uniform will be available on Gaulded Zero Twenty-one when you stop for repairs and supplies. The mission directives will be forwarded to your log along with the passcodes and cardkeys necessary for your task. Good luck, Captain."

"Thank you, Colonel."

Officer Hyrin pressed a button and the colonel's face disappeared from the screen.

"Congratulations, Captain," Officer Duncan said, his deep voice booming through the bridge. "We're grateful they gave you the position."

"Yes," Officer Shathryn said. "And who knows who they might've assigned should you have declined?" She patted her purple hair. "I'm sure they'd be dreadful."

"We wouldn't want that," Devren told her. He looked around at the crew. "Members of the SS Kratos, I swear to do my best to protect and serve you as a leader should. While I don't deem myself worthy to fill my father's shoes, I promise to be a fair and merciful captain and will do my best to complete our missions in a way that protects you and sees you safely home, wherever that may be."

"The Kratos is our home," Tariq shouted from the back of the bridge.

"That's right," Straham seconded.

Cheers and shouts went up from the other crew members. It seemed to Liora that she witnessed a tradition among shipmates. It made her happy to see Devren's acceptance, while at the same time, the fact that the captain who had been killed was also his father struck her hard. She respected the way Devren had stepped into control instead of dwelling on the loss at a time when his crew depended on him. There was much more to the young captain than he let on.

"Lieutenant Argyle, how are the repairs coming?" Devren asked.

A Salamandon with grease in his gills, on his black uniform, and caked in the nails of his long, skinny fingers, answered, "She's got three fried converters and the hull looks like Emmentaler cheese." He smoothed his bushy mustache. "Give us some time to jimmy rig it and we'll be able to limp to Gaulded Zero Twenty-one, but just barely. I'd recommend taking it easy."

"Thank you, Lieutenant," Devren answered. "Finish what you need to of the repairs and give us the green light when we're clear to take off."

"Yes, Captain Metis."

Devren gave the older lieutenant a wry look. "Captain Metis was my father, Sam."

"Better get used to it," Lieutenant Argyle answered. "I have a feeling it's going to stick."

At the lieutenant's motion, the other crew members not normally aboard the bridge left. The room felt empty without the press of bodies. Liora preferred it that way.

"Congrats, Dev," Tariq called before he ducked out of the room.

Devren sat heavily in the captain's chair. He stared at the screen for a few minutes as though he saw things beyond the black monitor.

"You always wanted to be a captain," Officer Hyrin said, breaking the silence with an encouraging smile.

"Not like this," Devren replied quietly.

The silence that filled the bridge lingered until the intercom beeped.

"Captain Metis, we're ready for take-off," Lieutenant Argyle reported.

Devren sat up straight. "Officer Shathryn, how does she look?"

"Like a wounded cavarian, but she'll fly."

Devren met Hyrin's eyes. "Officer Hyrin, let's take off."

"Yes, Captain," Hyrin replied.

The ship shuddered as it lifted into the air.

Hyrin threw a worried look over his shoulder. "Here's hoping," he said. He slid a bar toward the top of his control panel. A grating noise sounded, then the ship pushed forward.

Devren let out a breath and a small smile touched his lips. He looked back at Liora.

"Welcome aboard the SS Kratos."

Chapter 5

Gaulded Zero Twenty-one loomed on the starboard side of the ship. Liora studied it from near the captain's chair. A mass of debris, the hulls of spaceships, remains of old space stations, and battered pieces of transports had been welded together to create a trading post. As she watched, a giant cone from the nose of a rocket was hauled into a gap between two Aluminum Finches that looked as though they had seen better days.

"This is where you resupply?" she asked with doubt in her voice.

Devren nodded. "It doesn't look like much, but the Gaulded are owned by the Kristo Belanite family of independent traders from the Draco Dwarf Galaxy. When Coalition supply ships are too far away, we can count on fair trading and they deal in CSOs."

"CSOs?" Liora repeated.

"Coalition Standard Ounces," Officer Duncan answered from behind her. "It ensures fair trade across the Macrocosm. The Kristos have honored CSOs for the last century, and so they've gained the Coalition's loyalty."

Liora's gaze followed a ratty Tin Sparrow to its docking point on Gaulded Zero Twenty-one. "But anyone can trade here?"

Devren nodded. "Anyone smart enough to know not to cheat a Belanite. They're like living lie detectors." He glanced at her. "Keep on your toes. There's no telling who we'll see here."

"She can handle herself," Officer Straham said.

"Yeah," Duncan seconded. "Anyone would be better off facing a Belanite than a Damaclan."

He smiled at Liora. She forced a return smile past the knot in her stomach.

Hyrin guided the ship into an empty space at the dock. The landing of the SS Kratos jarred the crew aboard the bridge.

"Blame that on the fried converters," Hyrin glanced back at Liora. "My landings are usually like butter."

"That happened to be the worst butter of my life," O'Tule said, patting the green skin of her cheeks. "Now I know what butter feels like. It's like being smacked in the head and booted in the backside all at the same time. It makes me pity butter and want to be nicer to it, if you know what I mean."

Shathryn gave a knowing nod. "I know exactly what you

mean," she said as she attempted to pat down her frizzy hair.

Officer Hyrin smoothed a hand across his dashboard of buttons, switches, and levers. "Don't listen to them. We'll get you sorted out in no time."

Devren motioned for Liora to follow him out of the bridge. "Time to stretch our legs. Repairs might take a while."

"Yeah," Tariq said, catching up to them amid the hustle of crew members in the hallway. "Thanks to your owner, we became a pincushion for the Revolutionaries."

"He wasn't my owner," Liora snapped.

"You were his pet, were you not?" Tariq asked.

At that moment, the main door leading from the SS Kratos slid open. Liora's heart skipped a beat at the sight of Malivian leaning against the railing of the loading dock.

"I assume you're talking about me?" the reptilian Hennonite said with his lipless smile. "I was hoping you'd have to refuel soon, if you made it through the attack." His gaze swept the SS Kratos' hull. "Looks like it was a close one."

Devren paused on the deck. The Kratos crew bunched around their captain. It was clear by hands close to guns and the serious expressions on the faces around Liora that the Coalition members were ready to fight for Devren should the need arise.

Devren seemed to realize the same thing. He forced a smile.

"Interesting seeing you here," he said. "I thought we might get the chance to discuss particulars again." He tipped his head at Straham. "Officer, see that the crew gets their commission as well as four coppers for the pub. They deserve it after that last skirmish."

His words appeased the tension of his crew. They followed Straham down the loading ramp and past Malivian. He appeared to be waiting patiently, but Liora knew from the raptness of his gaze and the way his clawed fingers tapped against his thigh that he was barely holding himself in check. The knot in her stomach tightened.

As soon as the last crew member was gone, Malivian stalked up the ramp. All pretense of the camaraderie with which he had addressed the officers when they were aboard his ship had vanished.

Tariq stepped in front of Devren and crossed his arms, halting the Kirkos' owner.

"You have my property," Malivian demanded.

"I'm not sure what you mean," Devren replied.

Malivian's eyes narrowed. "You stole Liora from my ship."

Devren glanced at her.

Liora wanted to run, but the Gaulded didn't offer much chance of an escape, and her Damaclan heritage forbade her from such a cowardly act.

"Liora isn't property." Devren's voice remained calm.

Malivian sneered, revealing rows of pointed teeth. "She's a slave, *Captain*." He spat the last word. "I purchased her for a hefty sum, and have yet to recoup on the cost. You have no idea how expensive it is to obtain such a Damaclan beauty. Her face alone fills the stands of my circus with admirers."

Malivian's forked tongue ran across his teeth and Liora looked away.

The circus master continued, "I don't suppose you want me to report the fact that a Coalition officer stole such a priceless product from my ship when you were supposed to be protecting us."

"You left us to die out there," Tariq growled.

Devren put a hand on his friend's shoulder. "It's alright," he said quietly. "Let me handle this."

Devren met Liora's gaze. She couldn't read his expression.

The captain's jaw tightened and he looked away.

"Fine; she's yours. Take her back and end the risk to my crew."

Cold washed through Liora. She wanted to protest, to fight them all, to escape, but the sting of betrayal was too great.

Malivian stalked up the ramp with a triumphant smile.

"Handcuff her for me," he said, holding out a set of thick silver cuffs.

Devren took them without a word. He motioned for Liora to turn around. She faced the ship that she had briefly thought of as her salvation. Now, the fact that she had fought for the crew left a bad taste in her mouth.

"I'm sorry about this," Devren said, his words quiet.

"I'm sure you are," Liora replied dryly.

The familiar weight of the cuffs holding her hands behind her back made her heart beat quicker. Devren checked both cuffs to ensure they were secure. As he did so, Liora felt something slip into her palm.

"Come back to us," Devren whispered.

Before she was sure he had even said anything, Devren turned her back around.

"She's ready."

Liora glanced at Tariq as she walked past. The blue-eyed medical officer looked away.

"About time," Malivian said when she reached him. He grabbed her arm and steered her roughly down the ramp.

Liora looked back once, but Devren and Tariq appeared to be locked in a heated discussion. Tariq threw his hands down and stormed back inside the Kratos. Liora could feel Devren's gaze on her back until they turned past the closest starship and disappeared from view.

"Did you think they would save you?" Malivian asked, his voice low and mocking. "All humans are alike. Dangle money or the promise of punishment in their faces, and they back away like a whipped cur."

Liora saw him smile out of the corner of her eye. It sent a rush of terror through her. She wanted to fight and run, but his electric probes would reach her with lightning speed. The last thing she wanted was to be tortured on the ground of the docks like an animal. No one would step in to save her. Laws regarding property left no doubt what would happen to someone who got between a slave and their master. They would end up in a cage beside her with scars of their own.

"Speaking of whipped, I need to teach my own cur a few lessons in manners." Malivian's words hung in the air.

They reached the gaudily painted Iridium Osprey Kirkos nestled among several Copper Crows and a metallic painted Tin Sparrow. Posters for Malivian's next circus show plastered along the Kirkos' sides announced that the show would take place on planet Luptos in the Maffei One Galaxy. The poster closest to the loading ramp showed Liora crouched in her cage. It proclaimed, "Only the strongest souls dare to let a Damaclan into their mind!"

She turned away with a grimace.

"That's right," Malivian said. "You are going to earn your keep. I have already sold tickets to Venticans from Hoarth and the Talastan family of the Nebuton system." He glared at her. "The Garnick Talastans aren't known for their sense of humor."

She knew what he expected from her. If she didn't act remorseful, her punishment for running away would be that much worse. Forcing the words to sound somewhat sincere, she said, "I'm sorry."

"You will be," he replied.

There was steel in his voice and a tone Liora had never heard before. The anger she saw in his yellow eyes frightened her. Liora gritted her teeth and led the way through the massive belly of the Osprey Kirkos.

Creatures from across the Macrocosm lashed at the bars and glass of their cages. A purple-tongued lizard creature spit venom. It splattered on the glass and dripped down, misting when it hit the sand below. A feathered animal with piercing red eyes turned its head upside down to watch them pass. Spider-like creatures the size of Liora's head with two-dozen legs ran on the inside of their cages to keep pace with them. It looked like every member of Malivian's circus was out for blood.

The same showed on Malivian's face. The outrage he revealed sent tremors down Liora's spine. "Ungrateful," he muttered. "Unappreciative." He raised his voice and shouted, "Who else would dare keep a Damaclan mongrel? You'd be dead if it wasn't for me!"

Liora cringed at the spittle that hit her back as she reached her cage. He shoved her inside and locked the door before she could even turn around.

The sight that met Liora made her shake her head.

"You don't have to do this, Mal. Please don't," she pleaded.

He raised both sets of half-circle blades. She had never experienced four at once. Two was bad enough. She didn't want to know what double that would feel like.

I'm sorry, she said into his mind. *Please don't do this.*

Malivian's mouth twisted into a snarl. "It's too late, Liora. Stay out of my head."

He tossed the blades. Liora turned. Two of them bit into her back while the other two sunk into her right side. Malivian pressed the buttons in his hands.

Liora jerked backwards with the force of the electricity surging through her body. Her face hit one of the bars. She fell to the ground and lurched uncontrollably. The pain tore a sob from her lips. Malivian's previous torture had been nothing compared to this. It felt like every nerve ending was alight with fire, as if the lightning of the Cas One Galaxy surged through her body. Liora couldn't think, couldn't fight, couldn't do anything more than struggle at the bottom of her cell while Malivian watched, his expression cold. It was the last thing she saw before she passed out.

When Liora came to again, the lights were dim in the Kirkos hull and the myriad of creatures slept in their cages. The small squeaks and sounds of tiny pattering feet told her that the furry animals from the dark planets were up. It was their favorite time of night.

A sour taste coated Liora's mouth. She pushed up gingerly to a sitting position. Her head ached where it had hit the bars. Liora rubbed her face against her forearm and met the sticky coating of blood from right side of her forehead all the way down to her jaw. It felt as though the bars had split her eyebrow open. Her right eye was swollen and puffy, and it hurt to open her mouth.

She would survive.

Liora opened her hand that was still cuffed behind her back. Throughout the torture, she had kept her fingers clenched into a fist. At first it was on purpose, but by the end, her joints had locked and she couldn't have opened them if she wanted to. Luckily, that meant whatever Devren had given her was still there.

Her hands were shaky from the aftereffects of the electricity. Liora had to work carefully to keep from dropping the object. It was small and flat with two points on one end that pushed together with little effort. She realized it was the tweezers she had used to remove the bullet from Devren's side.

The irony twisted her mouth into a small smile. She opened the tweezers as far as they would go, then, using both hands, forced them further until they snapped into two pieces. The amount of effort it took let her know just how exhausted she was.

Willing her mind to concentrate, Liora pressed one piece of the tweezers against the solid floor and used her weight to bend the end of the metal. She tested the angle of the bend. Satisfied, she closed her eyes and focused entirely on the handcuffs.

Traveling in a circus gave one many opportunities to watch the escape acts of the men and women Malivian met up with. Circus nightlife was filled with the hustle and chaos of creatures, acrobats, disappearing acts, and life-risking tricks to wow audiences from across the Macrocosm. Daytime, however, was the time to hone crafts and practice stunts the next night would require.

Fortune had placed an escape artist's apprentice near Liora's cage one day. He practiced his art of escaping from chains, handcuffs, and a straightjacket so many times Liora felt like she could have done all three herself. Not one to allow any being to linger near his prize pets without paying the admission fee, Malivian had eventually chased the apprentice back to his master and Liora had locked the information away in her mind in the hopes that someday she would have her own chance to put it to use.

Now was that opportunity. Inserting the piece, Liora twisted the bent end inward until she felt the teeth slide free. She slipped the bar from the handcuff and let it fall off her wrist. In two more seconds, the other cuff was on the floor.

The lock of her cage proved to be more difficult. Luckily, Liora had the two pieces of the tweezers to work with. She bent the second one to match the angle of the first. Following the same steps the apprentice had done so many times, Liora pushed the bent end of the first piece into the lock opposite the pins. She turned it slowly upward until it was in tension.

Inserting the second piece, Liora raked it slowly along the pins. The small metal on metal sound set Liora's nerves on end. If Malivian found out what she was doing, she would be tortured again. The voice in the back of her mind whispered that perhaps she wouldn't survive a second round.

A subtle, metallic click sounded. Liora's heart jumped. She pushed at the bars. Her breath caught in her throat when the door swung outward. Liora stepped onto the cold floor and stumbled lightheadedly. She caught herself on the next cage, pushed upright, and ran down the hall.

The alarm sounded when she hit the button for the hatch to open. As soon as the gap was wide enough, Liora jumped out. Her feet, then her knees, hit the deck of Gaulded Zero Twenty-One. She shoved up to her feet once more and ran past the other starships.

Even at the late hour, the Gaulded's landing deck was filled with activity. It appeared the Kratos and Kirkos weren't the only ships who had been attacked. Blow torches, plasma cutters, and blazers filled the contained air inside the Gaulded's hold with the acrid scent of metal. The sound of mallets and hand saws sounded from every corner.

Crew members of the ships Liora passed turned to watch her go. She felt conspicuous and alone as she darted between space crafts and around repair gear. A giant pallet of artillery swung over her head. Liora ducked and made her way along the stripped hull of a Copper Crow painted to look like an iridescent fish. The name Space Poseidon glowed near the hatch.

Liora ran around the corner and slammed into Devren.

"I was about to come looking for you—" he began.

Tariq cut him off. "Dev, her face."

Devren gently pushed her back so he could see her better. Liora dropped her gaze at his gentle probing.

"Malivian did this to you?" he asked.

The anger in his voice made Liora look up. Devren appeared ready to kill someone.

"Calm down," Tariq told him. "Let's get her to the ship. It's the only place we'll have leverage."

Devren put a protective arm around Liora. Tariq walked behind them like a bodyguard. Liora felt as though she had entered some different reality. Somehow, even with the thought of Malivian coming after her, she felt safe between the two humans who had entered her life by accident.

Chapter 6

While Devren led the way to the Kratos, Liora had a chance to really look at it for the first time. The starship was shaped like a reverse arrowhead. The front of the ship was blunt and flat where the bridge sat. The two wings that swooped to either side made up the medical bay and living quarters. The protective hull beneath and the sides of the Kratos sloped together in a point at the back to form the landing deck, holding bays, and storage rooms. The ramp they hurried up came from the cargo deck where several officers loaded supplies and repair equipment.

Devren hit the button for the loading door to close.

"Don't let anyone in here," he told the officers.

"Yes, Captain," they replied as a group.

Liora felt their questioning stares as the humans rushed her past.

"We don't have time for the medical wing," Tariq said with apology in his voice. "We need to go straight to the bridge."

"What are we doing?" Liora asked.

Neither human answered as they rushed up the hall. The door to the bridge slid open and Duncan rose from his seat.

"What happened?" he demanded as soon as he saw Liora. The rest of the crew members stared at her.

"We'll discuss it later," Devren replied. "Swear her in."

"I, uh…" Duncan stared at Devren as if he had lost his mind.

"Now, Officer," Devren commanded.

"He's coming," Tariq announced.

Liora's heart slowed at the sight of Malivian storming up the ramp to the SS Kratos.

Officer Duncan picked up a book. "Put your hand on here," he directed.

Liora did so numbly, her attention on Malivian as he pounded on the door to the loading deck.

The Hennonite looked straight at the camera. "I'll get security," he warned, his yellow eyes flashing.

"Liora, what's your last name?"

Liora realized Duncan had asked the question twice.

When she focused on him, he gave her a kind smile. "I can't swear you in without a last name."

"Day," she said, her mind spinning. "Liora Day."

"Day?" Tariq repeated. He looked surprised. "I thought you'd have some Damaclan last name. Incendo, or Annihilo, or Decerpo, or something equally as disturbing."

Liora shook her head. "My mother was Damaclan, but my father was human."

Every crew member in the bridge stared at her.

"I'm coming back with security," Malivian yelled at the camera. "I'll show you what property rights mean to the Belanites."

"Right," Duncan said. "We have little time. Liora Day, do you swear to uphold the Coalition's oath of equality of race, exploration of the Macrocosm, and advancement of knowledge for the growth and understanding of mortalkind?"

Liora wasn't sure what was going on. Her mind still felt frazzled from the electricity, and her head pounded where she had hit it on the bars. What she was being sworn to made no sense. She wasn't part of the Coalition.

Devren put his hand gently to her cheek, turning her face toward him. Liora flinched, unused to any touch that was kind.

"Swear it, Liora," Devren said, dropping his hand. "It's the only way I can protect you."

Another pounding on the door brought their attention back to the camera. Malivian was back and with three Belanite security officers. How he had found them in such a short time baffled Liora. That was it. She was going back to the Kirkos.

"Swear it," Tariq urged.

Liora looked at them. Devren, Tariq, and Duncan watched her with equal expressions of worry. Shathryn and O'Tule nodded encouragingly. Hyrin looked from the security monitor back to Liora, his eyes wide. They were trying to protect her. How an oath could keep her safe made no sense, but Devren had gotten her out of the cage again. She owed him that much.

"I swear," she said.

"Yay!" Shathryn and O'Tule cheered.

A smile spread across Devren's face. He pushed the button to open the holding door. They could hear the pounding of steps as Malivian and the three officers ran to the bridge.

"Welcome, officers," Devren said when the door slid open.

Malivian snarled at them, looking more animal than humanoid. "Give me back my property."

"Your property?" Tariq looked devilishly confused, his head tipped to one side and his blue eyes creased at the corners. "We don't have any of your property here."

"They came onto my ship and stole her," Malivian spat, motioning toward Liora.

"I can reassure you that no member of my crew has been aboard your ship since we landed on Gaulded Zero Twenty-one," Devren replied. "Check your cameras. I'm sure you'll find it to be a fact."

Malivian glanced back at the officers. The three Belanites with orange scaled skin watched him closely.

"Officers, Liora is my property. I paid a heavy price for her. She's mine!"

"Is that right, Captain?" the Belanite with the moon crest on his chest asked.

Devren shook his head solemnly. "Sir, this Hennonite accosted Officer Day when she was away from my ship. He beat her and did foul things to her. I should press charges based on her condition alone. My chief medical officer was just checking out her injuries before we came to find you."

Tariq nodded. "I second my Captain's call for charges. Officer Day is no doubt suffering from a concussion as a result of the blow. The Hennonite has cost us the use of our officer for several days."

The title 'Officer' rang in Liora's head. She felt the Belanites' gazes on the tattered uniform shirt Devren had given her when he freed her from the Kirkos the first time. It was in poor condition after Malivian's actions, but the crest of the SS Kratos was unmistakable.

"Did you beat this young woman?" the first Belanite asked.

Liora remembered Devren saying that the Belanite were like living lie detectors. She thought quickly back through Devren and Tariq's words. They had been very careful not to say anything that wasn't true.

Malivian sputtered. Apparently he knew the same thing about Belanites. "I, uh, yes," he finally spit out. "But she deserved it. She's my property and I can do whatever I want with her."

The head Belanite turned to Liora. His words were carefully spaced when he asked, "Are you this Hennonite's property?"

Liora felt everyone's gaze turn to her. The stickiness on the side of her face itched, and her back and side ached where Malivian had tortured her. He had purchased her; that was true. The years she had spent in his possession would haunt her dreams. Yet Devren had given her a chance at a new life. The question was whether she believed it.

She met the Belanite officer's gaze. "I am an officer of the Starship Kratos. This Hennonite beat me, and he deserves to be punished."

"Point for us," she heard Officer Straham whisper behind her.

"She's lying!" Malivian said. "Can't you hear it? She's making it up."

All three Belanites grabbed Malivian. He tried to wriggle

free from their grasps. The head Belanite drew a club from his belt and slammed it across the back of Malivian's skull. The Hennonite's legs gave out and two of the officers dragged him from the bridge.

"Sorry for the trouble," the head Belanite said. "We'll see that he is appropriately punished. We don't allow cheating, lying, or stealing on any of the Gaulded. Please apologize to the Coalition for us."

"I will," Devren replied. "We value the working relationship we have with your family."

"Glad to hear it."

The Belanite left the room.

A few minutes later, they heard the loading door shut. Liora's eyes locked on the image of Malivian being dragged across the landing deck. When he disappeared from sight, relief fell over her in a wave. She wavered as her knees threatened to give out.

"Whoa," Devren said, catching her arm. He and Tariq led her to a chair.

"That's quite the blow," Duncan noted. "I'll get the bag."

Liora shook her head. "You don't need to worry about me. I'm fine."

She moved to stand up, but Devren put a hand on her shoulder, holding her down much more easily than he should have been able to.

"Liora, you've been through a lot today. I'd suggest letting Tariq see to your head, then Duncan can show you to your room. A good night's sleep is probably the best thing for you."

Liora stared at Devren. "My room?"

A smile touched the corners of his lips. "Each officer aboard the SS Kratos has his or her own quarters. They're not much, but…"

His voice died away. "Liora?" he asked gently.

She didn't know what to say. She had never had anything to call her own, and now he was giving her a room and a position aboard his ship. It was too much.

"I've got to go."

"Liora, no," Shathryn said, her tone hurt and confused.

"I'm sorry," Liora replied without looking at any of them.

She made her way to the door. Duncan grabbed for her arm, but Tariq's voice stopped him.

"Let her go."

Liora jogged down the hall and out the door to the loading dock. She kept running until she was far out of sight of the SS Kratos' cameras and anyone who might try to pursue her.

It was another trap, a cage, somewhere she might not have escaped from if Devren hadn't let her go. She had vowed during her captivity with Malivian that if she ever got the chance, nobody would capture her again. She would get far away from the Kratos, the Kirkos, and anything that resembled the hull of a ship. She would never belong to anybody again, ever.

Liora looked at Gaulded Zero Twenty-one, really looked at it, for the first time.

Her headlong rush had taken her from the loading docks to the inside of the strange supply drop. Hallways of ships had been welded together to make long, pressurized winding walkways around the outside of the mass. Huge pieces of scrap metal had been attached and sealed so that the interior of the Gaulded was air locked. The commotion that met her ears drew her to the edge of the railing.

All around her on various twisted and turning levels, people from all walks of the Macrocosm bartered, talked, laughed, and argued. Humanoid races she had never seen before discussed beads, weapons, cloth, dry goods, and metals. Copper coins, silver bars, and even phosphate rocks were being weighed and traded.

At one stall in which a variety of guns hung from the walls, a Salamandon argued with a horned Gaul. The Gaul gestured to the bars on the scale and shook his head. The Salamandon's gills worked overtime as he argued in the common tongue. The Gaul shook his head and picked up one of the silver bars. The Salamandon's eyes widened and he gestured quickly.

The Gaul bit the silver bar. It broke in half. He waved the fake bar angrily. The Salamandon backed away with his hands up. The Gaul grabbed the gun on the counter and shot the Salamandon. The gilled humanoid fell over the railing and plummeted to the ground far below. Everyone scattered. A few looked up for the body's point of origin, but they left the Salamandon alone. Soon, a pair of Belanites carried the body away.

"Harsh, isn't it?"

Liora glanced over at the hooded Zamarian who leaned against the railing a few feet away.

He gestured at the Gaul. The horned shopkeeper cleaned the gun and shoved another bullet into the chamber before he hung it back on the wall.

"It's life," she said quietly.

The Zamarian lifted his shoulders in a shrug. Blue streaks marked his face and ran down his hands in the marking of his people. Zamaria was a planet of blue and gray. The markings were a hereditary camouflage of the race. It was said they had the same metal running through their veins that they used to make their weapons. "It is? That's debatable."

He gave her a closer look. "You could use a place to clean up. No one should walk around the Gaulded like that. It'll mark you as a target."

"No, thank you," Liora declined.

The Zamarian tipped his head to indicate the shop behind them. A variety of weapons and armored clothing hung from the walls. "You don't have to trust me. My mother's in there. She'll see that you're taken care of."

Liora watched him closely. "That sounds ominous."

The Zamarian grinned. "You don't trust anyone. Someone as beautiful as you is smart to be wary." His gaze shifted to the tattoos on her neck and his eyes widened. "But you wouldn't trust people, would you, *Damaclan*."

The word was spoken as an accusation. The Zamarian's eyes narrowed and he lifted his hands as if expecting an attack.

"Leave her alone, Zran," a woman's voice said from the shop.

"Mother, she's a Damaclan."

"She's a girl," the woman replied; her voice carried a hint of steel. "Treat her with respect."

Zran shook his head and backed away. "I value my life," he muttered. He pushed through the shop and disappeared out the back.

A woman with the same blue streaks and a weathered face stepped into view.

"Don't mind my son," she said. "He most likely thought he was saving you until he realized he should probably save himself from you."

The woman's tone brought a small smile to Liora's face. "I wouldn't have hurt him."

She shook her head. "It's hard when yours is a race judged before you've spoken a word."

Liora turned her gaze back to the hectic marketplace. "Most Damaclans don't take the time to speak. Their words lie within the bodies that mark their wake." The mantra of her youth sent a shiver down her spine.

"Yet here we are having a perfectly normal conversation." The woman paused and gave a soft chuckle that lowered Liora's walls. "If you can call speaking of Damaclan normal. I can't recall the last time I saw one of your race."

"Me, either," Liora said without looking at her.

"Come inside and wash up," the woman urged. "Zran was right. You don't want to be seen as a target. There are few here who wouldn't balk at the chance to prove themselves against a Damaclan." She waved a hand. "Bragging rights and all that." She ducked back into the shop. "I have something that might fit you."

Liora hesitated in front of the shop. The woman's kindness was something she hadn't expected. Zran's reaction was normal; his mother's, unexplainable. Yet she was right. Wandering a Gaulded bleeding and bruised wasn't exactly a show of strength. If she was going to have a chance at survival, she would have to gain her bearings.

When Liora stepped into the shop, the older woman motioned for her to enter their living quarters. She held aside the curtain that separated a small sitting room from the washroom. Liora walked across the small floor of the ship and found herself at a sink with a mirror. She stared at her reflection. It had been years since she had seen herself in anything more than the tin plate upon which Malivian's servants brought her food.

Liora's brown hair hung nearly to her waist in a loose braid. Her dark eyes were guarded as she searched her face for any sign that the young girl she once recognized still existed. The Damaclan tattoos that marked her as a member of the clan ran from behind her left ear and down her neck.

Beneath the tattered uniform shirt, the tattoos had been crafted down her chest where the marks curled like the Gaul's horns below her collarbones; bold lines spiked away from the original tattoo and worked down both of her arms with the signets and rank markings of the Damaclan warrior training. The black triangles at her wrists and the red symbols above them told that she had completed the last ranking at age twelve. On the inside of her forearms, other markings that she wished she could forget proclaimed her clan name with the red seal of her bloodline.

"Here," the Zamarian woman said. She held out a rag and a bar of soap. "Clean up while I find something that'll fit you." She looked Liora up and down critically and a light appeared in her worn blue eyes. "I think I have just the thing."

She backed away and let the curtain drop before Liora could stop her.

Liora gave in and ran water over the rag. The soap stung when she used it to scrub her face. Scents of lavender, Earth aloe, and Martian sage touched her nose. Her eye was already black, but at least the swelling had stopped enough that she could see. The gash in her eyebrow could probably use a stitch or two, but it had stopped bleeding for the most part. She cleaned the rest of her face and then held the rag to her forehead. Bruises from hitting the bar colored her cheek and jaw. The skin was tender to the touch, but at least nothing was broken.

"Here we are," the woman said. She stepped through the curtain with several articles of clothing in one hand. She paused at the sight of Liora's clean face. "Much better," she said with a satisfied nod. "Now get these things on. We'll throw that Coalition uniform away before any Revolutionaries try to jump you. Unless that's already happened."

She let the question linger and ducked back out the door.

Liora looked through the clothing the woman had brought. A black shirt with long sleeves and a neck high enough to cover most of her tattoos zipped up the back. Matching black pants and boots made up the rest of the outfit. Liora fingered the material.

"Is this Ventican cloth?" she asked in surprise.

"Yes," the woman called from somewhere outside the room.

"I can't accept this," Liora replied. The cost of the cloth alone was worth far more bars than she had ever owned in her life. Ventican cloth was interlaced with supple metal strands so that the wearer was protected with a semblance of armor.

"Accept it," the woman replied from closer to the door. "I've been hanging onto it for no reason at all. Nobody shops here for Ventican clothing. A trader desperate to resupply his ship before the Coalition landed practically gave it away. It'd be a shame for it to go to waste."

Still feeling as though she should refuse the generous offer, but knowing the Coalition uniform made her a target, Liora pulled on the Ventican attire. She stared at herself in the mirror. The clothes fit as though they had been made for her. The boots, black serviceable gear, would work on the deck of a starship or the mines of Planet Tanus. The clothes covered most of her tattoos and would allow her to go unnoticed through the majority of the Gaulded.

Liora gave her hair a critical look. "Do you have a knife?" she asked.

Chapter 7

Liora couldn't help feeling as though she had been given a new chance at life. Though the woman protested Liora's many offers to help, she vowed to return and repay the Zamarian for her kindness someday. Liora walked through the Gaulded with the sensation that she was camouflaged. No one gave the girl dressed in black a second look. She wandered the many levels of the market with a confidence she hadn't felt in a very long time.

Liora's stomach growled at the scent of fried banarang hanging from the stalls of a smoke shop. Her steps slowed when she drew near. She was in the middle of contemplating whether she could snag a piece while the smoker's back was turned when a shout caught her attention. Liora leaned against the railing and studied the commotion below.

A pub made up the entire bottom of the Gaulded. Ship crews, welders, scrubbers, dockers, and craftsmen and women crowded the tables and bars. Until that point, everyone had maintained a fairly good-natured atmosphere. But at the shout, silence settled over the pub. The mixed crowd stared between two tables at the far end.

"That'll teach you to mess with the Kratos crew," Lieutenant Argyle said. It was obvious by the way he slurred his words that the lieutenant had drunk a few more than he could handle.

The entire table across from them rose to their feet. Horned Gauls and several hooved Calypsans towered above the Kratos crew members.

"What have you done?" Jarston, the Kratos' cook, demanded. "You don't throw anything at a Gaul!"

The Gaul he spoke of wiped beer from his soaked shirt. He snorted in anger and locked eyes with the lieutenant.

Even Argyle appeared sober enough to realize the enormity of his mistake.

"Back to the ship!" he yelled.

"Hurry!" Officer Straham shouted.

Everyone ran to the exit only to find it blocked by two Gauls with crossed arms and death stares.

"We're all going to die," Officer Hyrin gasped.

Shathryn shrieked as the men closed in.

Liora glanced around quickly. The mismatched ships and space rubble packed together for the body of the Gaulded made quite an obstacle course. She didn't know if she could reach them in time.

Liora threw herself over the railing. She caught an outstretched I-beam and shimmied down it hand over hand to the end. Swinging back and forth to gain momentum, Liora let go and plummeted toward the Gaulded pub. She grabbed a railing to slow her descent, jumped to another railing, and tore the back off a chair hanging over the final ledge.

Liora crashed on top of the two Gauls by the door, flattening them to the ground.

The crew of the SS Kratos stared at her.

"Liora?" Straham said in surprise.

"Hurry!" Liora commanded. She shoved the door open just as the other Gauls and Calypsans reached them.

Liora stepped aside for the crew to pass. Slamming the chair piece on her knee, she broke it in two. It was easy to fall into her training. Muscle memory didn't fade even with all the time in cages. The chance to fight sent a thrill of excitement up her spine.

"Come on," she said.

The two closest Gauls glanced at each other and charged.

Liora clocked the one on the left just below the ear, dropping him to the ground like a sack of rocks. The Gaul on the right swung at her. Liora ducked, brought part of the wooden chair up to connect with his jaw, and finished him with a backhand that spun him nearly around before he fell.

The others stopped. Everyone in the pub was completely silent.

"Who's next?" Liora asked.

"Come on!"

A pair of hands grabbed Liora by the back and spun her around. Liora stared at Tariq in surprise.

"Run or die," he said, motioning behind them.

Apparently watching four Gaul get clobbered by one small

woman was enough to rile the fight in the drunken pub members. They were climbing over each other as well as the chairs and tables to reach the door.

Liora took off with Tariq at her side. They followed the crew of the Kratos along dark ramps and through passageways to the loading docks. Eventually, the sound of pursuit faded.

"Thank…goodness," O'Tule gasped. "I think we almost died back there. My life flashed before my eyes and I've come to realize something very meaningful about myself." She paused for dramatic effect and concluded in her clipped tones, "I need to learn to run faster."

She leaned against Shathryn whose hair stood out in every direction.

"I'm so glad you were there," Shathryn said to Liora. "They were going to kill us!"

"I told you not to throw things at a Gaul," Cook Jarston said.

"How was I supposed to know they'd all come runnin'?" Lieutenant Argyle asked.

"Stab a Gaul in the back, prepare to face the pack," Tariq and Liora recited at the same time.

Liora fought back a smile at Tariq's raised eyebrows.

"They're a very close society," Tariq said.

"How was I supposed to know?" Argyle asked. "I didn't know the saying. How do you know the saying?" He looked at the other crew members. "Did you know the saying?"

Shathryn and O'Tule shook their heads.

"You shouldn't go throwing things at other people anyway," Shathryn scolded. "It's rude."

"They shouldn't talk about Hyrin like that. Of course he has yellow hair. He's a Talastan. He can't help it," Argyle said.

"They know that," Officer Straham replied. "They just

wanted to get a rise out of you."

"Accomplished. I hope they're satisfied," Argyle replied sullenly.

"At least four of them aren't going to be feeling very well tomorrow," Hyrin said, his eyes bright. "Did you see Liora take them down?"

"You took all four of them?" Tariq asked.

Liora didn't reply. She was debating whether it was smart to follow the Kratos crew back to the starship. The way she had left the pub meant she probably wouldn't be welcome much longer on Gaulded Zero Twenty-one.

Tariq must have read her expression. "Come with us. You don't have to be part of the crew. You can leave whenever you wish."

At the sight of their ship, the rest of the Kratos crew hurried ahead. Liora hung back. Tariq walked slower as well.

She tried to hide her surprise. "I thought you didn't approve of me."

Tariq glanced back at her. "I don't approve of Damaclans. They're dangerous and usually not team players." He looked her up and down as if noticing her new attire for the first time. "You seem to be pretty good at taking care of yourself. When Devren sent me after the crew, I didn't expect to find you defending them."

"I didn't expect them to need me," she replied.

Tariq looked at the ship. The hull had been repaired with huge scraps of metal welded over the previous scraps.

"Will it fly?" Liora asked uncertainly.

"It's an older ship, but she's strong. The repairs'll hold until we get back to Titus. Until then, we have a crew of surveyors in the Cetus Dwarf Galaxy to rescue from the Revolutionaries." Tariq shoved his hands in his pockets. "Devren received the documents regarding the mission.

Apparently, the surveyors crash-landed. They're sitting ducks unless we can get there." He paused as though debating how much to tell her. He gave her a searching look and continued, "I tend to distrust the easy answer. The Coalition doesn't generally send ships that far unless there's something valuable out there they don't want the Revolutionaries to get their hands on. I have a feeling it's going to be quite the fight."

"Are you always so untrusting?" Liora asked.

She saw the answer in Tariq's gaze before he turned away. "You made quite the mess back there. I wouldn't hang around to face the consequences if I were you." He paused, then said, "Plus, they let Malivian out. Apparently he has the ear of a few higher ups, or enough platinum to pad several pockets. I'd hate to see you in a cage again."

He walked up the ramp without waiting for her answer.

The thought of Malivian wandering the Gaulded in the hopes of finding her made Liora's hands clench into fists. She wanted to take him down and make him suffer like he had made her, but fear lingered in the back of her mind. If he had his torture devices, he could incapacitate her before she connected with a single fist. It had happened before. She would awaken in a cage, her chance at freedom gone for good.

Liora let out a slow breath and walked up the ramp to the SS Kratos. Somehow, stepping into the ship felt right and familiar. The sound of her boots on the clean floor almost brought a smile to her face. She passed Cook Jarston on her way to the bridge. He grinned.

"I'll have something made up special for you, Officer Day," he promised.

The thought of food made her stomach growl.

"Thank you," she told him.

When the door to the bridge slid open, Devren and Tariq

were the only two on deck.

Devren smiled. "Tariq told me he ran into you." He nodded appreciatively at her clothing. "You look ready for combat."

"The uniform was a bit torn after Malivian…" Liora let her voice fade away.

"His name won't be mentioned here again," Devren said. "I'm grateful for what you did for my crew. You are free to go whenever you'd like, and you have a place here for as long as you want to stay. Welcome aboard the Starship Kratos, Officer Day."

That brought a smile to her lips. "Thank you, Captain."

Tariq snorted. "I never thought I'd hear a Damaclan call you captain."

Devren shrugged. "I could get used to it."

"I'll bet you could," Tariq replied quietly. He refused to meet Liora's gaze.

Devren pressed a button on his console. "Officer Duncan, report to the bridge."

A few minutes later, the officer appeared at the door. "Yes, Captain?"

"The sooner we take off, the better chance those surveyors have. Also," Devren glanced at Tariq, "I hear we've made a few enemies. Let's not give them a chance to retaliate. Tell the crew it's time to leave."

At Duncan's announcement, crew members entered the bridge.

"Jarston saved you three some haffot stew and peach cobbler," Hyrin said as he took his seat.

"With fresh cream," Officer Shathryn echoed. "We won't have any more of that until we return from the mission. You'll want it while it's cold."

"Thanks for letting us know," Devren told her.

DAYBREAK

"On my way," Tariq said. At Devren's look, he grinned. "What? You expect me to let fresh cream go bad? You'd better hurry or I'll eat yours, too."

Devren's dark eyebrows lifted at the challenge. He glanced at Hyrin.

"I've got it, Captain. We'll call you if anything goes wrong. Currently, the path to the Arizona transporter is clear. We'll make the jump and it's smooth sailing from there."

"That's an optimistic outlook," O'Tule pointed out. "There are hundreds of things, and maybe even thousands, that could go wrong right now. You need to be prepared for the bad as well as the good. I'm not so sure optimism is the best thing for a pilot to have."

Hyrin gave her a smile that said he was used to her rants. "Peach cobbler has a way of making me optimistic."

"I'm going to tell Jarston not to give that Talastan any more cobbler," O'Tule said loudly to herself. "It could be bad for all of our health regardless of his culinary skills. The best thing would be for the rest of the cobbler to be eaten without delay and—"

"Dibs," Tariq called without waiting for O'Tule to finish her rant. He shoved Devren to the side and darted through the door.

"Hey," Devren shouted. He took off after his friend.

Officer Duncan met Liora's gaze. "The best kind of captains are those with a sense of humor." He winked. "You might want to catch up before they end up eating yours, too."

Liora walked down the hallway with a smile on her face. She couldn't remember ever smiling so much in her life, yet being aboard the SS Kratos with a crew that treated each other like family, and who seemed to include her in that family even though she had only just met them, made smiling seem like the right thing to do.

85

She paused in the doorway to the mess hall. Devren and Tariq were at a table eating cobbler like it was going extinct. A big bowl of whipped cream sat on the table between them. They scooped spoonsful like kids, spreading it on their cobbler before taking huge bites. Both men had it all over their faces.

"So this is what it looks like to eat in a mess hall," Liora said.

Devren sputtered and Tariq merely watched her, his smile gone.

"Grab a spoon," Devren invited.

Liora crossed the room and picked up the extra spoon waiting on the table. True to his word, Jarston appeared with another bowl of cobbler.

"Thank you for saving our lives," the cook told Liora when he set the bowl in front of her. "There would be fewer of us aboard the Kratos right now."

"Is that true?" Devren asked, watching her with interest. "Tariq said it was a coincidence that they ran into you there."

Liora glanced at Tariq. He studied his cobbler.

The intercom buzzed.

"Officer Tariq, your assistance is needed in the medical wing."

"What's going on?" Tariq asked.

"Officer Bonway nearly amputated his finger performing repairs in the engine room," came the answer.

Tariq rose. "I'll be right there." He took another big bite of cobbler, then rushed from the room.

Devren turned his attention back to Liora. "You're not getting off that easy. What happened on the Gaulded?"

She lifted her shoulders. "I happened to be changing a few floors above when I heard the commotion. I just have good timing."

"If good timing means flying from four flights up to clobber the Gauls barring our escape, then yes," Jarston replied from the kitchen with a hint of good-natured sarcasm. "That's good timing."

Devren sat back and crossed his arms. Jarston took it as his cue to close the windows to the kitchen.

The captain gave Liora a straight look.

"Why did you save my crew?"

"They needed it," she replied without looking at him.

"Liora."

She kept her attention on her cobbler.

"Officer Day, look at me."

Liora set her spoon down. When she met Devren's gaze, the want to understand nearly broke through the walls she kept around her emotions. She closed her eyes.

"I shouldn't have come back here."

"But you did," Devren said gently. "So this is where you should be." He was quiet for a moment, then he said, "Liora, I trust every single crew member aboard my ship. I need to know I can trust you, too. What brought you back here?"

Liora met Devren's gaze. "I'll show you."

Devren nodded.

"Close your eyes," she said.

Liora brought up the memory she wanted. Her breath caught in her throat as she pushed it to Devren. His hands gripped the edges of the table.

"I'm sorry," Liora whispered.

Flames were everywhere. Liora hid beneath the blankets in her mother's house. Screams and cries for help sounded from the cement paths of the village. The living pulse of fire showed beyond the curtains as it devoured their neighbor's home.

"They'll destroy everything," Chief Obruo shouted from their kitchen.

"*We can stop them,*" *Liora's mother argued.*

"*Not like this,*" *Obruo replied.* "*Not without losing everything of value to us.*"

"*We are Damaclan. We'll fight back and rebuild.*"

"*We don't have to fight back. We can sacrifice one life for many. That's the way it has always been,*" *Obruo said.*

"*But not her.*"

"*She has the blood,*" *Obruo pointed out.*

"*But not your blood,*" *Liora's mother replied.*

"*That's why she's got to go,*" *Obruo argued.* "*She'll tear us apart, Tenieva. She's already done it.*"

Liora covered her head beneath the blankets.

"*Don't make me go, don't make me go, don't make me go,*" *she chanted over and over, pushing it toward them.*

Chief Obruo burst into the bedroom and grabbed her by the arm, dragging her from the bed. "*Enough with the mind tricks!*" *he shouted.* "*Take your black magic and rid this place of evil!*"

He pulled her kicking and screaming from their home. Liora glanced back once to see her mother standing in the door, tears streaming down her face and her arm outstretched.

"*Help me, mother!*" *Liora cried.*

"*I'm sorry, baby,*" *her mother called in a sob.*

"*Accept our sacrifice!*" *Obruo yelled.*

His Damaclan tattoos stood out in stark contrast amid the flames. Blood and carnage lined the cement and tile paths of the village. The dark shadows, the nameless ones, raped and murdered. Liora glanced at the body of a boy she knew sprawled beneath a land cruiser. She turned her head, burying it in Obruo's side.

Chief Obruo dropped down to his knees next to Liora. He grabbed her arms tight and forced her to look at him.

"*Liora, your clan needs you.*"

"*You said they're not my clan,*" *she replied, her voice shaking.*

The chief shook his head. "*Damaclan blood runs in your veins. Even though it isn't pure, we raised you as our own. You completed the training." His hand touched the fresh tattoo on the side of her neck. "You are worthy. Go protect our village from the shadows."*

Liora's eyes filled with tears. "I'm afraid."

A shriek pierced the air. Flames began anew on the far side of the village.

"If you don't go, the clan will be lost," Obruo said.

Liora turned slowly. Glass crunched beneath her bare feet. Obruo gave her a little shove in the direction of the screams.

"Save us, Liora. Repay your bloodright."

Liora walked numbly between the burning houses. The clan had always praised themselves on simplicity and beauty. The paintings along the sides of the gray houses melted in the flames. Liora knew how the paintings felt.

Shadows with red eyes and clawed hands raced ahead, tearing apart the only home she had ever known. Liora wanted to cry, to stop, to run, to do anything other than keep walking, but the chief had told her to go. She was the chosen sacrifice. If they accepted, the clan would be saved. But what about her?

A shadow rushed by close enough that Liora felt the pull of its black mass against her skin.

"Take me," she said as she had been taught.

The shadow slowed and turned. Ice ran through Liora's veins when its demon eyes met hers. It made a little sound, a half-shriek, half-whistle, and hundreds of shadows surrounded Liora.

Claws dripped the blood of her people as they circled her. She could smell the carnage on them, shadows without form, but with a hunger so great it showed in their bared fangs and reaching hands.

"Taste," one of the shadows whispered.

"Taste," the word rippled through the rest of them like a summer breeze rustling the grass.

"Taste." The word sent a shiver down Liora's spine.

Fangs flashed and sunk into her throat opposite the tattoo. Liora screamed and struggled at the pain. It shouldn't have mattered, it shouldn't have changed things. Yet the shadow reared back, its fangs slick with black instead of red.

"They tried to trick us," the shadow shrieked, its voice so terrible Liora had to cover her ears.

"They tried to feed us half-blood," another said.

"They have sealed their fate."

"No!" Liora cried.

All of the shadows looked at her.

"I-I'm the last one," she said, her voice shaking. "I'm the last initiate. The rest of the girls are gone." She bit back a sob. "You've taken them all. I have to be enough."

"So sad," one shadow said.

"Impure," another echoed.

"Her bravery shall be her only salvation," a third whispered, its clawed hands brushing through her hair.

"End this."

The word of the final shadow sent them back through the village. Liora was frozen to the ground as she watched each villager be killed and every home destroyed. Tears streaked her face when the two suns rose and revealed her mother slain in front of the biggest home. The shadows had left, and instead of taking the clan's final sacrifice, they had left her as the only witness.

Crew members burst into the mess hall.

"I told them you were here!" Hyrin exclaimed.

"We're so glad you came back!" O'Tule said. She gave Liora a huge smile. "You're a crewmate, which means now you're our sister. We can't lose sisters; we have to look out for each other. It's one of those things that comes along with being sworn in, you know?"

Liora stared at her, not sure she understood the words the woman said.

"Yes, we need another girl aboard; the testosterone gets a little overpowering," Shathryn told her with a kind smile.

"You're the one with the gun obsession," a man with a large mustache pointed out.

"I like guns more than I like men, Sicily," Shathryn replied with a wink. "They've never let me down."

Liora blinked, still caught in the tail end of the push. Her thoughts were torn between the past and the present. A glance at Devren showed the same. Maybe she had revealed too much. She didn't know why she trusted him.

When Devren's gaze met hers, she knew why. There wasn't judgement or pity on his face. All he showed was understanding and kindness.

"I'm sorry," he mouthed beneath the commotion of his crew.

She didn't trust herself to speak, so she settled for a nod.

He took a breath as if centering himself and turned to the others. The smile that touched his lips at his crew's raucous descent into the cafeteria let her know how he felt about the members of the SS Kratos. They were a family, a noisy, chaotic, slightly dysfunctional one, but a family just the same, and he had invited her to join it.

"Did you like the cobbler?" Straham asked, his eyes bright. "Jarston makes it best."

"It was amazing," she replied.

"I heard that," Jarston called from the kitchen. "She can stay."

"Do you hear that?" Hyrin said. "You know what that calls for, right?"

"Kratos oil!" Straham and Sicily said at the same time.

"What's Kratos oil?" Liora asked.

A volley of groans and chuckles went around the table.

Devren smiled at her. "I'll leave you to your initiation."

"What initiation?" Liora asked. She watched him walk from the room. "Don't leave me with them!"

"You'll be fine," he called over his shoulder.

"Don't worry," O'Tule said as soon as the door to the mess hall shut. "We've all done it. You have to be initiated as a new officer. It's a tradition, and tradition can't be ignored. It's the glue that holds us all together, and glue is very important because, well," she paused, then concluded, "It holds us all together. It's a tradition."

"Tradition!" Jarston called from the kitchen.

He burst sideways through the sliding door as if unable to wait for it to open all the way. There was a cup in his hand balanced on a white platter. Dark liquid coated the sides.

Jarston set the cup in front of Liora with a flourish.

"Kratos oil."

Liora eyed the cup suspiciously. "Am I supposed to drink this?"

"Drink, drink!" Straham called. The others took up the chant.

Shathryn winked at her. "It won't kill you, hon. We've all survived it."

Liora picked up the cup. The liquid inside was thick and sloshed in one piece. She lifted it to her nose and sniffed.

"Don't sniff it, drink it!" Hyrin said, his sideways eyelids blinking rapidly in his excitement.

Liora put the cup to her lips and took a deep gulp.

"That's good!" she said in surprise. "What is it?"

Jarston grinned at her. "Real earthling chocolate with a dash of swarthan honey and a single drip of oil from our good ship. I keep it for special occasions."

"It's the best thing I've ever had," Liora said. She drank the rest down.

"Initiation complete!" Hyrin called.

A cheer went up through the crew members. Liora couldn't help the smile that touched her lips at their enthusiasm. Everyone patted her shoulders.

"The Kratos doesn't get new crew members easily," O'Tule said. She gave Liora another big smile and said in her clipped way, "When we do, they become family, and family is priceless. I don't know what I'd do without my family. We're a team, a group, we fight for each other and we make sure everyone is taken care of. You can always use more members to your family, you know?"

A warm feeling settled over Liora as O'Tule continued her rant about the importance of being one of the crew members. She didn't fight it. As much as she was afraid of settling into life aboard the Kratos, for the moment, it felt good to belong somewhere.

Shathryn touched Liora's hair. "Did you do this yourself?" she asked.

Liora met the humanoid's questioning gaze. "It was in the way."

"Hmmm," Shathryn said, her tone showing her distaste. "Did you do it with a blunt knife? It looks like a zanderbin's been grazing here." Light sparkled in her purple eyes. "I think I can help with this."

"Oh, yes!" O'Tule said. The small woman danced around as if she couldn't contain her excitement. "Let us, please! Shathryn is amazing with a pair of scissors, a force not to be trifled with! Let her take over and you won't even know what happened to you."

"She did this for me," Sicily said, smoothing his mustache with two fingers. "I'd trust her if I was you."

Liora didn't know exactly what she was being asked to let them do, but she couldn't deny the enthusiasm on both women's faces.

"Alright," she gave in.

Shathryn and O'Tule steered her out of the cafeteria and up the hallway to the living quarters. Liora was taken to a room with paintings all over the walls that matched those on the corners of the halls.

"You did those?" she asked Shathryn.

The purple-haired woman shook her head and pointed at O'Tule. "Those are this little lady's creations. Beautiful, aren't they?"

O'Tule smiled as Liora ran her hand over a highly detailed scene of a moondu grazing with the rings of Saturn in the background.

"You see, sometimes I feel like I can't get all the words out I need to," O'Tule explained in her fast way. "It's like all of the scenes are bottled up inside me and if I don't let them out, I'm going to explode all over the place!"

"We don't want that to happen," Shathryn said. She pulled a small fold-out seat from the wall beneath a mirror and motioned for Liora to sit down. Liora did so with her gaze on the beautiful pictures, amazed that they had been created by the little woman at her side.

"Exactly," O'Tule rushed on. "If that was to happen, it wouldn't be a pretty sight. You'd see little old me all exploded and nothing left but splattins all over the place. Instead, Captain Metis, bless his soul, allowed me to paint whatever I wanted along the hallways and in the rooms as long as it was beautiful." She winked at Liora. "And of course it's always beautiful. It comes from me!"

Shathryn pushed on a handle and a small drawer slid open. She withdrew a pair of scissors and a comb, then met Liora's gaze in the mirror. "I promise I'll be careful," she said, her purple eyes warm. "Trust me. I know plenty about the connection between a girl and her hair."

"She really does," O'Tule began.

It was clear she was about to go off on another tirade, but Shathryn beat her to the punch.

"As it is, I'm going to just even things out a bit." She smiled at Liora. "Damaclans are the most beautiful, terrifying race there is. I've always wondered how beings so gorgeous can be the heart of a race so deadly." She winked at Liora in the mirror. "You're no exception, my dear. In fact, you're the loveliest Damaclan I've ever seen in my life. How do you keep the menfolk away from you?"

The question brought a sudden blush to Liora's cheeks. She stared at herself in the mirror. She had never blushed in her life. She shook her head as Shathryn ran a comb through her hair.

The woman paused as though waiting for an answer.

Liora finally went with, "I'm not quite sure."

"Of course you're not," Shathryn replied with another purple-hued wink. "The gorgeous ones never are. You carry this sort of dangerous, I'll-kill-you-if-you-look-at-me-wrong air. It must drive the men crazy. They don't know whether to kiss you or shoot you."

"That's got to be quite the conundrum," O'Tule acknowledged. "I've seen the way the captain looks at you. You know, he is quite eligible. Devren's always been kind to women and would never dream of hurting anyone. He has a huge heart. It's like he's his father all over again, only Devren's still young enough to believe in the goodness of mortalkind. He only wants to help, you know, but he could do it so much better if he had a good woman at his side."

O'Tule paused and stared at Liora with a horrified expression on her green face. "Not that I don't mean you're not a good woman. You're an amazing woman. It's just that Dev's sort of innocent and I don't know if he'll know quite how to handle a Damaclan of your, um, ferocity." She gave Shathryn a pleading look.

The other woman's smile was kind. "What Frayn means is that while our captain is an experienced man as far as life, he's still a bit on the naive side when it comes to women." She lowered her voice conspiratorially and said, "He tends to think all women are good creatures. We're just hoping no one will break his heart and prove otherwise."

She measured a length of hair and gave a snip with the scissors. Liora felt strands fall onto her shoulders. It was strange to trust someone with a deadly weapon so close to her head and yet not be tense. Even though O'Tule's high energy filled the room with the vigor that seemed to fuel her life, both women set Liora at ease as much with their actions as their words.

O'Tule settled into a dialogue about how the painting around the mirror symbolized her friendship with Shathryn and how their meeting upon the Kratos was one of both kismet and necessity. Shathryn smiled and nodded at the appropriate places, allowing Liora to fall into a lull of security in which only the shear of the scissors and the gentle pull of the comb through her hair seemed to matter.

Near the end of the haircut, Shathryn set the scissors on the edge of the drawer to reach for something. The scissors dropped and the woman tried to catch them. In doing so, she bumped the pitcher of water on her small pull-out table with her elbow and sent it plummeting toward the floor. The actions surprised her enough that she let go of the comb as well.

Liora's hands shot out by pure reflex. She caught the scissors by the handle and tossed them up to give her time to snatch the comb out of the air before it could hit the ground. With her right hand, she grabbed the pitcher and jerked it to the left to catch the water that sloshed out at the abrupt stop. She set the comb on the table and reached back with her left hand in time to catch the scissors by the tip. She twirled the small blades in her fingers and held them out to Shathryn.

Both women stared at her as if she had sprouted two heads.

"How in the Macrocosm did you do that?" Shathryn asked in a hushed voice.

Liora didn't know how to answer the question.

O'Tule spoke in quiet tones on the verge of reverence. "I've heard about that," she said, her eyes wide. "It's the Damaclan training. It speeds up the reflexes so that to the Damaclan, it's almost as if time itself slows down. Liora can react that much faster than us because she is, in fact, operating on a faster time frame. To her, though, the pitcher, scissors, and comb fell at a slower speed, enabling her to respond at what feels to her to be a normal reaction rate."

"Is that true?" Shathryn asked, turning her attention back to Liora.

"I guess so," Liora replied, thinking it through. "We train for speed and agility so that when anything happens, our instincts are ready to react without us thinking about it."

"Incredible," O'Tule said with a shake of her head. "I'd never spill anything again. The captain would let me bring drinks back to the bridge."

"No, he wouldn't," Shathryn replied. At Liora's questioning look, she explained, "Frayn once spilled an entire goblet of drak berry juice on the console. It took us weeks to get the stickiness out. Since then, all drinks have been banned from the bridge." She gave O'Tule a dry look. "It's something we have never forgiven her for."

O'Tule rolled her eyes. "At least I didn't get caught wooing a man on the captain's chair."

"For your information, he was a Zamarian captain. They are rare and far in-between." Shathryn winked at Liora in the mirror. "I'm not about to let one get away if I can help it." She gave one more snip, then stepped back with a satisfied nod. "Done. What do you think?"

Liora gave her hair a critical look. The longest dark brown strands reached her chin while the rest was shorter so it wouldn't get tangled. It looked much better than the rough cut she had given it with the Zamarian's knife. It would be easy to work with, and gave her appearance a bit more edge.

She still wasn't used to seeing her reflection. In the back of her mind, she searched for the young girl of her memories. She may not have been carefree with the way Obruo had raised her, but at least with her mother she had been happy.

For the first time in her life, she saw a glimmer of that happiness again.

"I really like it," she said past the tightness that formed in her throat. "Thank you."

"It was my pleasure," Shathryn replied.

"Mine, too," O'Tule seconded. "Come back anytime."

Chapter 8

Liora joined the other members of the SS Kratos crew to pay final respects to those who had fallen in the skirmish with the Revolutionaries. Three dark caskets of recycled vogum wood from cargo crates sat behind one blanketed in the blue and yellow flag of a Coalition captain.

Devren stood next to the captain's casket, his head lowered and his hands held behind his back. He spoke quietly, whispering words nobody else could hear as he said farewell to his father.

Liora saw light catch on two iridescent tears that dropped

to the coffin lid and faded into the flag. Devren held his eyes with a gloved hand for a moment.

Tariq walked to the new captain's side. He said a few quiet words. Devren nodded. Tariq motioned to Officer Duncan.

The older officer pushed a button on the side of the loading deck. A small square panel slid open near the middle of the wall. Several crew members walked over to carry the captain's coffin. Devren reached for the front. Tariq tried to gently persuade him to let the others handle it, but Devren refused.

Liora saw him wince slightly when he bent to slip his hand in one of the handles on the side of the coffin. The other crew members took their places and they walked their fallen captain to the square in the wall.

"Equality of race," Devren began. The rest of the crew took up the words. "Exploration of the Macrocosm, and advancement of knowledge for the growth and understanding of mortalkind."

Devren concluded, "Captain Metis, you gave your life for the Coalition, and you will always be remembered. Thank you."

He lifted his end of the coffin to the square. The pressurized door pulled the wooden coffin through. A slight popping sound was heard and the door slid back into place. The hum of a furnace roared to life, cremating the captain's ashes along with the coffin. A few minutes later, a small panel at the back of the furnace opened and the cinders were released into space.

The sight of the captain's ashes floating through the black vastness gripped Liora's heart. The coffins of the three crew members soon followed. Tears showed on the faces of the Kratos crew as they watched their friends fade away into the vast darkness.

Jarston cleared his throat. "This calls for a drink."

"I second the notion," Lieutenant Argyle said.

In twos and threes, the crew members made their way toward the mess hall. Liora held back. She hadn't known the fallen Coalition officers. It didn't feel right to participate in a remembrance toast.

"Do you have that blood ready?" she heard Devren ask Tariq.

She turned in time to see the young captain's eyes roll back. Tariq grabbed him before he could hit the floor.

"Help me," Tariq commanded.

Liora rushed to his side. Tariq quickly checked Devren's wound. Blood coated Tariq's hand when he pulled it away.

"He refuses to listen," Tariq grumbled as Liora helped him carry the captain to the medical wing. "I told him to take it easy. Does he do it? No. He gallivants around the ship like a captain who hasn't just taken a bullet in the side. I'm going to have to sedate him this time."

"He'll be mad," Liora pointed out. She helped Tariq set the captain gently on a table.

Tariq gave her a frank look. "Do I look like I care? I'd rather him be mad than dead. Here. Hold this."

She took the tray he handed her and watched the medic cut open the bandages. Blood poured from the wound.

"That's what I thought. He tore all the stitches." Tariq glanced at Liora. "He couldn't leave one or two for good measure. Nope. Had to make sure every single one was torn through." He shook his head and reached for the staple gun. "He'll be mad as a swarthan when he wakes up, but at least he'll wake up."

Liora watched the medic swab the wound and staple it closed. Devren barely moved during the procedure. The captain's eyes finally opened as Tariq was wrapping the last of the bandages.

"What…happened?" Devren asked.

"You passed out on the holding deck after the funeral, that's what happened," Tariq replied. He shook his head. "You always take it a step too far, Dev."

Devren glanced at Liora. "Was anyone else there?"

"They went in to toast their fallen comrades," she replied. "It was just me and Tariq."

Devren sat back on the bed with a sigh. "At least there's that."

"At least?" Tariq sputtered. "I almost pulled out the blood this time. If you don't go straight to your quarters and rest, I definitely will."

Tariq ducked under Devren's arm and walked with him down the hall. Liora cleaned up the medical equipment and threw the dirty bandages into the incinerator. When Tariq came back, Liora was glad to see that the human appeared somewhat mollified.

"He promised to sleep. Dev's going to be the death of me someday." He glanced at Liora. "Come on. I'll show you to your quarters."

"How long have you and Devren known each other?" she asked as they made their way down the quiet hallway.

"Since birth, pretty much," Tariq replied. A smile stole across his face. "We got into a fight over a toy gun. The squib room teacher resolved it by giving us another. It was the beginning of a beautiful friendship."

Liora smiled. "And now you're on the same ship."

Tariq nodded. "His dad was practically my dad. We shared everything. So, naturally, when he wanted to join the Coalition and follow in his father's footsteps, I was right beside him." His voice quieted and he said, "I didn't think he'd end up taking over the same ship. I know it's been hard on him."

They reached a door and Tariq gestured to the panel beside it. "Place your hand on the reader and I will record your palm." He put his hand on the palm reader next to Liora's, and a moment later a buzz sounded. The door slid open to reveal a room with the same layout Shathryn's had been.

"It's not much, but it's yours." Tariq rubbed his eyes tiredly. "I'll think I'll talk to Jarston about that drink."

He ducked back into the hallway. The door slid shut.

Silence filled the air. Liora looked around the first room she had ever had. It was spotless and designed with utility in mind. The blankets of the simple bed had been tucked in tight over a small pillow to prevent anything from floating away in zero gravity conditions.

The drawers of a small dresser were embedded in the wall and slid open with a simple touch. A glance inside showed uniforms already folded along with some small clothes and a pair of loose clothes Liora assumed were for sleeping.

A mirror with a pull-out seat below reminded Liora of getting her hair cut. She had a lingering urge to ask O'Tule to paint colors on her white walls as well. There was a tiny washroom that branched off to the right complete with a pull-out toilet and a small pull-out sink that kept the water contained until use was necessary.

Exhausted from the day's events, Liora settled on the bed. It was soft to the touch and gave beneath her body. Liora closed her eyes and concluded that she could get used to the feeling. Anything was better than the hard cage floor.

A few minutes later, Liora gave up and crawled off the bed. It was difficult to accept that she had slept on a hard surface for so long that being on the bed made it feel like she was sinking. She spread the blanket on the floor and put the pillow beneath her head. With a sigh, she settled on her back and closed her eyes again. The claustrophobic sensation went away and her muscles were finally able to relax.

She was about to give herself up to sleep when footsteps pounded up the hallway. They reached her door and it slid open. Liora sat up, caught disoriented between sleep and awake.

"Why are you on the floor?" Tariq asked in surprise.

"Why are you here?" Liora replied. The scent that clung to him touched her nose. "You've been drinking."

"It's been a rough day. Devren needs you." Tariq moved as if he was going to help her up, but shoved his hands in his pockets instead.

Liora rose to her feet. "What's going on?"

"He's in shock. I think it was something with the bullet and blood loss, and losing his father, and becoming captain all in the same day." Tariq hurried down the hall with Liora at his side. "He's having some sort of breakdown. I've never seen it before. He said you could help."

The look Tariq threw her said he was trying to figure out what she could possibly do. Liora wondered the same thing.

At Tariq's touch, the door to Devren's room slid open. The simple gesture let her know how much Devren trusted him.

Liora's eyes focused in the darkness and she made out the form of Devren hunched over in the bed with his elbows on his knees. Tariq sat next to him and touched his shoulder. "She's here. Liora came back with me."

Devren glanced at her. The light that spilled from the doorway illuminated the haggard look in his dark gaze. His face was pale and exhaustion showed in the bruises beneath his eyes.

"I can't do it," he said.

"Can't do what?" she asked.

He shook his head and his hair spilled forward to hide his face from view. "I can't be what they need. I can't be my father."

"You don't have to be your father," Tariq told him quietly in a tone that said he had repeated the statement more than once. "Your father would want you to be your own person. He always said that."

"I can't hold a candle to the man he was."

Liora saw that Devren's shoulders were shaking. His fingers trembled and his breaths came out in a shudder. She met Tariq's gaze.

"He's been like this since I found him," he told her, his eyes wide with concern for his friend. "Please help him if you can."

Liora nodded. She took a seat on the bed.

"Devren, can I try something?"

"Yes," he said, his words muffled in his hands. "Please."

Liora set a hand on Devren's back. She glanced at Tariq. Pushing always left her vulnerable. It took energy, especially when she was attempting to do what Devren seemed to need. Tariq was too busy watching his friend to notice her questioning look. The concern on his face was enough of an answer. She would be safe with him in the room as long as she was helping Devren.

Liora closed her eyes. She let go of the strangeness of the ship, the courage it took to attempt a new life, the way her face ached after Malivian's beating, and the uncertainty that filled her when she thought of the course her life had taken. With a breath, she put it all aside and concentrated on Devren.

She found his torrential thoughts the same way she had felt his pain. It bombarded her on each side, sorrow, frustration, grief, heartache, and a feeling of utter loss.

Let me cover it, she said. *You need to rest.*

Devren hesitated, then gave a small nod.

Covering emotions felt almost the same as she had with the pain. Liora pulled instead of pushed, and the emotions cascaded over her in a tidal wave.

Tariq was right. The loss of blood had been a factor, weakening Devren's body until he could no longer keep the emotions at bay. The feelings of loss from his father shook through her to the point that she could barely breathe. She could feel how much strength it had taken him to step into his father's shoes and see his crew through the attack.

Breathe, she said into his mind. *Sleep.*

She could feel Devren's muscles loosen. Tariq helped him lay down while she concentrated. She lost track of time until Tariq touched her on the shoulder.

"He's sleeping," the officer whispered.

Liora carefully released her hold. The emotions eased, settling from her into his resting state. The relief of letting go escaped her lips in a sigh.

"Come on," Tariq said in a hushed voice.

He helped her from the bed and led her down the hall. The batter of emotions had left her exhausted. He kept a gentle grip on her arm as if he guessed as much, but when she glanced at it, he dropped his hand.

"What did you do?" he asked.

She looked at him from the corner of her eye. "It's nothing."

"Don't do that."

At his frustrated tone, she met his gaze. "Do what?"

"Act like that was nothing." He motioned back toward Devren's room. "He's asleep. I've been up with him for half the night. I didn't think he'd ever sleep again the way he was.

He said he thought you could help him, and you did it without saying anything."

Devren had taken Liora speaking in his mind without overreacting. For some reason, she worried about what Tariq would think. He was cut from a different cloth than his friend. He seemed more practical, yet stronger in other ways. She didn't know what he would say, and it bothered her that it worried her. She never cared what anyone thought.

The best she could do would be to tell him the truth, but that was the last thing she wanted him to know. Far too often people had come to see her act at Malivian's circus, to feel her mind push at them on Malivian's command, to surprise and scare them with her strange ability, only to have their awe turn into terror. She didn't want Tariq to look at her like they did when she was done. The fear and loathing she thought she had gotten used to were something she didn't think she could handle from him. Admitting that scared her.

"Tariq, I…" She lowered her gaze. "Can we talk about it later? My head is pounding."

It was the truth. Between Malivian's beating and helping Devren, she had ended up with a headache the size of Titus.

Tariq watched her carefully for a moment. "Sure," he finally said.

He walked with her quietly back to her room and waited outside for the door to close. When it did, Liora leaned against it. Her whole life had changed. She had started over completely when she stepped back on board the Kratos. It left her open and vulnerable in ways she had never been. It was a scary thought, and one that spun in her mind when she settled back on the blankets on the ground.

"Liora?"

She sat up again at the sound of Tariq's voice.

"Yes?" she asked.

"Can I come in?" He paused, then asked, "Are you decent?"

She looked around quickly, but there was nothing to hide and no reason to do so. She wore the only clothing she owned, and there wasn't anything else in the room.

Feeling foolish, she said, "Yes."

The door beeped when Tariq set his hand to it, and the officer stepped in. His eyebrows pulled together at the sight of her on the floor.

"You know, the beds here aren't so bad."

Liora lowered her gaze at the question in his voice. "It's too soft," she said.

He sat on the edge of the bed and looked down at her. "I guess after the floor of a cage, anything would be too soft."

It was hard to tell the direction of his thoughts by his tone.

Silence settled between them.

Liora finally broke it. "Did you need something?"

"Huh? Oh, yes." He held out the object in his hand. "I brought you this."

She accepted the bag of frozen drak berries and gave it an uncertain look.

"You shouldn't have," she said.

That brought a small smile to Tariq's lips that quickly disappeared. "It's for your bruises. Here." He took the bag and pressed it carefully to her face. "It'll help the swelling go down."

"It looks pretty bad, huh?" she asked, reaching up to hold the bag on her own.

"Like you ran into a wall. You really should watch where you're going."

Liora laughed and caught herself, surprised at her reaction. "They appear out of nowhere."

"Like trained Damaclans." Tariq's blue eyes showed a

spark of humor when he said, "It's a different sort of joke when a Damaclan is actually in the room."

"I've never heard it as a joke before."

"Really?" He sounded surprised. "It's used when someone's being super stealthy and…" He paused. "Now you're the one joking."

She leaned back against the bed with a smile. "Gotcha."

He huffed and rose to his feet. "Yeah, you did." He ran a hand over his face, pushing his tangled black hair back from his eyes. "I'd better get some sleep or I'm going to be no good in the morning."

"Same here," Liora replied. She glanced at him. "Although, I've got no idea what I'm actually doing here."

"On this ship?" Tariq asked. At her nod, he said, "Wall security. Keep them from jumping out at people."

She shook her head. "You're ridiculous."

He nodded. "I've been told that." He walked to the door and waited for it to slide open. He glanced back at her, his expression indecipherable. "I'll make sure the palm reader gets reprogrammed in the morning so my print is removed. You should probably keep the riffraff out."

The door closed behind him. Liora laid back on the blankets and pressed the frozen berries to her face. It was a long time before she fell asleep in the strange room that was now hers.

Chapter 9

Liora awoke to Duncan's voice over the intercom.

"Officer Day, your presence is requested on the bridge."

"I'll be right there," she said.

She splashed water on her face and ran the comb she found in the bathroom drawer through her hair. She liked how much easier it was to handle since Shathryn had cut it.

Devren and the rest of the bridge crew were already there when she arrived.

Devren gave her a grateful smile and gestured toward the monitor.

"The planet matching the coordinates from the Coalition missive is in sight, but Officer O'Tule found a ship near our drop point," Devren told her. "We relayed the information to Colonel Lefkin. He ordered us to destroy all Revolutionaries with extreme hostility."

Liora wondered what that had to do with her summons. She didn't have any expertise in neutralizing enemies or planet surveillance.

Devren nodded at O'Tule. "Pull the ship up on the screen."

The craft appeared to be a Copper Crow in poor repair. The name 'Star Chaser' had been painted in a fine hand along the hull. The ship sat heavily to one side and battle damage was evident along the starboard flank.

"Do you see anything you recognize?" Devren asked quietly.

Liora studied the sides of the ship as O'Tule made a sweep. There was nothing special to make the Revolutionary craft stand out, except—

"Wait, go back." Liora pointed at an image on the screen. "Can you focus on that?"

O'Tule brought up the symbol painted near the loading doors. The screen focused on the red pickax with a circle around it.

Memories of the same symbol tattooed on the forearms of heavily muscled men surfaced in her mind.

"I remember them," she said quietly. "They aren't soldiers."

Devren waited beside her without speaking.

"They came to the circus once." Liora thought of the wonder in the eyes of the children who ran through the tents as if they couldn't get enough of what they were seeing. Mothers followed close behind with the men lingering to

111

view the stranger exhibits. "They're a huge family. I wonder what brought them out here."

"Pull back," Devren told O'Tule.

She did so and swept the area around the craft. The camera paused on indentations in the sandy ground.

"A group left the ship." Devren's brow furrowed. "We haven't found any sign of them."

"What do we do?" Hyrin asked.

"The Colonel said to blow up the ship," Officer Shathryn said with a hint of uncertainty.

The door next to the loading deck of the craft they watched opened and a form stepped out. Liora realized why the crew members appeared reluctant to follow their colonel's orders when the small atmosphere suit of a child landed on the sandy ground, then held up a hand. A slender form joined the child. Two other small children climbed down beside the first.

"Have you seen any men?" Liora asked.

"Not yet," O'Tule replied. "It doesn't make any sense."

"Why would they travel in a family group clear out here?" Shathryn asked.

"That's what we need to find out."

Hyrin glanced back at Devren. "What about the surveyors?"

"If they're down there like the Coalition suspects, the Revolutionary presence is a threat to them as well. We'll send down a Gull to investigate. The last beacon from the surveyors is only a few clicks off. With a little luck, we can check out both areas before a decision is made."

The intercom buzzed.

"Captain, the Colonel is trying to contact you," Hyrin said.

"Put him through."

Colonel Lefkin's face appeared on the main screen.

"Captain, report."

"The Revolutionary ship appears to carry women and children, Colonel. I'm sending in a Gull to investigate."

Disapproval showed on the colonel's face. "Captain Metis, your orders were to destroy the ship with extreme hostility. Their presence proves a threat to the survey crew."

"Colonel Lefkin, I understand," Devren replied. "The Gull is already on its way. I just want to ensure that none of the survey crew is being held captive aboard before we blow the ship. We're close enough to the surveyor beacon's last signal that they might be related."

That appeared to mollify the colonel. He nodded. "Very well. Secure any cargo aboard the surveyors' ship. This is to be your highest priority. Report to me with your findings." His face disappeared from the screen.

Hyrin let out a whistle. "What was that about?"

"I don't know." Devren studied the ship. "We need to get to the bottom of whatever's going on here."

"I didn't enlist with the Coalition to kill women and children," Hyrin said.

"Neither did I," Devren agreed. "There's more to this mission than they're letting on. Let's get aboard that ship."

The crew followed their captain from the bridge.

"You're going?" Liora asked on their way down the hall.

"Yes," Devren said, "And so are you. Officer Duncan will man the ship until we return. My crew is small and we took on heavy casualties in the last attack. Several members of the investigation team were injured. Until I add more personnel, our missions will require all hands to go above and beyond."

"That's nothing new," Hyrin said quietly.

Devren glanced back at him.

"What, Captain?" the Talastan asked, his eyes blinking sideways. "It's not like any of us do exactly what it says in our job description."

"They gave you a job description?" Shathryn asked.

Officer O'Tule grinned at her. "Mine just said, 'Do what the captain tells you to.' So that's what I do."

Shathryn snorted. "Not me. I have to argue about it a bit." She patted her fluffy purple hair. "Lets me feel like I have an input into the proceedings."

Liora glanced at Devren. He looked like he was trying to hold back a smile.

The captain motioned down the hall. "Secure your weapons and meet me in the loading bay."

Liora followed Shathryn and O'Tule into a door marked 'Armory.' A crew member shoved clips into guns and handed one to each of the officers.

"Fully automatics?" Liora asked in surprise.

Shathryn gave her a knowing nod. "We don't know what we'll encounter. Better to be safe than sorry. These MP Twenty-fives have proven to be effective in almost any type of atmospheric condition and gravity level. They shoot at a higher rate without jamming, and," she accepted the gun and took another clip for the pistol in her holster, "They're extremely handy for letting men know when you're just not interested in them. Thanks, Branson."

"Anytime, Officer Shathryn," the man replied. He held a gun out to Liora.

"I'd take it," Hyrin said from behind her when she hesitated. "The captain won't let you on the Gull without the ability to defend yourself."

"I'm not sure a gun is necessary," Officer Straham said, following them. "With her, we might not need any weapons."

Liora took the gun Branson held out.

"I noticed your lack of sidearm," he commented. "Can I interest you in a Beretta or Glock? They shoot the newest

R.I.P. bullet technology to expand and shred anything they touch. Your enemy will be dead before he or she knows what hit them."

Liora couldn't help comparing him to the food merchants who hawked their wares at Malivian's circus stops. It seemed getting a gun aboard the Kratos was as easy as buying a cocoa-covered stano leaf or fried and powdered vogum cane. His smile was just as inviting as though she would receive the same pleasure shooting a hostile Revolutionary as eating overly sweet confections.

"I'm good," she said. "I don't have much experience with guns."

His eyes narrowed thoughtfully. "I think I have just the weapon. Hold on."

He pushed a finger to the print reader on one of the drawers behind him and pulled it open.

After a few moments of rummaging, he said, "Here it is." He held out a harness with a blade nestled inside.

Liora withdrew the blade from the sheath. The metal was mixed in jagged sections, some parts light, others dark. It was serrated with wrapped finger grooves that fit her hand.

"Is this Zamarian steel?" she asked in amazement.

Branson nodded. "The darker part. I've run it through the analyzer, but it can't tell me what the lighter parts are made of."

"That's a beauty," Hyrin noted. "Why don't you ever give me anything like that?"

"You'd cut yourself," O'Tule and Branson said at the same time.

Hyrin glanced at Liora and nodded. "Yeah, I would." He double-checked the clip of his gun and slid it back into the holster on his hip. "Giddy up."

"Give him a gun and he thinks he's a cowboy," Shathryn

said with a shake of her head.

"I really can't accept this." Liora tried to give the knife back to Branson, but he crossed his arms and refused.

"I'm the Kratos Armorer for a reason," Branson replied. "I may have failed officer's training," he gave an embarrassed smile, "But Captain Metis knew my true calling. Guns, knives, stars, bayonets, laser pulse rifles, grenades, you name it, I've worked with it. Weapons are more than my job, they're my passion." He speared her with a look. "That knife was found during one of our runs. It was meant for you. I won't take it back."

Liora debated whether she should try to match stubbornness with the Coalition cut, brawny little man.

"Come on," O'Tule urged. "We're going to be late. You don't want to answer to Dev, I mean the Captain, if you're tardy. He might give you a week of latrine duty, and you do not want to know what goes into keeping those things clean!"

"Alright." Liora wrapped the sheath around her thigh. She tried to ignore how comfortable the blade felt near her hand as they walked down the hallway. It had been a long time since she had owned a similar weapon. The fierce urge to fight welled up in her chest and she had to shove it back down.

The group turned left into a room she hadn't been in yet. Small spaceships, aircraft, and landcraft took up the majority of the area. At one end, officers were pulling on atmosphere suits and helmets near a small ship while Devren gave them instructions. He nodded when he saw the bridge crew and made his way over. Tariq walked at his side. The medical officer's eyes narrowed when he saw Liora.

"Do you think giving her a gun is wise?" Tariq asked Devren.

Liora pretended not to overhear the question Tariq made

no effort to soften. His mistrust hurt and confused her. After all, he was the one who had practically convinced her to come back to the Kratos, he had trusted her to help Devren during the middle of the Captain's breakdown, and he had even brought her something for her face after Malivian's beating. Now, the look of suspicion on his face when he saw her holding a gun felt like a stab in the back.

"She's an officer of this ship," Devren replied in a tone that left no room for argument. "I will not have any of my crew setting foot on a hostile planet unarmed."

"She should stay here."

Devren met Tariq's gaze. "She knows what kind of people are on that ship. She may be the only resource we have."

"Then I'll consider this mission doomed to fail," Tariq replied. He walked away without giving Devren a chance to reply.

"This one's for you."

Liora turned to find O'Tule holding out an object to her. The green-skinned woman said, "It's your atmospheric pressurized oxygen recycling dome guard."

At Liora's blank look, O'Tule grinned. "Your space helmet."

"Oh. Thank you," Liora said, her thoughts still on the conversation between Devren and Tariq.

"I snagged the best three. Sicily spits when he talks, and Cassidin has a tendency to throw up when we land." She pulled her helmet over her green hair as she spoke and her voice became muffled, "You'd think he'd need windshield wipers to see anything."

"That's gross," Shathryn said.

"Tell me about it," O'Tule replied. "Last time he ate ramo stew. Hopefully this time he went with something clear."

Liora slid the zipper of the form-fit atmosphere suit. It felt like a second layer of clothing and was made of stretchy material that didn't hamper her movements at all. According to O'Tule, it would protect her from pretty much any atmospheric conditions they might find on the red planet.

Liora picked up her gun and followed the others into the Gull, which turned out to be a small spaceship made for surface missions. Her heart thudded in her chest. She had never landed on a hostile planet before, or shot a gun for that matter. The presence of the knife she had moved to the outside of her atmosphere suit was reassuring. At least if the worst scenario happened, she could fight her way out.

Hyrin guided the ship from the belly of the SS Kratos. Liora watched the surface of the red planet draw closer through the window.

Devren's voice crackled over all of their headsets from the co-pilot seat. "Officer O'Tule, give us the breakdown."

The green-haired officer held up a small screen. "This planet is a Class F." She glanced at Liora and explained, "Planet F One Zero Four of the Cetus Dwarf Galaxy is marginally able to support life. There's a somewhat stable atmosphere with large percentages of nitrogen and oxygen. You should be fine for a few hours with your helmet off if necessary." She lowered her voice and said, "Though I don't recommend it. You never know what kinds of bacteria you might find in the air. When in doubt, keep the helmet on."

"Got it," Liora replied.

"The survey team reported hordes of what they called giant flesh-eating worm-like creatures, but they said they only come out at night. We should be long gone by then, right Cap?" There was a hint of worry in O'Tule's voice.

"Right," Devren replied. "In and out. Let's make this quick. Our goals are for Team Alpha to investigate the Revolutionaries and terminate any possible threat to the surveyors while Team Beta heads to the source of the surveyors' last beacon. We need to secure whatever their cargo is and get it back to the Kratos. Everyone clear?"

A chorus of 'clear' went around the Gull.

"I'm setting her down about a click from the Revolutionaries. That should give us some breathing room," Hyrin called over his shoulder.

The Gull shuddered as it entered the red planet's atmosphere. Liora realized she was holding her breath. She let it out in a slow rush. It fogged the shield of her close-fitting helmet, but fresh oxygen pulsed, chasing the fog away.

"I never get used to that," an officer buckled into a seat across from Liora said. He looked rather green, and Liora was pretty sure he wasn't a Roonite.

"Keep it together, Cassidin," Shathryn implored. "Give us a touchdown without fireworks."

"I don't mean to," the young officer protested.

"Count to one hundred," the gilled Salamandon next to him suggested.

"Ninety-nine," Cassidin began.

The Gull landed with a thud that shook everyone inside the ship. Cassidin immediately threw up.

"Great," Shathryn muttered. "Windshield wipers."

"Cassidin, catch up to Team Beta after you get cleaned up. Officer Hyrin—"

Whatever Devren was about to say was cut off by the percussion of bullets against the side of the Gull.

"We're under fire!" Hyrin shouted.

"Strafe them; protect the hull," Devren ordered. "We need the ship in good enough shape to get us back." He hit the button for the door. "Tariq, take Team Alpha and sweep left. Team Beta, follow me. Draw fire from the Gull and eliminate all hostiles."

Liora didn't have time to think. She jumped out of the door after Officer Cassidin and followed Team Alpha to the left. As soon as Hyrin shut the door, the fire turned from the ship to the crew.

Gunfire rained down on all sides. Bullets hit the red dirt around Liora. She dove to the right and rolled behind a pile of rocks.

"Can't...breathe..."

Liora glanced back and found Officer Cassidin crouched next to her. He had his helmet off and was desperately trying to clean out the throw up.

"Get your helmet back on!" Liora said.

She grabbed his helmet and was about to shove it back on his head when a bullet hit his skull. The officer slumped to the side.

Liora froze. She held the helmet and stared numbly from Officer Cassidin's fallen body to the bullets that hit the rocks around her.

"Liora, down!" a voice yelled.

Liora was tackled to the ground. The blow knocked the wind from her. She rolled to the right and unsheathed her knife. It took her a moment to realize she had pinned Tariq and was holding the knife to the throat of his atmosphere suit. There was a gouge and cracks spider-webbing across the front of his helmet as if a bullet had barely missed killing him. His eyes were wide and he fought for breath.

Liora backed off quickly.

"Do you have any sense?" Tariq demanded. He pushed up to his knees and peered around the rocks. Four bullets sent shards into the air. Tariq ducked. He glanced around and his gaze settled on Officer Cassidin. A string of muttered curse words caught Liora's ears.

"We're pinned," he said. He leaned against the rocks and

fought to catch his breath.

Liora scanned the area. The next clump of rocks was bigger and a hole showed close to one end. The cave looked promising.

She nudged Tariq.

"Get away from me," he growled.

Frustrated at their situation and the way he treated her, Liora grabbed him by the helmet and turned his head to face the cave.

"That would be defensible," she shouted above the gunfire.

Tariq glanced behind them. Random shots sounded among the rocks. Nobody else was in sight. A volley of bullets hit the rocks near his head. He ducked back.

"I'll cover you," he said. "Get ready to run for it."

Liora's heart pounded. Part of her wondered if he would use her as a distraction to get away. She didn't like the thought of being peppered with lead.

"Go!" Tariq shouted. He showered the rocks behind them with bullets, keeping the Revolutionaries under cover.

Chapter 10

Liora ran across the space of dirt between the two patches of rocks. She had less than a second to peek in the cave before bullets hit the rock where her hand had been. She dove inside and spun on one knee to face the opening.

Liora's heartbeat thundered in her throat. She fought to catch her breath. Someone yelled in pain. She was half-tempted to go back out and track down the crew when a closer cry sounded.

Tariq dove heavily through the entrance and landed with a thud at her feet. Blood showed from several places in his atmosphere suit. Two forms appeared in the hole after him. It took Liora less than a second to verify that they were hostiles. She pulled the trigger on her submachine gun. The bodies fell on top of each other.

Tariq scrambled up faster than she thought he was able to and shoved the bodies into the opening of the cave, blocking out further attacks. When he was done, he slid to a sitting position on the sandy cave floor facing the hole.

"Tariq, you need help," Liora said.

She reached for his bleeding leg, but he yanked it out of her grasp.

"Leave me alone," he snarled.

Anger flooded through her. "What have I ever done to you?" she demanded.

"I can't stand Damaclans," he said. "They're savage, vile, disgusting creatures more ready to rip a person's beating heart out of their chest than solve things civilly."

The assessment hurt. Liora pushed the emotion away. "I'm only half Damaclan."

"Yeah, well, I feel bad for the human who slept with the Damaclan that made you. Or was she raped?"

Liora dove for his back. He dropped his shoulder and spun, slamming her to the ground. Liora grabbed his knee when he tried to pin her and rolled to the right, throwing him against the cave wall. Tariq whirled with an elbow out. She blocked it and turned in, using his momentum to throw him off balance. She dropped and spun on one knee, catching his legs with hers. He fell heavily to the ground.

Liora landed on him when he tried to get back to his feet. She shoved a knee in his back and wrapped an arm around his neck. She resisted the urge to slide the knife from her sheath and end him once and for all.

The sound of their breathing was loud in the cave. In the

distance, muted gunfire continued.

"Are you going to kill me?" Tariq asked. His tone was tight with pain.

Liora held him for a moment longer, then pushed him away. She climbed off his back and stepped to the hole, afraid the distraction might have allowed Revolutionaries to sneak up on them.

The sound of gunfire continued near the ship. An occasional shot hit the rocks near their cave, but no Revolutionaries were in sight, or other Kratos crew members, for that matter.

"It's clear," she said after a moment.

She turned to find that Tariq had rolled onto his back. His eyes were closed, but his chest moved beneath the atmosphere suit. A closer look showed blood leaking through the suit at his shoulder and lower leg. The crack in his helmet was letting in air from the red planet. O'Tule's warning about not breathing in the air if possible stayed in the back of Liora's mind.

She dropped cautiously to her knees next to Tariq. He didn't open his eyes. His breath fogged the inside of the helmet. The amount of blood from the shoulder wound alarmed her.

"If we don't get that stopped, you'll bleed out," she said.

Tariq didn't answer.

"Where's your med kit?"

Silence met her question.

Liora bit back a comment about stubborn males. Realizing he must have lost the kit in the fray, she crawled to the bodies of the slain Revolutionaries. A glance showed them to be older males with battle-worn, weary faces. Red sand had been caked into the creases of their skin. She wondered how long they had been shipwrecked.

"Maybe I can go for help," she said. She pulled the top body back. Bullets immediately peppered the rocks. One tugged past the shoulder of her atmosphere suit, tearing the fabric. Liora ducked back.

"They've got us pinned down."

Trapped inside the cave, Liora knew her options were limited. Survival instincts took over. She used her knife to cut strips from the rebels' shirts where they appeared to be the most clean. She worried about infection, but with Tariq losing blood so quickly, she was more concerned about him dying at her feet.

She returned to him and knelt in the dirt. His face was pale and his breathing shallow. The unclean air wouldn't help his body any. Liora figured she could stand an hour. She touched the control pad on her arm and turned off the oxygen to her atmosphere suit to conserve it.

Tariq opened his eyes. "What are you doing?"

She pulled off her helmet and set it carefully on the ground.

"Giving you my helmet so you can breathe some clean air while I work on you," she explained without meeting his gaze.

Using both hands, she turned his helmet to the right to slide it free of the catch, then lifted it clear. Tariq moved so that his head rested on a rock outcropping. She felt his gaze on her when she picked her helmet up.

"Air will still come in through the bullet holes."

Liora nodded. "Not as much. At least without a cracked shield, it'll be cleaner."

She lifted the helmet toward him, but he shook his head. "Too claustrophobic. Give me a minute."

"We don't have much time," she replied. "The Revolutionaries could be here any second, and if you don't let me do something about your wounds, I might be fighting them next to a corpse."

She held his gaze, her own defiant, angry, and with a touch of fear at the thought of being trapped alone on planet F One Zero Four.

He grabbed his shoulder against a surge of pain and his jaw locked tight. When he moved, the wound in his leg left a dark streak through the sand.

"Fine," he finally breathed out through gritted teeth.

She pulled off her gloves and set them next to the helmet. Able to work more nimbly with bare fingers, Liora unzipped the top of Tariq's atmosphere suit. Blood coated his shoulder and ran down his bare chest. Liora eased Tariq back slightly to check for an exit wound, but there wasn't one.

"The bullet's still in there," she said quietly.

Tariq's words came out tight. "You'll have to remove it before you bandage the wound."

Liora shook her head in protest. "I don't have any supplies, my knife is dirty, and our bandages are made out of shirts from the rebels I killed." She forced her voice to remain steady when she said, "I'm not prepared for this."

Tariq lifted his good arm to indicate the cave opening. "I don't know where the others are, but they've got us cornered in this hole. It doesn't sound like we're getting out any time soon." His voice lowered and he said, "Remember what O'Tule reported about the flesh-eating worms? I'd like to be able to hold my own against those."

"And if my hand slips?" Liora asked, only half-joking.

"Then you'll prove I'm right about Damaclans," Tariq replied with his eyes closed.

Liora wiped the blade of her knife carefully on the inside of his atmosphere suit where she judged it was cleanest. She pressed a shirt strip below the wound to catch what she could of the blood so it didn't fill Tariq's suit even further. With an outlet of breath, she touched the tip of the knife to the injury. To Tariq's credit, he didn't wince.

Liora's hands shook. She wiped her head with her arm and put the knife to his skin again, but she couldn't make herself cut into the bullet wound.

"You've got to do it."

Liora's gaze locked on Tariq's. His forehead shone with sweat and pain showed bright in his eyes.

"Take a breath," he instructed, his voice tight. "And just go for it. You've got this."

"I don't think I do," she replied, her words shaky.

Tariq put his hand over hers. Before she could stop him, he pushed the tip of the knife slowly into the wound. The muscles in his chest flexed with the pain, but he didn't make a sound. Fresh blood welled from the injury. His hand fell away.

"Your turn," he said, his eyes half-closed.

Liora eased the knife in further, opening the bullet hole so she could find the slug. Blood spilled out, making it harder to see. The knife grazed something hard. She drew it back. There were no medical instruments she could use to search for the bullet.

Liora wished she had the pieces of the tweezers Devren had given her to escape the Kirkos. That felt like an eternity ago. Without other options, she slid her fingers into the wound. Tariq gave a gasp of pain. The hole was warm and slick. She gritted her teeth and forced herself to probe for the slug.

Tariq's muscles relaxed. A glance showed that he had passed out. Liora breathed a sigh of gratitude and searched deeper. Her fingers grazed the hard sides of the bullet and her breath caught in her throat. Using more force than she wanted, Liora was able to work the slug up to her fingers and pull it free.

More blood welled out of the wound. Liora let it bleed for a moment, hoping it would help carry out any bacteria from the bullet and her fingers. The hole would need to be stitched, but not before she had a chance to flush it properly. She packed the strips of cloth into the wound, then tied others around his shoulder and chest to hold it in place.

With Tariq still unconscious, she quickly checked his leg. Luckily, a bullet had only grazed it. The gash was nasty, but shallow. She wrapped it as well and bound strips around the outside of his atmosphere suit to help hold it in place.

She was tying off the last strip when Tariq muttered something. The words 'dirty Damaclan' caught her ear. Liora shook her head, telling herself it was only the shock. She couldn't blame him for what he said. He had a right to say whatever he wanted given his condition.

Liora's hand strayed to Tariq's forehead. She told herself she just wanted to check for fever, even though spiking one so quickly would be a stretch. She wouldn't push or cover his pain. He hated her. He wouldn't be forgiving if she tried.

Yet she needed him. He was her only partner on the red planet. With the sounds of gunfire intensifying as the two suns lowered, Liora didn't dare wait alone. Tariq could help her if she assisted him with the pain.

Intending to cover his shock as she had done for Devren, Liora touched his forehead. The feeling of his cool skin beneath her palm sent a shiver up her arm. Liora closed her eyes, opened her mind, and drew inward.

Instead of the pain she expected, something else hit Liora full force. Images and thoughts rushed over her, stealing her breath and making her mind reel. She tried to stop it, but she couldn't take her hand away.

Tariq walked down the hallway of the homestead spaceship. He looked younger, his rare smile fresh and his blue eyes clear. It was night and Titan, Saturn's largest moon, showed through the closest window. The hall lights were on and tiny bugs whistled as they flew around it, their yellow halos casting patterns on the hallway floor. He wondered how bugs always found a way to survive. Despite all the cleaning protocols, the creatures eventually returned.

The third-person view took Liora into the apartment. After two steps, Tariq froze.

Blood streaked the floor and along one wall as if someone had tried desperately to escape, only to be pulled back. Liora's eyes focused in the darkness. Someone stood in the living room. He held a knife and an object.

"No!" Tariq yelled.

He barreled into the room, all sense of self-preservation gone at the sight of the slain child.

The Damaclan, his tribe tattoos clearly visible on his pale skin, tossed the body aside and grinned.

A shudder ran through Liora's body. She knew that grin.

Tariq glanced to the right. The other body on the ground had been cut open from navel to neck. Her beautiful face was frozen in a rictus of pain, and her empty eyes stared beseechingly at him as though begging him to avenge her.

"Dannan!" he yelled.

The Damaclan met him halfway across the living room. Liora felt the deep stab of the warrior's knife as he sunk it into Tariq's stomach and pulled it to the right, a killing wound.

Tariq turned at the last minute, his knees buckling as he pulled himself from the blade. He swung at the Damaclan. The warrior blocked the weak swing and let the human fall to the floor.

"It is done," the Damaclan said.

Tariq's eyes closed and the memory vanished.

Liora staggered to her feet. Tears streamed down her cheeks. She told herself that perhaps it was just a dream. No one had ever pushed anything back at her. Maybe instead of a memory, she had just viewed whatever nightmare Tariq was caught in.

There was only one way to know for sure. It took every ounce of Liora's willpower to kneel by the human once more. She reached for the zipper on his atmosphere suit. With shaking fingers, she pulled the zipper down.

Liora's stomach tightened when the suit slipped away to reveal the white puckered scar across Tariq's stomach. Liora touched the scar, remembering the way the Damaclan's knife had buried into the flesh. The hilt had been black with the scaled head of the Tessari Dragon engraved into the burnished bone.

"Your fingers tickle, Dannan," Tariq slurred. A smile pulled at the corners of his mouth.

His eyes opened. Liora watched the emotions change from pained humor to anger and loss when he remembered where he was. She stumbled back.

"Tariq, I—"

A rumbling sound filled the cave. The floor dipped, then fell away. Liora dove and caught Tariq's hand.

A giant head reared out of the cavern where the ground had been. One white, blind eye sat at the top of a face a palm's width above the gaping mouth made of a circle of fangs. The name worm fit in that the creature had no arms, and its head was merely an extension of its long body. Rough red, slimy skin covered it completely. The creature let out a rattling, guttural moan, revealing crooked, needle-like teeth that ran in rows down the inside of its throat.

Tariq pulled up toward Liora. The creature lunged for his

body. She yanked him as high as she could, but he was heavier than she, and the blood on her hands made her grip slippery.

"Tariq!" she cried.

"Hold on," he said, his eyes fever-bright.

The creature hit the side of the cave so hard the rocks around them vibrated. Liora's footing slipped. She reached for a better handhold. The worm hit the side of the cave again. Liora slid down. Tariq's free hand scrabbled against the rocks.

The creature lunged forward. Tariq's foot disappeared into its mouth.

He let out a yell of pain.

It yanked his hand from Liora's.

"Tariq!" she yelled again.

The worm pulled back with terrifying speed. Tariq disappeared from view.

Liora stared at the hole where he had been. Her heart hammered in her chest and her mind tried to deny what had happened. Tariq was gone.

The memory of what he had gone through surfaced in her mind. She again felt the devastating loss when he looked at Dannan's slain body and saw his child's lifeless body thrown to the side. He had been wronged, so very wronged, by her people. The sheer mindless fury that had filled Tariq when he attacked the Damaclan surged through Liora's veins.

Tariq was injured and caught in the jaws of a deadly creature. Liora would not let the worm win. Tariq's rage multiplied with her own, creating a rush of wrath the likes of which she had never felt before. Fueled with fury and armed with the blade Branson had given her, Liora jumped into the hole.

Chapter 11

Tariq's yells drove her on. She knew he would fight, but given the shape he was in and the number of teeth that held him captive, she knew his odds were slim to none. She ran through the tunnel, slipping a few times on the slimy path the creature had left. Strange vibrations filled the dirt, pulsing around her in palpable waves the closer she got.

Liora reached the end of the tunnel and slid to a stop.

Hundreds of the flesh-eating worms writhed in a huge chamber far beneath the surface of the red planet. Their moaning, guttural sounds echoed through the air. Small, glowing beetles lined the walls, lighting the room. Red, dangerous-looking stingers tipped the ends of the worms' long tails. The remains of bodies that they had devoured littered the ground. Liora saw several Revolutionary helmets beneath the thrashing creatures.

Tariq was nowhere to be seen. The voice in the back of Liora's mind warned her that he might already be dead. She refused to listen. Reason warred with her anger. If he was in the stomach of one of the creatures, she would cut each of them open to see if there was a chance to save him.

"Tariq!" she yelled.

A hundred white eyes turned in her direction. Liora gripped her knife tight and leaped into the fray.

It took only a few dangerous moments to find out that the worms' sightless white eyes weren't for vision. They were the way the creatures sounded their vibrations, a sonar of sorts. When Liora stabbed the eye, it debilitated the worm. The creature would thrash around, spraying blood and white sludge everywhere. Liora could then slice the worm's throat down to the belly, spilling the contents onto the ground.

She lost track of how many bites she defended and lunges she ducked. She stabbed half a dozen eyes at a time and sliced through their stomachs after they were incapacitated. Bodies from eaten rebels, strange planet creatures, and two members of Devren's crew fell lifeless to the red sand, but Tariq was nowhere to be found.

When Liora had killed all of the worms in the cave, she took off up the closest tunnel, following the vibrations that meant a worm was ahead of her.

A muffled scream sounded as she neared the surface. Liora reached the worm and cut off the red stinger. The creature let out a thundering bellow and tried to back up. Liora only had one choice. She sliced the worm's belly and dove to the side, letting the contents spill back down the tunnel.

After checking to make sure Tariq's body wasn't included in the disgusting mess, Liora cut her way up the body until she reached the worm's head. With a backwards slice, she removed the neck completely and shoved the head out of her way.

"What on…Liora?"

Liora stared at the humans around her. Officer Shathryn was huddled against two other officers from the Kratos Liora didn't know. Shathryn's arm was bleeding in long tracks as though she had just been freed from the worm's mouth.

"That worm got me and I thought I was ashes in the Macrocosm," the purple-haired humanoid sobbed. "I was saying my prayers and everything, then the worm screamed and let me go. You saved my life! We tried to get to the others, but they're trapped."

"Where are they?" Liora demanded.

"The worms? They come from underground and—"

"The others," Liora corrected her urgently. "Where is Captain Devren and the rest of the Kratos crew?"

Shathryn tried to explain, but tears flowed from her eyes and Liora couldn't make out a word of what she said.

"They're that way," one of the other officers told her. He waved his arm. "They're with the rebels. Devren radioed us and we were trying to reach them when the worms appeared."

Liora was already running. Shathryn called her name, but she left them far behind.

Her sharp gaze made out the boulders and pits caused by the worms. She darted around them, her attention locked on the sounds of commotion in the distance. Sporadic gunfire and yells filled the air. She ran down a wash and followed the sounds to a small valley between two dirt mountains.

Devren, Straham, and Sicily fought beside four rebels against a dozen worms. The creatures lunged then drew back. Sicily fired a few shots, but the others appeared to be out of ammunition. Devren and a rebel held knives they used to push back the worms. Blood streaked the ground, remnants of someone who had fallen to the creatures' bloodlust. She counted seven slain worms, but others appeared as soon as the officers dropped their companions.

Liora ran around the hill, circling the worms. The light of the biggest sun showed on the horizon, lighting the valley below her in shades of red and gold. The creatures on the ground lunged and pulled back, their slimy trails catching in the dawn light.

Liora launched herself off the hill. She landed on top of three worms, stabbed their eyes, fell to the ground, and cut through the three necks with a short spin. She dodged a stinger and sliced, severing the appendage from another worm's body. When it twisted to retaliate, she sunk her blade deep in its eye. Two other worms attacked at the same time. Liora ducked and they slammed into each other. She drove her knife up, sending it deep into the first worm's throat before she tore the knife free and finished the second.

Liora heard yells as Devren and the other officers joined in. Worms fell left and right. Those who dove through the tunnels to enter the fray were cut down. Blood and carnage slicked the ground. Liora felt caked in death and devastation. All the while, the thought of Tariq injured and possibly dead haunted her mind, driving her to further destruction to ensure that none of the other Kratos members followed.

"Liora!"

She stood in the middle of the fallen worms facing the holes in the side of the hill. All around, slain worms twitched in the final throes of death.

"Liora," Devren yelled.

Several vibrations hit her. More worms were coming.

"Get ready," she called over her shoulder. "There's more of them on the way."

A hand touched her shoulder. She glanced to the right.

"It is you," Devren said, his eyes wide and face streaked with blood. "I thought you were dead."

"We got pinned down," she replied, fighting to catch her breath. "They took Tariq."

Devren's jaw tightened. He wiped the blades of his knives on his atmosphere suit and turned to face the tunnels.

"They'll pay," he said with steel in his voice.

"We take them together." Straham took up position on Liora's other side.

The four rebels fanned out, their weapons ready and gazes on the tunnels. Liora looked from the Revolutionaries to the Coalition officers. All of them were covered in blood from the worms and their own wounds. Each had the same determined expression on their faces. They would avenge those who had fallen from the worms, or die trying.

"Hold your ground," Devren told them. "We're stronger together. Protect each other's backs."

The vibrations grew louder. The number of worms sounded like far more than they had already faced. It was a losing battle, but the rebels and officers faced it head on.

A dozen worms dove out of the holes with more forcing through behind them. The mass barreled down on the humans and humanoids.

The worms moved with a speed that was terrifying. Their bodies glistened in the rising sunlight and their blind white eyes glared ominously. The fanged holes that made up their mouths opened in anticipation. Liora braced herself.

An ear-splitting, shrieking cry tore through the air. A

creature so big Liora couldn't see its entire body landed on the worms. Huge claws tore into the thrashing bodies. The worms let out guttural protests as they were shredded by a huge multi-beaked face. Every worm that appeared from the tunnel was slain and eaten in a matter of seconds. Within moments, even the bodies of the creatures that had been killed were gone.

The beast turned its many-eyed face toward the humanoids. The five beaks opened and a rumbling roar sounded so loud the officers and rebels had to cover their ears. The creature glared at them, its lizard-like features covered in worm blood. It flapped its leathery wings. Scales and spikes covered the beast from its back to the tip of its three tails. Eyes blinked in every direction from the beaked face. It lowered its head, intent on finishing its meal.

Liora spun her knife so that she held it point down. Her goal was the eyes, though there were so many she doubted it would have the same effect it did for the worms. The creature could eat half of them in one swoop. Its huge mouths opened. Hot breath washed over the group.

Gunfire spattered into the beast's chest and head. The sound of the Gull's engines echoed against the hillside. The beast reared back and swiped at the spacecraft. Hyrin maneuvered the ship out of reach and the Gull spun, revealing the open hatch.

Liora's breath caught in her throat.

Tariq stood on the loading bay with a rocket launcher on his shoulder.

"Get out of there!" he yelled.

The officers and rebels fell back. The beast lunged after them as if it couldn't resist the chase. The rocket soared through the air. It slammed into the creature's chest. The explosion knocked Liora off her feet. She rolled to her knees, her knife raised in case the beast attacked.

The creature flapped haphazardly into the sky, its chest torn open and cries of rage sounding from its beaks. Its wings blocked out the rising sun for a moment. It gave another shriek and turned, soaring into the distance.

The Gull landed.

"There are more of them coming," Tariq said. He leaned heavily against the rocket launcher. "Get in, quick!"

The rebels hung back. Devren waved his arm.

"Come on; we'll drop you at your ship."

The rebels looked at each other. Liora couldn't blame them. Setting foot on an enemy ship after the battle for their lives must have felt like diving out of the frying pan into the fire.

Devren understood the same thing.

"I'm the captain of this crew. You have my word that you will be protected and delivered to your people safely. Do you really want to hang around here for another of those animals to attack?"

"The family might need us," one of the men said quietly to his comrades.

"You've got to hurry up. I can see more demon birds on the horizon," Hyrin called over his shoulder.

A rebel with blood-streaked long gray hair met Devren's gaze. "We have your word?"

Devren held out a hand. "As captain."

They shook. The rebels climbed cautiously into the Gull. Hyrin closed the loading bay and swung the ship southwest.

Liora took a seat across from Tariq. Other crew members from the Kratos who had been rescued sat and lay in the small ship's hull. Everyone appeared to be in the same state of wounded but surviving. The crew barely blinked an eye at the appearance of the Revolutionaries. The rebels took the seats closest to the door. If they felt any anxiety when it closed, they didn't show it.

Everything that had happened in the past few hours threatened to crash down on Liora. She sheathed her knife and crossed her arms over her chest in an effort to maintain a hold on her emotions. She had never set foot on a hostile planet, been shot at by Revolutionaries, watched one of her comrades die at her feet, and gone into a rage so deep she slaughtered an entire horde of flesh-eating creatures without a second thought. She was covered in the blood and carnage, a reminder of the beast she had become.

Her gaze met Tariq's. He looked as beat up as she felt. The leg of his atmosphere suit had been shredded. Blood showed beneath the tattered cloth. He leaned awkwardly to one side, his arm resting in his lap.

"How are you doing?" she asked just loud enough for her voice to carry over the Gull's engine hum.

"I'll survive."

His eyes traveled over her body. She suddenly felt the bite wounds and bruises beneath the sludge that covered her from head to toe.

"How about you?" he asked, his tone unreadable.

She wasn't sure how to put into words what she felt.

Before she could answer, Hyrin called back, "Has anyone seen Shathryn or Veras? We lost radio contact with them."

Liora rose and walked to the front of the Gull. Devren studied the ground from the co-pilot seat while Hyrin steered the ship over the hills and valleys of the red planet.

"They're west of here," Liora told them. "I ran into them and they told me where I could find you."

"Perfect," Hyrin replied. "Maybe we can get to them before more of those bird beaks show up." He turned the ship to the west. A few minutes later, they made out the forms of Officer Shathryn and the two other crew members in the valley where Liora had left them.

Hyrin landed the Gull in a cloud of red dust.

"Oh, thank goodness!" Shathryn exclaimed when the loading door opened. "I was worried more of those worms would show up."

"It's not the worms you have to worry about," Officer Straham told her, his worried gaze on the sky as though he feared one of the beaked beasts would drop on them without warning.

"Well, the worms were bad enough," Shathryn said as the other officers helped her inside. She held her arm close. "If it wasn't for Liora, we'd be underground right now." She gave Liora a beaming smile when she was helped to the seats behind Devren.

The officer who limped up behind her nodded. "When that worm came up, we thought we were done for. We were out of ammo and Shathryn had already been attacked and was bleeding. The worm surfaced and Liora cut it open from inside the tunnel. Its head fell off, and there she was."

"The most gruesome angel I've ever seen," Shathryn said. "Blood everywhere and nothing but her knife against those monsters. It was amazing." She dove into a moment by moment recounting of the attack as Hyrin maneuvered the Gull into the sky once more.

Liora leaned her head against the back of the ship and closed her eyes.

"You ran into them?" Tariq repeated.

Liora kept her eyes closed. "I was looking for you," she said, forcing her tone to remain steady.

Silence filled the air between them. The images of Tariq's memory flashed through Liora's mind. No wonder he hated Damaclans with such intensity. His hatred had fueled her rage against the worms as much as her own anger. Her stomach twisted at the thought that he would distrust her even further if he knew the whole story.

Chapter 12

"If what you're saying is true, the Revolutionaries aren't responsible for the Coalition surveyors' beacon."

Liora focused on Devren's voice in an effort to push her thoughts away.

Devren's words were a quiet counterbalance to Shathryn's near-hysterical voice. An officer named Clell moaned with pain while Tariq patched his stomach. Liora felt claustrophobic in the small ship surrounded by so many people. She closed her eyes and listened to Devren in an effort to stay calm.

"Perhaps if we can find the reason for their distress signal, we can get to the bottom of what the Coalition wants us to do here."

"You'll have to meet with Stone about that," the gray-haired rebel replied.

"Will he be at the ship?"

"I'm not sure. We lost track of our men when the worms attacked." His voice lowered. "We've been here three days and haven't seen them before. I don't know what brought them out."

"All I know is that huge worms make for even bigger predators." Officer Straham leaned his head back and gave a weary sigh. "If I never see one of those bird dragon things again, it'll be too soon."

"I second that," Hyrin agreed.

He settled the ship onto the sunlit sand a click away from the Revolutionary spacecraft.

"Give us a few minutes to talk to them," the rebel told Devren. "We'll smooth things over so they don't come out shooting."

"I appreciate that," Devren replied.

As soon as the rebels were off the ship, Officer Straham put his palm to a reader near the back. A panel opened to reveal a hidden cache of weapons.

"It pays to be cautious," Devren told his crew while Straham handed them out. "Don't have itchy trigger fingers, but stay on guard. We're enemies, but something's not right here. Until we get to the bottom of it, I don't want anyone making any rash decisions." He looked at Shathryn. "Understood?"

A wave of surprise filled Liora at the Humanoid's embarrassed look. "I understand."

"Did you shoot someone?" Liora asked her.

Shathryn lifted her shoulders in a little shrug. She looked so fragile with strings of worm entrails in her hair and her gun held in the crook of her bandaged arm, it was hard to imagine her hurting anyone.

"I may have shot the commander of a rebel force we were supposed to question a few years back," she admitted.

"You also shot the heir to the Belanite secondary line," Hyrin said from the front seat.

"He was a jerk," Shathryn told the pilot.

"We're lucky they still let us land on any of the Gaulded," Hyrin reminded her.

"How about the Salamandon princess. What was her name? Cry...cray...Cratonista?" O'Tule asked.

"She not only had a stick where the stars don't shine, she was hitting on Devren," Shathryn said with a spark of protectiveness in her gaze.

"I told you I could handle myself." Devren shook his head. "It's not like I would have done anything."

"I'd hope not," Shathryn replied. "She was up to no good."

"You've really got to stop shooting people," Tariq told her. "One of these days it may have consequences."

"Don't worry. Everyone I shot had it coming." Shathryn winked at him. "Want to give me a reason?"

Tariq cracked a smile. "I thought you had a book full of them by now."

She laughed. "I have a bad memory. Remind me."

"No thanks," Tariq replied.

"Here they come."

Everyone fell silent at Hyrin's warning. Two of the Revolutionaries they had rescued from the worms approached the loading ramp.

"Stone is willing to meet with you," the gray-haired one

said. "No weapons. Out in the open. Man to man."

"Captain, I don't think that's a good idea," Straham began.

Devren removed his pistol and submachine gun. He handed both of them to the disapproving officer.

"You can bring two unarmed crew members," the man continued. "Stone will have his advisors with him."

Tariq handed his guns to Straham without waiting for Devren to say his name.

"Officer Day, you too," Devren said.

It took Liora a moment to realize he was talking to her.

"Me?" she asked.

Tariq nodded.

Liora wordlessly handed the gun back to Straham. The officer looked a bit flustered at the amount of weapons he held.

"The knife, too," Devren said.

Liora had forgotten she still wore it. It felt as though the weapon was something she had always had. She couldn't have fought the worms without it.

She hid her reluctance when she unbuckled the blade. Shathryn held out a hand for it.

"Don't worry," the purple-haired officer said. "I'll make sure it gets right back to you." She lowered her voice and continued, "You've got to be ready if someone needs a little jab. There's a lot of deserving people out there."

She winked at Liora.

Liora fought back a smile and followed Tariq and Devren down the ramp. Leaving their crew members and weapons gave Liora a feeling of vulnerability she had never experienced before. She had never depended on anyone else for comfort, companionship, or security. The fact that the steps she took away from the ship were so hard bothered her. She glanced back, trying to puzzle it out.

"Given some luck, we'll get the information we need and return to the Gull within the hour," Devren told her. "We don't want to be out here when that hits."

Liora followed his gaze to red storm clouds massing in the distance.

"Maybe that's why the worms were so restless," she said quietly.

Devren's eyebrows pulled together and he nodded with a thoughtful expression. "You might be right."

A man with a white streak in his black hair stepped down the ramp from the Copper Crow. Liora vaguely remembered him from the circus. Two other Revolutionaries, a Salamandon woman and a male Gaul with huge horns followed. Faces peered from the doorway after them.

"Captain Metis, I presume," the rebel leader said. He held out a hand. "My name is Stone; I own the Star Chaser."

Devren shook his hand. "I appreciate you meeting with me."

"And I appreciate you rescuing my men," Stone replied. "It takes a certain kind of man to save an enemy."

"'The enemy of my enemy is my friend'," Devren quoted. "The worms and flying beast were the greater danger."

Stone gave an appreciative nod. "A proverb from Earth, if I'm not mistaken."

"You're correct," Devren told him. "My dad used to study Earthling international policy. He always said we must learn our history or be bound to repeat it."

"A wise man," Stone conceded. "I'd like to meet him someday."

Devren's lips tightened for the briefest moment before he said, "He was slain in a skirmish a few days ago."

"With Revolutionaries." Stone guessed the words the captain left unspoken. At Devren's nod, Stone's voice lowered. "We have all lost loved ones in this war. The sooner we can live in peace, the better for all."

"Peace as Revolutionaries?" Devren asked, his tone level.

"Peace as mortalkind," Stone replied.

Aware that they had reached an impasse, Devren glanced at Tariq. The medical officer stepped forward.

"Stone, we were sent here by the Coalition to investigate the beacon from a survey crew a few clicks away. I don't think your presence so close by is a coincidence."

Stone crossed his arms. The torn elbows of his coat showed signs of the battle with the worms and the Coalition officers.

"I suppose we'll both get out of here faster if we work together." Stone glanced at the growing storm in the distance. "If those worms and the winged creatures are any sign, this planet is about to get a lot less hospitable." He nodded at the Gaul behind him. "Jedredge, tell him what we know."

The Gaul took up the report. His deep voice rumbled when he said, "You came here following a beacon from your survey team. Apparently, they weren't alone. We were sent here on orders to locate one of our ships that had crashed on route to uncover a discovered object."

"Do you have the coordinates of the crash?" Tariq asked.

The Gaul shook his shaggy head. "The orders were encrypted. Unfortunately, Warlum and Tates disappeared during the worm attack. They hold the encryption keys."

"We're in the process of attempting to locate them," the Salamandon explained. "But their location beacons disappeared below ground."

"How long would it take for someone to hack the orders?" Devren asked.

Stone lifted his shoulders. "We don't have anyone left with those skills."

"Hyrin could do it."

Everyone looked at Liora. For the first time, Stone met her eyes. She felt his gaze on the tattoos running down her neck.

"You have a Damaclan on your crew?" he asked with a hint of surprise.

"Officer Day has proven herself," Devren replied simply.

Stone's gaze didn't leave Liora. "I was under the impression that the Damaclan had fallen out of favor with the Coalition, if they were ever in favor in the first place."

"My father was human," Liora told him. She hoped to appease his suspicions and move on. The need to clean the carnage from her body and have a moment to rest after the battle shortened her patience. "I feel like there are far more important items to address than my lineage."

Stone gave a noncommittal sound at her abruptness and had the tact to change subjects. "Who's Hyrin?"

"Our pilot," she replied. "From what I've seen, he has the skills to hack your system."

"Is this true?" Stone asked Devren.

The captain of the Kratos nodded. "He might be our best bet."

Liora could see the wariness Stone felt at the thought of allowing a Coalition officer access to his ship's computers.

"Captain?"

Devren glanced back at the Gull. Hyrin ran down the ramp and hurried across the dirt toward them. Puffs of red dust rose from each step.

"Captain," Hyrin gasped when he reached them. "There's been a development."

Devren glanced at Stone. "This is the man of whom we speak."

"Good to know," Stone said. "I've never met a Talastan I didn't get along with."

Hyrin straightened up when he realized he had interrupted their meeting. The fact that he didn't leave said multitudes about his concerns. He waited breathlessly for permission to continue.

"Report," Devren said.

Hyrin's words were rushed when he said, "Captain, Officer Duncan just radioed from the Kratos. There are ships, sir."

"What ships?"

"Ships coming in," Hyrin replied. "They've been using the Arizona transporter nonstop. Duncan thought at first they were just passing through, but since we're at such a distant location and there's such a variety of ships…"

"It's too great to be a coincidence," Devren finished.

Both leaders' attention was on Hyrin completely.

"What kind of ships have you seen?" Stone asked.

"All kinds; Crows, Eagles, Sparrows, junkers. Duncan's identified Revolutionaries, mercs, and salvagers." Hyrin looked at Devren. "Captain, whatever we've stumbled into, it's a lot bigger than we thought."

Devren glanced at Stone.

Stone nodded. "Let's get to the bottom of this. Officer Hyrin, you have permission to board my ship with two officers and attempt to hack the encrypted orders that sent us here."

"Encrypted?" Hyrin replied, caught off guard. "You don't have the key?"

"We're attempting to locate it," Tariq told him, "But for now, you're our best bet."

"That could take hours," Hyrin said.

A crackle sounded in the distance. Everyone's attention was caught by the sight of lightning flashing across the red storm front. Jagged green and yellow lines hit the ground at least thirty times.

149

A moment later, thunder unlike anything Liora had ever heard before hit them with the force of a wave. The wind knocked everyone back. Liora staggered and covered her eyes against the onslaught of sand that followed. For a moment, she couldn't see anything. Her crew members and the Revolutionaries were lost from view. Thoughts of the man-eating worms and multi-beaked birds toyed in her mind.

The percussive echoes died away. Liora wiped her eyes and glanced around. The other members of the group looked as shocked as she was.

"Let's go find those encryption codes," Stone said. "Jedredge, Faye, take Hyrin and his officers inside so he can get to work on the orders." The Gaul didn't look thrilled at the command. Stone gave him a stern look. "Officer Hyrin and the crew members of the SS Kratos are under our protection as long as we are working toward the same goal. The incoming ships may prove to be a far bigger threat than our little skirmish, no matter who we've lost." He glanced at Devren. "'The enemy of my enemy is my friend', right?"

Devren nodded. "Exactly."

"Captain?" Liora waited until Devren motioned for her to speak. "I know where the worms come from."

"You've been there?"

The thought of going back into the tunnels made Liora's muscles tighten, but she nodded. "I can show you."

Both commanders brought weapons out. Stone and four other Revolutionaries joined them on the Gull while Shathryn and O'Tule followed Hyrin to the Star Chaser.

Liora directed Devren to the place she had slain the worm to rescue Shathryn and the others. The body of the worm was gone; deep claw marks and shredded flesh showed evidence of the creature that had eaten it.

Liora peered into the tunnel.

"You sure this is a good idea?" Straham asked.

"If we want to find whatever is drawing the other ships, we need the encryption codes. We don't have the hours Hyrin says it'll take to break the orders. We need those keys." Devren motioned toward the tunnel. "Let's go."

Liora stepped into the darkness. Behind her, Stone's rebels and the Coalition officers turned on the lights mounted to their guns. Even though she held the submachine gun in her hands, the presence of the blade fastened around her thigh gave her more comfort. Liora slung the gun over her shoulder and drew the blade. No matter what happened on planet F One Zero Four, she made a vow to thank Branson for the weapon.

The footsteps behind Liora slowed when she reached the huge chamber. Her stomach turned at the odors wafting from the bodies of the worms and their victims. Now that the rage had faded, seeing the devastation she had caused felt like stepping into another reality. She could barely believe it had been her hands that had torn the creatures apart, leaving the mass-scaled massacre beneath the planet's surface.

"You did this?"

Liora looked at Tariq. The officer leaned against the side of the cavern. Fresh blood showed through the shoulder of his atmosphere suit, reminding her of their moments in the cave. "I was searching for you," she said.

Stone shook his head, his eyes on the quantity of slain bodies. "Nothing can match the rage of a Damaclan. Beware he who wrongs the worshipers of the Tessari Dragon."

Liora turned away from the rebel leader's searching gaze. She followed Straham down to the floor of the cavern to look through the bodies of the red planet's victims.

Chapter 13

"I found Tates," one of the rebels yelled. She paused, then said, "Or what's left of him."

Everyone made their way between the slain worms. Stone rummaged through the man's shredded atmosphere suit.

"Sorry, Tates," he said, his words quiet. A relieved look spread across his face and he pulled out a laminated card. "This is what we're looking for."

As soon as they reached the rebels' ship, both the Coalition officers and Revolutionaries waited anxiously for Hyrin's report. He typed quickly, entering the information from the card and letting it run the decryption. The anxious faces of the mixed group crowded behind him on the Star Chaser's small bridge would have been laughable if it wasn't for the extreme situation.

"Oh no," Hyrin breathed.

"What is it?" Devren asked.

Hyrin looked up at his captain. "It's worse than we could've imagined. No wonder so many ships are here."

Stone set a hand on Hyrin's shoulder. "What did you find, son?"

Hyrin glanced back at the screen. "It appears the crew of the SS Cerus accidentally stumbled upon an Omne Occasus, a galaxy imploder."

"How would that work?" Devren asked.

Hyrin studied the screen. "This imploder magnifies energy by a quadrillion, simulating the collapse of a star on such a magnitude that anything within the event horizon, or the boundary of the black hole, would be absorbed, destroying all forms of energy." He looked up at Devren. "Captain, anyone with that kind of power would control the Macrocosm."

"Who has that kind of technology?" Stone asked, his face intent.

"I'm not sure," Hyrin replied. "It doesn't say. Experiments of that magnitude were outlawed ages ago."

The screen in front of him beeped.

"Captain, we have a transmission from Officer Duncan."

Devren looked at Stone. "Duncan is aboard the Kratos. I'd like to take the transmission if you don't mind."

At Stone's nod, Hyrin pressed a button.

"Captain!" Duncan said, his voice high with worry. "Two scavenger ships are inbound on your location. I've moved the Kratos to the opposite side of the planet to shield us from attack, but it'll take the Gull longer to reach the ship. I'm not sure what to do."

"Scavengers," Stone growled. "I hate scavengers. Filthy vultures without morals or a conscience to cloud their judgement." He motioned to the Gaul. "Jedredge, take Jenkin and Viarie to the ground. Set up a three-point alert. I want to know when those ships come into view."

"Done," Jedredge said with a nod of his huge head. He left the bridge with a speed that belied the huge Gaul's size.

Stone turned to Devren. "You're welcome to stay aboard my ship. We're in this for the long haul. Keep the Kratos safe behind the planet. We can put aside our differences until the Omne Occasus is dealt with."

Devren watched him closely. Liora knew he was trying to decide whether the rebel leader was trustworthy. None of them had much of a choice in the matter. If they could band together, perhaps they would have a chance to survive.

It seemed Devren came to the same conclusion.

"Thank you," the Kratos' captain replied. He looked at the screen. "Officer Duncan, keep the Kratos hidden until we contact you. Maintain radio silence. If there is need for an emergency evac, you might have short notice."

"Got it," Duncan replied. "I'll keep constant vigil on this channel. Kratos out."

The screen went black.

Stone addressed Hyrin. "How long before you have the coordinates of the imploder?"

"It might take me a little bit. This message has a few glitches. Did you say you know the origin?"

"It came from Command Seven. They're stationed near the Sculptor Dwarf Galaxy."

"That might account for the magnetic interference. I'll let you know when I have it cracked." Hyrin centered his chair and started typing intently on the keyboard in front of him.

Stone motioned for them to leave the bridge. O'Tule and Shathryn stayed behind in case Hyrin needed anything.

"Take some time to clean up and rest," Stone said.

"We can go back to the Gull," Devren replied. "We'll give your crew their space."

"Nonsense." Stone ran a hand through his long streaked hair. Sticky goop covered his palm when he pulled it away. He made a face. "We could all use a chance to shower. We have plenty onboard and you won't be able to until you make it back to your Iron Falcon."

Stone looked at the Kratos members. "You have plenty of reasons to distrust me and my family." His gaze landed on Liora and his eyes narrowed slightly. "And I've plenty to distrust you. Keep together. While I can't promise friendliness from my crew, they'll be under orders to give your members their space. If there's any trouble, let me know."

"Thank you," Devren replied. He watched Stone walk away down the hall.

"I don't like this," Tariq said quietly.

"Neither do I," Devren admitted. "But we don't have much of a choice. We can't risk the Revolutionaries getting their hands on the Omne Occasus before us, and the best way to do that is to stick together. I don't trust Stone any further than I can throw a haffot, but we're here, so we'd better make the most of it." He studied his crew. "Clean up in pairs. Guard each other's backs. We'll meet back here in twenty minutes unless Hyrin cracks the coordinates before that or we see signs of the salvagers."

A girl with long blue tentacles instead of hair made her way down the hall. A male Ventican followed, his gray fur offset by tailored black armor.

"Captain Metis, Stone has asked me to escort you and your

crew to the secondary lounge. Stone has ordered for the lounge and facilities to be emptied for your access."

"I appreciate that," Devren replied.

Liora glanced down every hallway they passed. The fact that they were in hostile territory wasn't lost on anyone. The Kratos crew stuck together and moved in a tight-knit unit. Even the chance to clean up and rest after the long night didn't chase away their caution.

"Here you are," the girl said, indicating a common area with couches and an open door that revealed a clean washroom and branching shower area. "Stone also wanted me to let you know that he will have food sent over shortly.

"Thank you for your hospitality," Devren told her.

As soon as the door closed, Tariq and Straham maneuvered a couch in front of it. Tariq fell heavily onto the cushions.

Devren gave his friend a worried look. "You need medical attention."

Tariq lifted his shoulders and couldn't hide the wince the movement brought. "I'll survive."

"You should clean up. You look like you came from the belly of one of those worms."

"I pretty much did," Tariq replied offhandedly. "Let's just say it realized its error in not relieving me of my weapons before it swallowed me."

Straham gave a visible shudder. "That's gross."

"Or cool because you survived it," Officer Veras, the other officer from the Kratos, said.

All three men gave him an incredulous look. Liora would have found their reaction amusing if she wasn't so tired. The thought of showering off the slime and carnage that covered her and the chance to settle her nerves after the battle was one she couldn't resist. She rose and made her way to the washroom. If the officers wanted to argue who went first, she would take advantage of the opportunity.

"What?" the young human said. "It's not like you're still in there. We survived."

"We're still fighting to survive," Straham reminded him. "As it is…"

Liora chose one of the walled showers and stepped inside. Pulling the door shut behind her, she stripped off the clothes the Zamarian woman had given her on the Gaulded Zero Twenty-one. She was amazed to see that the Ventican cloth barely showed signs of the fierce battle. After the dozens of teeth and multiple stab attempts from the worms, Liora had been sure the armor was ruined.

As it was, only light grazes in the black shirt and pants showed where the armored clothing had saved her life. The bruises on her skin that coincided with the bite marks revealed how lucky she had been. Liora had vowed to repay the Zamarian for her kindness, but how did someone pay another back for saving her life and the others Liora was able to protect when she survived?

The hot water stung. Liora scrubbed her clothes until the last of the worm guts swirled down the drain. She hung the clothes beside her weapons and quickly washed in the water, aware that the other members of the crew would want to clean up as well. When she was done, she was surprised to see that the Ventican cloth was already dry. Pulling it on, Liora ran her fingers through her hair to straighten it out.

She felt like she could breathe again. It was as if washing off the guts and blood helped to erase the harsh edges of the memories from the night.

Straham and Veras already occupied two of the other stalls. Liora made her way back into the crew lounge.

Devren and Tariq sat at one of the tables. Both glanced up

when she entered. She had the distinct impression that she had interrupted an intense discussion.

"You look like you feel a lot better," Devren noted. He gave her a kind smile.

"I do," Liora replied. "There's something about hot water." She glanced at Tariq and found him watching her. She closed her mouth without commenting how truly long it had been since she had set foot in a shower. Somehow, the vulnerability of such an admission was more than she wanted to admit in front of both men.

Liora sat on one of the couches. The soft cushions beckoned to her.

"Take a nap," Devren suggested. "You saved lives today. Heroines deserve the chance to rest."

A small smile touched the corner of Liora's mouth. "It didn't feel so heroic. I was covered in so many worm pieces I felt like I was one of them."

Devren chuckled. He leaned back in his chair, balancing it on the back legs like a child. It made him look younger, more carefree. Liora had no doubt every woman the captain encountered found him incredibly attractive. His dark eyes sparkled teasingly when he said, "Your knowledge of the tunnels was incredible. Are you sure you're not part Terrarian?"

The thought of sharing kindred with the mole men from planet Tanus made Liora smile. "Unfortunately, no, but I'll bet they would have had quite the feast today. At the circus, there was a Terrarian who ate whole plates of worms to amuse a crowd. He made quite the killing."

Devren chuckled. "You do have a humorous side," he said with a pleased expression. "I thought we'd get it out of you yet."

Liora glanced at Tariq. The human watched her with his

gaze guarded and expression unreadable.

Liora's smile faded and she ran a hand over the couch cushion. It was becoming more beckoning than she wanted to admit. Damaclan training forbade her from letting down her guard around possible enemies, yet the Kratos crew members had fought and bled beside her. If she couldn't trust them, she was alone in the world. She had been solitary long enough to admit that she didn't want it anymore.

"I think I will take a nap," she conceded.

She rolled over so that her back faced the men. Despite the angry protests of her instincts, she would rather risk getting stabbed than feel Tariq watching her as she slept. Guilt flooded her with the knowledge of how he would feel if he knew the truth.

Liora rested her head on one arm and closed her eyes.

The dream that swept her away took on a threatening edge the moment she fell asleep. Dark shadows raced beside Liora. She was a child again, running away from the nameless ones who had just destroyed her village. Blood showed in her footprints and tears for her fallen mother streaked her cheeks.

"Let her go," a shadow hissed.

"She'll bleed planets dry," another whispered.

"More for us," the first said. "Souls are not long for this universe."

"Give her a blade."

"Show her the way."

"She'll be the key to end it all. The girl from the stars; the girl without a soul."

The last voice was louder. Its shadow appeared in front of her, looming, encompassing. Liora couldn't stop running. Her feet took her inside the nameless one. She became lost in the shadows.

The dream shifted and Liora found herself standing in a

hallway. Bloody footprints showed where she had walked from the door. The blood matched the fingermarks on the walls and the sound of a woman's cries for help.

Liora didn't want to go toward the sound, but her feet moved anyway. She tried to not look at the streaks of red below the pictures that lined the hallway, pictures that showed a young couple smiling at each other as they stood beneath the halos of white flowers on Isonoe, the Jupiter moon made popular for its marriage dome carved out of the interior.

Another photograph showed a young man with black hair and blue eyes smiling down at a newborn baby. The baby's dark hair stood up, refusing to be cowed by the pink bow stuck to one side. The name Lissy was written in an elegant hand along the white bassinet. In the background, medical equipment and other babies could be seen. A green hand with a band around the wrist poked from inside the next bassinet.

Liora couldn't tear her gaze away from the third frame. In it, the wife and husband watched their little girl play. Lissy was older now, her black hair a mass of curls as she chased butterflies inside an artificial terrarium. There was a smile of pure contentment on Tariq's face as he held his wife close. Her head was on his shoulder; an expression of loving adoration showed in her gaze as she looked up at her husband.

Another cry tore Liora's attention away. Unbidden, her feet carried her forward into the doorway of the living room.

The woman from the photographs cowered away from her attacker. In one corner, little Lissy sat with her knees pulled up and tears of fear streaking her cheeks. There was a red mark across her face as if she had been slapped.

"Leave them alone!" Liora yelled.

The Damaclan warrior didn't seem to hear her. He

advanced toward the woman. The blade of the bone knife he held glittered dully in the apartment's lighting. Liora knew what it would look like when it was covered in blood. There was nothing she could do to stop the warrior or save Tariq's family. Her feet were frozen to the ground and her shouts went unheeded.

The blade sunk deep into the woman's stomach. The little girl gave a cry. Sobs tore from Liora. She wanted to save them. She wanted them to be alright. She wanted the Damaclan warrior to be dead like he was supposed to be; except the Damaclan was caught in Tariq's memory and haunting her dreams, a living nightmare that would never stop plaguing her reality.

The Damaclan turned his head and met her gaze. "Liora." His lips pulled back in the rictus of a smile, revealing bloodstained teeth.

"Liora."

"No!" she yelled.

Hands grabbed her wrists.

Liora struggled. She knew her knife was on her hip. If she could just reach it—

"Liora! Stop!"

She opened her eyes.

Liora stared into Tariq's blue gaze. Her left hand was pinned beneath them while her right fought to reach the blade. Tariq's chest was bare and wet as if he had rushed out of the shower and only had time to pull on pants. A few drops of blood showed from the wound in his shoulder. His chest heaved as if he had fought a hard battle.

"You were having a nightmare," he told her. He held her wrist for a moment longer as though worried letting go might mean his life.

The thought of the knife made Liora's eyes sting. Tears

welled up and streaked her cheeks before she could stop them.

Tariq's expression softened. "It's okay," he said, his voice quieter. "You're okay."

He sat on the couch next to her and lifted his arm, pulling her to rest against his chest. His gentle fingers pushed her hair back from her face.

"I've got you," he said, his voice a soft cadence. "You're going to be just fine."

Liora closed her eyes against another rush of tears. She had never felt so on the verge of losing control. It was too much. Being comforted in his arms after all that had happened overwhelmed her emotions.

"I know who killed your wife."

Tariq had been softly wiping the tears from her cheeks with the backs of his fingers when her words stopped him.

His tone was a mixture of uncertainty and loss when he asked, "What did you say?"

Liora didn't want to repeat what she had said. Every part of her being screamed for her to shut her mouth and accept his kindness. But she couldn't face the guilt, and she wouldn't live a lie.

She opened her eyes. "My clan killed your wife and child."

Tariq's muscles went rigid. He studied her face for a moment, his eyes searching hers as if willing himself to believe that it wasn't true. There was pain in his gaze as if her saying the words had taken something valuable from him.

The truth was in her eyes and she couldn't look away.

"Damaclan."

The word was spoken as a curse.

Liora pulled back from Tariq.

"There's no way," he said, his voice level and deadly.

"The knife that killed her had the Tessari Dragon carved

into the hilt, did it not?"

Tariq nodded without speaking.

"Only Damaclan chieftains carry such a weapon." She didn't want to say the next part, but she had already gone too far to go back. "The Damaclan who killed her had this clan tattoo on his neck."

She swept her hair to one side and pointed to the tattoo just below her ear. It the symbol of her clan, a blade in the center of the Eye of Tessari.

Tariq rose slowly from the couch. The tenderness that had been in his eyes when he comforted her had vanished completely. His hands opened and closed. Another drop of blood trickled from the wound in his shoulder, but he didn't appear to feel it.

"Damaclan filth," he growled. "Why are you here?"

"I'm a runaway like you," Liora replied. His words stung. She knew it was the only reaction she could have expected, but she wished it was otherwise.

"You're a murdering savage," he spat.

"Tariq, I had to tell you," she said. She took a step back in the face of his vehemence. "I couldn't pretend."

"You're a liar and a coward." Tariq stepped forward, following her retreat. His hands opened as if he wished to throttle her.

Liora took another step back. "I saved your life," she reminded him, hoping he would calm down so she could reason with him.

"I'd rather have my wife and daughter here," he replied, his blue eyes flashing with anger.

"I didn't know what to do," she said. "I know you loved them. I know how much you cared about them."

"How do you know?" he demanded in a yell. "How can you even begin to comprehend? You're nothing but a merciless half-breed murderer."

Liora's legs met the back of another couch. Tariq's hands closed around her throat. Muscle memory begged for Liora to punch him in the stomach, elbow him in the back when he bent over, and drive her knife into his kidney when he hit the ground, severing his artery so he would bleed out in a matter of seconds. Instead, she didn't struggle.

Tariq's hands tightened. Liora couldn't draw in a breath. The rage she saw in his eyes matched the fury that had fueled her to dive into a cave of worms and slay hundreds of them in her search for him. She didn't want to care for him, and she hadn't wanted to hurt him, but fate was cruel and as merciless as he had accused her of being.

Black danced at the edges of her vision. She struggled to say his name, to calm him, but there wasn't anything she could do. For the first time in her life, when she was faced with a fight, Liora gave up. She didn't know if that made her a traitor to her clan, but given what the Damaclans had done, she didn't want to belong to them anyway. As Tariq's hold tightened, her only regret was that the one gentle thing in her life had been his same hands wiping away her tears.

Chapter 14

Tariq suddenly released her.

Liora gasped for air.

His eyes were accusing when he said, "You call yourself a member of the Kratos? You're not even worthy to scrub the sewer dump. I don't know why Devren allowed trash aboard our ship, but you'll never be an officer to me. Get out of here before I do something I truly won't regret."

Still struggling to breathe through her bruised throat, Liora ran for the door. Tears burned in her eyes. She told herself over and over again not to cry. The door slid open and she burst through, nearly upending the tray Devren carried.

"I brought you some...Liora, what's wrong?" he called as she rushed down the hall. "Tariq, what did you do?" she heard him demand before she rounded the corner.

Liora grabbed a Kratos atmosphere suit from the utility room and hit the button for the door.

"Liora, wait!" Devren entreated.

Liora ducked outside and didn't slow her run through the sandy hills until she reached the harder packed dirt that would hide her footsteps. She ran uphill with the knowledge that most would take the easier downhill route. She turned at a twisted, brittle-looking tree and slid down the side of a gully.

Sure they would never find her, Liora took the time to pull on the atmosphere suit. Her cheeks were dry and jaw clenched. She wouldn't cry. She refused to let the emotions get the best of her. She had been a fool to pretend she fit in with the Kratos crew members. For a time, it felt almost too good to be true to fight beside a team and feel like she actually belonged. A Damaclan didn't belong anywhere but with his or her clan, and hers had been destroyed.

Liora leaned against the side of the wash and let herself catch her breath. She knew deep down that was the only way her confrontation with Tariq could have gone, so why did it hurt so much? She had lost friends before, but this felt different. Even though she had only been aboard the Kratos a short time, it felt like she had just lost a family.

But they weren't family. Liora pushed the thought away. The Damaclans had been the closest thing to family she had ever had. She strapped the knife to the outside of her atmosphere suit as she thought the facts through.

If Tariq's memories showed his age accurately, his wife had been killed less than two years ago. The nameless had wiped out Liora's clan when she was twelve. Obruo should have been dead. The blood of the clan ran through the streets. By Damaclan law, he should have fought and died beside his people the way Liora had wanted to. She had been too terrified to act on the laws when she was twelve, but the chief's death was certain. If the nameless ones didn't kill him when his clan fell, his own knife to the stomach should have for, as the chief, he had failed to protect them.

Liora buried her devastation at being cast from the Kratos in plans for what would happen if she found Obruo. The Damaclan had made sure that her training was as brutal as possible. After what he had done to Tariq's family, he deserved to die the same way.

A memory surfaced that she had almost forgotten.

"What are you doing?"

Liora, her small arms trembling beneath the weight of the water jugs, spoke even though she knew she shouldn't.

"I'm so tired. The other kids went to bed a hand's-breadth ago. Can't I?"

She refused to cry. She was supposed to be strong. Her mother always said she needed to be stronger than the other children to prove her Damaclan blood. She wouldn't break character even if he punished her for speaking.

Liora's fears came true. Obruo grabbed the mastery staff. The needles that lined the bone club glinted in the lights that hummed softly overhead. Liora turned her head so she didn't have to look at him. She met her gaze in the mirror and held it.

"Your human blood is weak. You need to fight through it." Obruo slammed the staff across her back.

Liora bit her lip at the pain. She stared at herself in the glass, telling herself not to break.

"I train you harder because it's the only way you'll become

a Damaclan warrior. If you want the tattoos, you're going to have to earn them."

Obruo brought the club across the back of her thighs.

Liora's teeth cut into her bottom lip. The taste of blood centered her.

"If you were my real daughter, there would be no tainted blood in the clan." He grimaced and brought the club across Liora's low back. "If your mother had been faithful."

The Damaclan law of clanship required any member with Damaclan blood, no matter how faint, to be raised as a pureblood child. If they survived the training, the bloodline allowed them to undergo the rituals and tattooing. However, the law never said one couldn't push the child to the point of breaking.

Liora knew that was Obruo's hope. Her mother had no chance to defend her when it came to training. As chieftain, Obruo had all say in Liora's instruction. If he wanted to force her to hold water jugs all night, Tenieva had to let it happen. Though Liora's mother stayed up with her when she couldn't sleep because of the pain from the mastery staff, she wasn't allowed to be there when Liora was beaten.

"You won't survive training," Obruo said.

It was the first time he had actually voiced his intentions aloud.

It was apparently a night for more firsts.

Liora met his gaze in the mirror. "I will survive it and I'll wear the clan tattoos."

Liora had never challenged Obruo in such a way. As she held his gaze, her arms gave out. The jugs fell to the ground and broke, spilling water across the training room floor.

Fear made Liora's arms shake from more than the stress of holding the heavy containers. The look on Obruo's face was one of triumph.

"You'll fail if I have anything to do with it," he vowed. "You'll never receive the clan marks."

He raised the mastery staff above his head. Liora forced herself not to cower away from the coming blow.

A drop fell on Liora's helmet shield, bringing her back to the present. She stared as the small bead of liquid started to smoke. Adrenaline pulsed through her at the implication and she wiped it away quickly with her gloved hand. Green and yellow lighting struck around her as thick reddish-hued clouds massed overhead.

"The salvagers have landed." The sound of Shathryn's voice was loud with fear over the headset.

"How far away are they?" Devren asked.

"Jedredge says two clicks. They'll be here soon."

"Keep me informed," Devren said. "Stone has men hidden in the hills. The rest of you, grab your guns and head outside. If we can pick them off before they attack in force, we'll hold the upper hand."

The radio crackled, then a voice Liora hadn't heard before spoke. "Captain Metis, this is Viarie from the Star Chaser," he said in a thickly accented voice. "The salvagers have landed and I count nineteen of them heading this way."

"Nineteen is a lot," Hyrin noted.

"Just concentrate on the coordinates. We've got this," Devren told him.

"The storm is overhead," O'Tule called. "There's no end to it in sight."

"The ground is smoking," another officer said. "It's heading this way."

"Get to cover!" Straham's voice yelled over the headset.

Someone shrieked.

"Acid rain," Shathryn cried. "It's eating through my suit!"

"I've got you," Tariq told her. "Everyone, into the Gull or the Crow. This rain is deadly."

"Liora's out there," O'Tule said with heartbreak in her voice. "Tariq, you selfish brute, what did you say to make her run out there like that? It's a death sentence!"

Liora turned off her headset before she could hear his response. The last thing she wanted was to listen to his disdain again.

A rushing sound touched Liora's ears. She scrambled out of the wash as more raindrops fell, burning little holes into her atmosphere suit. As soon as her foot cleared the edge of the gully, a rush of acid water flooded past, carrying debris and several half-melted creature carcasses. The partially disintegrated skull and front claws of a bird beast bobbed in the acid wash.

Liora tore her gaze away and looked around for cover. A wormhole lay open on the side of a dirt mound not far from her. She ran toward it and leapt inside. She used the dirt to wipe away the liquid on the outside of her space suit. A quick check showed that though there were small burn holes, no damage had been done to the inner lining. The atmosphere cycling system still worked, providing her with clean air to breathe.

The ships were under attack. If the rain wasn't proving a hindrance to the salvagers, maybe their atmosphere suits weren't affected. If that was the case, the members of the Kratos and the Star Chaser would be helpless in a battle. If they took off from the planet, they would run into the salvagers Duncan said were orbiting above. Their only option was to fight a ground battle, especially if they had any hope of finding the Omne Occasus.

Liora pushed to her feet. She wished she had grabbed a gun. As it was, she was armed with a knife and her Damaclan training. It would have to be enough. She took off through the wormholes.

Liora reached the cavern that had become a worm tomb and darted to the left. The tunnel took her to a viewpoint near the northwest of the Gull and the rebels' Copper Crow. Several of Devren's officers hunched beneath the Gull shooting off into the storm. Spats of lighting lit up salvagers wearing what looked like some sort of protective armor over their atmosphere suits. The acid rain didn't appear to slow them at all.

Two salvagers fired and a Coalition officer fell. Liora ran back into the tunnels. She took a branching path and appeared behind the assailants.

Liora attacked without warning. Her knife sunk deep into a back where the right kidney would be. She spun to the left and buried her knife to the hilt at the base of the next attacker's skull. Before the two bodies hit the ground, Liora blocked a gun with her forearm and shoved her knife up through the bottom of another salvager's helmet.

Bullets whizzed past her. Liora dove to the right and rolled. She came back to her feet, sunk her knife into a salvager's stomach, and ducked behind his body to shield her from another volley of gunfire.

As soon as the clip ran out, Liora shoved the salvager forward, rolled after the body, and threw her knife. It shattered the glass of the last salvager's helmet and dropped him where he stood. Liora yanked the knife out on her way past and dove back into the wormhole just before a fresh cascade of bullets hit the ground.

A quick check of her atmosphere suit showed acid holes that had burned through, but it was still holding for the most part. Liora ran up the tunnel and circled around. From the trajectory, the bullets were being fired from a higher vantage point. She took a branching tunnel, darted to the right, and exited behind the hill.

Four salvagers stood on top firing down at the ships. One of them motioned. They turned their aim to a point further on. Liora ran quietly up the slope.

She hamstringed the closest shooter and slammed her knife into the chest of the second when he turned at her attack. The third salvager was ready. He dove at Liora, barreling her off her feet.

She rolled down the hill with the salvager. Her helmet rebounded off a rock and the radio crackled on.

"It's Liora!" O'Tule yelled. "Liora's alive! Fire, Straham; save her!"

"Shoot up the hill!"

"There's a pack of them to the west," Shathryn called. "Viarie's injured and we lost Officer Smythe. They've got us pinned down. I don't know how long we can hold off!"

"Hang in there, Shathryn," Devren said, his voice tense. "We've got a band headed your way. Straham, protect Liora. She's alone up there."

The salvager landed on top of Liora and knocked the knife from her hand. She punched the side of his helmet so hard she felt her knuckles split inside her glove. It knocked the salvager off. She grabbed her knife and was about to end the man's life when a bullet hit her helmet.

The impact threw her backwards and shattered the glass. Stunned, Liora managed to maintain her grip on the knife. The salvager drove a knee into her side and grappled for the weapon. Liora shook her head, trying to clear the glass while at the same time keeping her hold on the blade.

The salvager gave up trying to rip the knife free and instead shoved it toward her chest. Liora pushed back with both hands in an attempt to keep the serrated edge away. The salvager was a Calypsan. He outweighed her by at least double if not triple. The feet of his atmosphere suit had been altered to fit his hooves. His hands inside the gloves were thick, beefy, and shoved down with far more strength than Liora could defend against.

The blade pierced her atmosphere suit just below her collarbone. She let out a yell of pain.

"Liora!" Tariq yelled. "Liora, shove him up! I can't get a shot!"

Liora swung her right leg up and over, catching the Calypsan around the throat and forcing him backwards. She put her left foot against his chest and thrust him away from her.

Bullets peppered the salvager's body. He jerked to the side and fell lifeless to the ground.

A drop of acid rain landed on Liora's cheek. The burn shocked her with a fight or flight rush of adrenaline. She wiped it away quickly.

"Devren!" Shathryn yelled.

Liora forced herself to her feet and picked up the knife that had fallen to the red ground. She stumbled into the closest wormhole.

It took a moment to get her bearings.

"I have the coordinates!" Hyrin called over the headsets. "It's close to here. No wonder the salvagers are landing!"

"Oh no!" O'Tule cried, her voice crackling. "Shathryn!"

Liora ran through the tunnels. The route forced her down to the cavern and across to a series of tunnels with worm bodies she had to sidestep. She charged up the path and burst into an intense firefight.

Salvagers had Shathryn, Officer Straham, and a rebel she assumed was Viarie pinned in a shallow cave. Coalition officers shot from the hill above, but more salvagers must have landed because Liora counted at least twelve of them hiding behind the rocks across from the cave. Any time one of the three so much as peaked out, the gunshots drove them back.

"I can't get a good shot," a Coalition officer said into the headset. "They're under cover."

"Another ship is landing," Hyrin reported. "We're about to be surrounded."

"We need to get them out of there," another called.

Liora knew she couldn't take out twelve quickly enough to save Shathryn and the others. If she could find a tunnel close enough, maybe she could get them out another way.

A body lay a few feet away. The fallen salvager had an oxygen tank strapped to his back. Liora dove for his gun. Bullets struck the ground around her. She lifted the semi-automatic and fired at the other salvagers. Reaching the oxygen tank, Liora pulled it free and ducked back inside the tunnel.

She ran up to where she guessed Shathryn and the others to be. She could hear gunfire through the dirt tunnel. There was no way to gauge how thick the wall of soil was.

"Shathryn, can you hear me?" Liora called.

"Liora, is that you?"

Grateful that the headset still worked at the base of her shattered helmet, Liora replied, "Get the others as far from the back of the hole as you can. I'm going to get you out of there."

"Be careful," Straham told her. "These salvagers have us pinned."

"Viarie's going to bleed out if we don't get him out of here," Shathryn said. A small squeak sounded, then she cried, "They're closing in."

"Cover the best you can," Liora called.

"Liora, what are you doing?" Devren asked.

"Thinking like a Terrarian," Liora replied.

She shoved the oxygen tank into the dirt and ran back down the tunnel. She spun and shot from the hip. The bullet hit the top of the tank. The cylinder exploded and shot backwards, creating a gaping hole in the dirt.

Liora sprinted through the dusty air.

"What was that?" Stone demanded.

"Are you guys alright?" Liora called.

O'Tule sounded scared when she asked, "What just happened?"

"We're okay," Shathryn replied.

Tariq's voice came over the headset. "The explosion surprised them. If you move now, you might get them out."

Liora worked through the hole. Shathryn, Straham, and Viarie were covered in dirt where they huddled near the front of the small cave.

"Come this way," Liora said.

She grabbed Viarie beneath the armpits and helped Straham drag him to the tunnel. Gunshots sounded. Shathryn dropped to the ground.

"I've got him," Straham said. "Go back for Shathryn."

Liora left Viarie in the tunnel. She shot right to left, laying down fire so she could reach Shathryn.

She dropped to her stomach next to the officer. "Are you shot?"

Shathryn shook her head, but her shoulders shuddered.

"I can't do it anymore," she said. She tipped her helmeted face to look at Liora. "I'm so tired of being shot at."

Liora forced a smile. "You're almost out of it. All you need to do is go back through that hole."

Tears showed in Shathryn's eyes. "I can't do it."

"You can," Liora told her. "You've got to. You need to

help Viarie. He won't get out of here if you don't."

She hesitated, but Liora could tell the thought that someone needed her was important.

"Go help Straham. We don't have much time. I'll cover you," Liora urged.

"Shathryn, this is your captain," Devren called over the headset. "Get to Officer Straham and help him move Viarie out of there. That's an order."

Shathryn nodded. Resolve filled her face. "Got it, Captain." She pushed up to her hands and knees.

Liora fired out of the shallow cave mouth to cover her retreat. Shathryn had just reached the tunnel through the hole when the ground shook.

"It's collapsing!" Shathryn called.

Liora glanced back. The tunnel was falling quickly.

"Get out of here," she told them. "Run!"

Another rumble shook the ground. Dirt collapsed, filling the hole. Liora's heart pounded in her chest.

"Shathryn? Straham?" she called.

Bullets impacted the side of the cave, sending her back against the lip where she was protected by a tiny shelf of rock.

"We made it," Straham answered breathlessly. "We're at the mouth of the tunnel."

"We've got you covered," Tariq told them. "You're clear to the Gull. I'll meet you there. Liora, what's your plan?"

"You need to find the Omne Occasus and get it out of here. If more ships land, we'll be surrounded. We can't let them have it," she replied. "They might have me pinned, but they can't move without becoming my target. I'll hold them down so you can get out."

Silence met her words.

Devren broke it. "Liora, that's a death sentence. There're

too many of them out there. We're not leaving you."

"You don't have a choice," she pointed out. "You've got to get to the galaxy imploder."

"She's right," Stone replied from the Star Chaser. "If they reach it before we do, we've lost the war."

"I'm not leaving a crew member behind," Devren argued.

Liora fought back a wry smile. "I decline my station on the Kratos. You're no longer my captain. Go protect your crew."

"Liora," Devren tried to argue.

"Devren, they need you," she replied, cutting him off.

"It's true, Captain," Hyrin said. "If we can get the Omne Occasus out of here and let the salvagers know we have it, they'll chase us instead. It might be Liora's best chance."

"It's not a good idea," Tariq disputed.

"We don't have a choice," Devren replied. A bang sounded as though he hit something. "Fine. Let's go. Everyone to the Gull." He paused, then said, "Liora, we're coming back for you."

"When the coast is clear," she replied.

"Whether it's clear or not," Devren told her. His tone was firm.

Chapter 15

Liora strafed bullets back and forth to cover the Gull and the Star Chaser. According to Hyrin, the Omne Occasus' coordinates were in the next valley. The silhouettes of three other ships showed in the sky.

"Come on," Liora yelled. "Is that the best you've got?"

Bullets from the salvagers answered. A lighting strike hit the middle of the dirt valley so close that Liora smelled the acrid scent of electricity in the air. Strike after strike drove into the ground, shaking the earth with its ferocity.

Liora ducked, sure of what was to come.

Yells sounded along with a wind so strong Liora felt like someone was trying to pry her fingers off the rocks of the cavern she hid inside. She held on by sheer strength of will until the aftermath of the lighting subsided.

Moans and cries of pain reached Liora's ears. Realizing she had just been granted the element of surprise, she dove out of the cave and came up with her gun ready.

Liora was caught by the surreal moment.

Most of the salvagers had been thrown around by the storm. The rocks, the sand, everything looked different than it had when she blew up the hole. The acid rain had stopped briefly, a calm in the center of the storm. Red clouds swirled above them but didn't touch the ground. A shudder ran down Liora's spine and she glanced up.

A ship, a salvager's Tin Sparrow by the looks of it, was caught in the maelstrom created by the strange lighting. It was being thrown around like a child's toy. Another burst of lighting struck the craft. It twirled as it plummeted to the ground. There was no way the pilot would be able to slow its descent in time. The ship disappeared behind the next mountain of sand.

A sound caught Liora's attention. She spun to the right and shot. A scavenger grabbed his chest as he fell. Two more bullets meant two more fallen scavengers. Shots answered. Liora rolled up behind a big rock. She shot twice more and two other scavengers hit the red dirt. She was about to look out from behind the rock again when the hair on the back of her neck rose.

Liora glanced behind her just long enough to verify her suspicion. Sure enough, the eye of the storm was passing. Sparks of light crackled through the clouds that were nearly overhead once more. Liora grabbed the body of the closest scavenger and pulled him back to the cave.

She quick changed out of her atmosphere suit and dressed in the scavenger's. There was blood across the chest where she had killed him. She worried that it would mix with the knife wound in her shoulder, but given her current situation, that was something she would have to deal with later.

As lightning struck the ground and the acid rain began to fall in sheets, Liora returned from the cave wearing the protective suit and with both guns blazing. She ran to the left and shot behind each rock she passed. A few bullets replied from surprised scavengers, but they quickly dropped beneath her attack. When her guns ran out of bullets, she threw them down and picked up others.

Blood pulsed from shattered helmet shields. Any scavenger she didn't kill with a headshot received a follow-up one as soon as she reached him or her. Bullets tugged at her atmosphere suit, but by the end, she was left standing with the bodies of scavengers littering the ground around her.

Lighting flashed through the air. Liora followed the light, feeling more Damaclan than human. She wanted something else to kill and she felt the need to protect the crew of the SS Kratos. She threw down the guns and unsheathed her knife. Using the lightning as her guide, Liora ran through the crackling, surreal half-night created by the red storm.

She reached the valley sooner than she expected. Two other ships had landed beside the Gull and Star Chaser. In front of the four ships sat a half-entrenched starship of a make Liora had never seen. It rivaled the size of the Coalition's carrier ship, the Platinum Eagle. The nose of the ship was buried deep in the sand. Red dust swirled around it, burying and unearthing the craft in twirling whirlpools.

Beside it, a smaller ship similar to the Gull looked as though one side had been blasted completely open from the inside. Coalition markings and the name 'Gull-SS Cerus' had been painted on the hull.

Liora knew better than to rush into a battle blind. She made her way silently to the Kratos' Gull and hit the palm reader for the door. It slid aside and she stepped into the ship.

The door shut behind her, blocking out the swirling dust, raging wind, and blasts of the lightning strikes. After all that had happened, standing inside the Gull felt like coming back to sanity. She leaned against the wall and closed her eyes, soaking it in for the few precious moments she dared to spare.

"Who are you?"

Liora's muscles tensed and her eyes flew open. In the dim lighting she made out the form of someone spread across the middle row of seats. He had raised himself up on his elbows and was watching her warily with a gun aimed at her chest.

Liora carefully raised her hands.

"Put down the knife."

She set it slowly on the ground. When she straightened, she removed her helmet with deliberate, unhurried movements. She set the reflective dome on the ground and stood back up.

"Liora!"

Viarie, the rebel soldier she had helped Straham rescue, watched her with an expression that was half-amused, half filled with pain. "They didn't think you'd survive that cave." He looked at the blood on her atmosphere suit. "Were you shot?"

Liora gave him a half-smile. "I'm harder to kill than that. Most of this blood isn't mine."

"You've got a dozen lives," he said with an approving nod. "It's good to see you again."

"I came back for a headset. I need to know what's going

on in there," she told him.

She grabbed one of the atmosphere suits hanging near the door.

"When we landed, there were already salvagers," Viarie reported. "Your pilot Hyrin was radioing back for a while, but they've gone silent. You need to be careful."

"Thanks for the warning," she said.

She was about to take off the salvagers' suit when the rebel stopped her.

"You should wear it. Take a communicator from the Coalition headset, but keep wearing the salvager suit."

At Liora's questioning look, he explained, "Salvagers hate each other, but there's nothing they hate more than a Coalition officer. Everyone thinks you're either dead or still trapped in that hole. Use it to your advantage. Stay in disguise and take those salvagers down."

Liora gave a nod of approval. "You're a good strategist."

"Why do you think Stone keeps me around?" he asked. He gave a chuckle and winced. "That's an inside joke. I just hope he comes back so we can laugh at it again."

"They'll be alright," Liora said. "I'll get them out of there."

"And the Omne Occasus."

She nodded. "That's the goal."

"That's the only option," Viarie told her. "Without it, everything we hold dear could be lost. How easy would it be for the salvagers to destroy all galaxies that oppose them? The Milky Way Galaxy would be the first to go. Take out the Coalition base on Titus, control the homestead ships, and everyone will do their bidding."

The thought sent chills across Liora's skin.

"I won't let that happen," she promised.

Viarie nodded. He gave her a tired smile before he settled back on the chairs and disappeared from her view. "Go get them, little Damaclan warrior."

Liora grabbed a headset from the closest atmosphere suit and slipped it inside her helmet. She switched the earpiece to silent. She would be able to hear them, but they wouldn't hear anything from her end. It would help to give her the element of surprise.

She pushed the button and the door slid open. The wind shoved her from side to side, buffeting her as she crossed between the ships. The feeling of being watched tightened her muscles and her grip on the knife. She debated whether she should have grabbed a few guns from the Gull, but stealth was her strongest ally. Anyone who attempted to sneak up on her would regret it very quickly.

Someone had forced open a door half-submerged in the sand. Liora stepped into the darkness and waited a moment for her eyes to adjust. Many footprints showed down the hallway. The mismatched tread of the salvagers covered the thicker, standard sole of the Coalition. She followed them, her senses straining for any sign of salvagers.

Strange markings lined the walls in a language she had never seen before. The architecture was foreign, sharp and jagged. Some branching hallways appeared to lead to nowhere, while others trailed off so far into the darkness that she couldn't see the end. The strange construction style set her on edge. Liora couldn't help but wonder what kind of creatures had built such a ship.

Hyrin's voice came over the headset. "We've got to be close."

"How do we know they don't have it?" O'Tule asked.

"They wouldn't be fighting so hard if they did," Devren replied. "Stay alert. They might be hiding in the next corridor."

"If there is a next corridor," Shathryn said. "This place

gives me the creeps. It makes no sense."

Tariq's voice was quieter when he spoke. "Hopefully the salvagers are as confused as we are. Keep to radio silence. We don't know who might be on this frequency."

Liora wished she had some way to track them. The footprints from the sand had stopped a ways back. She was following without any way to know which of the many paths they had taken. Liora focused on the walls, wondering if there was a chance to figure out how to get to the Omne Occasus before the others.

The symbols at each corner looked vaguely familiar. She tipped her head to the side in an effort to view them differently. Her heart slowed.

The markings were similar to those of the Galian language, an older, rough tongue used by simpler races. She often heard it in the seedier planets Malivian stopped at during his circus circuit. The fliers had been printed in both languages to attract several types of crowds. If she looked at it just right, it appeared that the letters were the same, but backwards.

The Galian word for 'Control' jumped out at her. The jagged etch on the side could substitute for a direction arrow. The crude sideways N was the beginning letter for the Galian word for 'path'.

Liora ran in the direction of the jagged marks. At each hallway, she checked the row of words. Recognizing the marks for the control room became easier. She took a hallway to the left and felt the floor rise as she sprinted; two more turns, and she reached a closed door. The word for control was written to the side.

There was no doorknob, handle, or palm reader. Liora's heart pounded with urgency. Being able to help her crew depended on her getting into the room.

She scanned the words quickly. It had been a while since

she had heard the language. With Liora as the main act, Malivian's show had eventually reached the upper, better paying classes, taking him away from the low-level shows. Liora had to flip the letters in her mind, translate them from the rough Galian to the common language, and figure out what the loose meaning was.

It felt like it took way too many precious seconds before she found the word for speak.

Not sure how to pronounce the Galian word with the backwards letters, she went for the common tongue. "Open," she said aloud.

The door slid to the side.

Grateful that whatever command system that controlled the ship had been programmed using multiple languages, Liora ran into the room.

A single chair occupied the center of the bridge. There were no buttons or panels, merely screens. Liora was at a loss as to how she should proceed.

"They're up ahead," O'Tule said into the earpiece.

"Quick, cut left," Devren commanded.

"It's a dead end," Shathryn replied. "We'll be trapped."

"I don't think they have the imploder. Otherwise they would be heading straight back to their ship." Tariq's voice was quiet. "Lay low. Maybe they'll pass us."

The thought of the crew in danger spurred Liora forward.

"Control on," she said.

To her relief, the screens around her flickered to life. Instead of monitors, the images were projected so that they appeared around her. She scanned them quickly. Scenes from outside the ship and inside flickered past. Star systems and a map of galaxies she had never seen before appeared above her.

There was an image of the Gull and several scavenger

ships. To her surprise, two other Coalition ships had landed. Troops stood in front of the Gull's door, but it appeared Viarie was denying them entrance. By the looks of things, it was going to get heated very quickly.

"Internal security," she called out.

Images inside the ship appeared. She waved her hand, pushing several aside. She found Stone's crew engaged in battle at the far end of the ship. They appeared to be holding their own. Liora moved past the scene. She paused on a room with a big transparent box inside. It was the only object visible. Two orbs, one red and the other blue, glowed from the translucent material. Metal rods, glass vessels, and a temperature gauge linked the two orbs together.

Liora scanned the other images. She found Devren and his crew crouched in a dark hallway as a cluster of scavengers hurried past. They definitely appeared to be searching for something.

Liora put her hand to her headset.

"I've located the Omne Occasus," she said.

"Liora?" Tariq replied immediately.

"Where are you?" Devren asked.

"Inside the control room of the same ship you're on. I found the imploder using the security system. I can guide you there."

"Thank goodness!" Shathryn said. "I thought we were completely lost!"

"Yeah," O'Tule seconded. "It's like a maze and we're the rats, only there are people waiting to kill you around every corner. And if you find the cheese, it can kill you, too."

"Quiet," Devren said. "We don't have much time. Liora, which way should we go?"

Liora verified that the scavengers were gone, then pulled the crew's image back so she could see the hallway layout.

"Go to the left, then an immediate right. There should be a slight decline."

She watched them on the screen as she flipped through the cameras to check their path. Her heart skipped a beat.

"Hold on. There're scavengers ahead."

"How many?" Tariq asked.

"Five," Liora replied.

"I'll take care of it."

"Wait," Liora told him. "They're armed and waiting. I think they might have heard you coming."

"Even better," Tariq said.

Devren took a step forward, but Tariq shook his head. "I need to do this."

Devren nodded as if he understood.

Frustrated that she couldn't help Tariq, and sure she was watching someone she had come to care about walk to his death, Liora stared at the images. She had no idea why Devren would let his friend go on by himself. She had thought they looked out for each other like brothers; now, she wasn't so sure.

Tariq dove into the next hallway and came up shooting. Three salvagers dropped before they even realized they were under attack. One salvager managed to get off a shot, but it sunk into the wall near Tariq's head. He fired two more times, and the last two salvagers fell.

"Clear," Tariq reported.

Liora's relief was short-lived. Ten more salvagers appeared in the hallway behind Devren's crew.

"Run," she said. "They're closing in. Take a left, go straight, then say 'Open' at the door marked with the backwards Galian for Cargo."

"Backwards Galian?" Devren asked as they ran.

"It took me a while to figure it out," Liora replied, "But

the writing on the walls makes sense once you realize the edges are straight instead of looped, and backwards."

Hyrin paused to study one of the markers on a branching hallway. "I see it!" he said excitedly.

Tariq grabbed his arm and pushed him forward. "We don't have time. Figure it out later."

"That's way too complicated," Shathryn complained as they ran. "Why couldn't they keep the galactic imploder on a nice, easy to navigate Sparrow or Finch? We'd be done by now."

Gunshots rang out behind the crew.

"Open!" Devren shouted at the door.

It slid to the side. Tariq returned fire, covering for his crew as they ducked into the safety of the cargo room.

"How do you close this thing?" Tariq asked into the headset.

The door slid shut.

"Oh," he said.

Pounding sounded on the door as the salvagers fought to get in. Tariq stood at the entrance, ready to take them on should they figure out the key to opening it.

"So that's what an Omne Occasus looks like." Hyrin's voice was filled with awe.

Chapter 16

Everyone stared at the box. It was huge. At least two of the crew would be required to lift it.

"It looks like it'll explode if you touch it," O'Tule said.

"Great. Just what we need. An exploding box." Shathryn's sarcasm was colored with fear.

"It won't explode," Hyrin told them. He examined the box closer. "The vials have to break, allowing the energy from each orb to mix." He paused, then sighed. "I wish I knew what the orbs were made out of. It'd be easier to disarm it."

Metallic clangs hit the door, but it stayed closed against the bullets the salvagers used.

"If we can't disarm it, what do we do?" Straham asked.

"Take it with us."

Everyone stared at Devren.

"It's the only way. If we can't disarm it here, we need to give Hyrin time to figure it out. Getting the Omne Occasus to the Kratos is our best chance to deactivate it and end the threat. That's the only way we'll lose the scavengers' interest and protect our galaxies."

Gazes turned to Tariq. Liora realized they viewed Tariq's opinion with as much respect as their captain's.

He studied the imploder with distrust clear on his face.

"Are you sure you're going to be able to disable this thing?" he asked Hyrin.

"I'm not positive, but I'd much rather try than let it fall into the wrong hands," Hyrin replied.

Tariq nodded. "As much as I don't like the thought of this thing on board the Kratos, Dev's right. Let's get it up."

"How do you plan to get out the door?" Shathryn asked.

"I'll create a diversion," Liora told them.

"You shouldn't come over here. There's too many of them," Tariq said.

"I know how to get around this ship. I'll be fine," Liora replied. "Besides, how else are you going to get out of there? We can't risk them shooting the imploder."

Liora jogged down the hallway. Looking through the screens had made navigating easier. It wasn't long before she heard the sounds of commotion near the cargo room.

Liora crept up to the junction. The salvagers looked as though they were prepared to wait the Kratos crew out. With only one exit from the cargo room, it wasn't a bad idea. Liora debated how to catch their attention without getting herself filled with bullet holes.

She glanced down at her atmosphere suit and an idea began to form in her mind.

Liora grabbed the chest of the scavenger suit where it was bleeding and staggered into the view of the scavengers. Several of them hurried up to her. She was grateful the reflective shield hid her face from view.

"It's a decoy," she said, stumbling against the wall. "They have the imploder. They ran that way." She pointed down another hall she knew led to a dead end.

"What are you doing?" Tariq demanded. "Are you crazy?"

Liora kept quiet in the hopes that the scavengers would believe her.

"They've got the imploder!" a scavenger said. "We've got to stop them before they reach the ship!"

Several scavengers ran up the hallway.

"You're coming with us," the one who had spoken said.

"I'll slow you down," Liora protested. She had hoped being wounded would make them leave her behind, but apparently chivalry did indeed exist among thieves.

"We'll carry you back to your ship," the first replied. "Come on. Help me."

At his command, a scavenger ducked under her other arm. They jogged after their comrades down the hall.

"Now," Liora said.

"What was that?" the lead scavenger asked.

"Open," she heard Devren say.

"Uh, now we'll stop them," she continued, making her voice tight as if she was in pain.

"Just hold on. We'll get you medical care as soon as the imploder is found," the leader promised.

Liora wished he was cruel so she could kill him without remorse. Instead, he actually seemed to care about his fellow scavengers. It was the last thing she had expected.

"I see it," Hyrin said with excitement over the headset. "Liora's right! Backwards Galian! Who would have thought?"

"So where do we go?" Tariq asked with a hint of impatience.

"Right," Hyrin said. "We need to take the route marked like this. It's a rough translation of loading dock."

"We'll take your word for it," Shathryn replied.

Liora could hear the labored breathing of the crew members who carried the box. She wished she was back inside the control room so she could guide them safely. The thought of a bullet hitting the Omne Occasus was a scary one.

The scavengers turned down the next hallway and reached the dead end.

"Hey," one of them exclaimed. "She lied to us!"

Liora unsheathed her knife and stabbed it into the shoulder of the scavenger on her right. He stumbled against the wall and she landed on her knees. Another scavenger lifted his gun. She threw her knife. It sunk deep into his chest. Liora dove at him, ripped out the knife as he fell, and rolled over his body to plunge the knife into a third man.

Bullets followed her as she fought to survive. Wherever she landed, another scavenger was there. Time seemed to slow with the falling bodies. She used their forms as shields and turned their own guns against them. Liora's Damaclan training took over entirely until she became a spectator in her own body, watching her hands break the neck of one salvager and then use the helmet of another to bash in the skull of a third.

The violent rush died away to leave her standing amid the bodies. It was the second time she had been left to view the effects of her wrath. She felt disgusted by the savagery she was able to channel, and loathed the blood that dripped from the fingertips of her gloves.

It took Liora a moment to realize that the leader of the scavengers was still alive. For some reason, she hadn't killed him. His helmet was off and he stood watching her, his eyes wide with shock and horror at the sight of his men and women broken and piled at her feet.

"What are you?" he asked.

Liora pulled off her borrowed helmet with numb fingers that left streaks of red across the shield.

"Just a girl?" he said as though he barely dared to believe it. "My daughter's around your age. You can't be older than twenty-five."

Liora shook her head, but couldn't bring herself to speak.

"Liora, get out of there," she heard Tariq say over the headset of the helmet in her hands.

"You shouldn't be able to do that," the scavenger continued. "You killed them." His eyes filled with tears. "All of them. They were good people."

"Good people have to die," she said softly. It was a phrase Obruo used to say when she questioned him about killing. She had hated learning the art of death. She would rather grow things the way her mother did in the garden on their roof. Instead, Obruo had forced her to train in the Damaclan art, and he had never failed to hide the hope that the training would kill her.

"You're wrong," the scavenger leader said with heartache in his voice. "You're so very wrong."

He lunged toward her with his hands outstretched. Liora sunk her knife into his stomach. At the same time, something pierced her skin where the side of her throat met her shoulder. She shoved the leader back and pulled the small, pointed object from her neck. It looked like a thorn and the end of it glistened darkly.

193

The scavenger slid down the wall holding his stomach tight with lifeblood flowing out between his fingers.

"You're finished," he said. "Your days of killing are at an end."

Fire ran from Liora's neck in both directions. A level of pain she had never felt before flooded her veins.

"What was that?" she demanded.

It was too late. The scavenger's eyes glazed over. He slumped to one side, joining his companions in death.

Liora shoved her helmet back on.

"They're everywhere!" Hyrin said. "How do we get around them?"

"They're Coalition," Shathryn pointed out. "Shouldn't we just give them the imploder and have it done with?"

"No," Devren answered firmly. "We can't let it fall into the wrong hands."

"Are you saying the Coalition is the wrong hands?" Straham asked.

"Possibly," Devren said. "Until we know their motive for certain, we need to get it as far away from everyone as we can."

"That's treason," O'Tule said with worry in her voice.

"It's survival," Devren replied. "With this kind of power, we can't make a hasty decision. We need time to figure things out."

Liora stumbled up the hallway.

"How do we get the Coalition to leave the Gull alone?" Hyrin asked.

Stone's voice came over the intercom. "Like this."

The sound of gunfire and people yelling answered.

"He's shooting at them!" Shathryn said.

"They're scattering," Tariq called. "Now's our chance."

Liora broke into a shambling half-run. Every heartbeat felt

like it pushed more of the thorn's toxin through her system. Pain pulsed against her lungs and her heart. Each nerve ending burned with fire. She didn't want to be left behind. The thought of staying in the foreign ship filled with scavengers terrified her as much as the pressure closing off her throat.

Liora collapsed against a wall. Her legs stopped working. She felt like she was suffocating. She threw off her helmet and curled into a fetal position. Everything hurt. The light piercing her eyes felt like acid rain burning her retinas. The floor against her side punished her body with a thousand daggers. Every breath was torture.

Liora realized something in that moment. Since losing her mother and the rest of her clan, she had thought the worst thing was to live when her loved ones had died. She had survived life with bitterness driving her to the next danger, and when she was imprisoned in Malivian's circus, she had hoped it would be the key to her eventual demise.

But now that death was an impending reality, Liora realized that she wanted to live. The worst thing would be to throw her life away without realizing her full potential. She wanted to see a sun again and truly appreciate its warmth. She wanted to fly in a spaceship once more and really feel the wonder of racing through the stars. Most of all, Liora wanted to love.

The emotion that had been so lacking in her life since her mother died made her heart ache with such fierceness it kept her mind alert despite the pain. She needed to remember what it felt like to love something and fight for it, to have a purpose, a drive, to belong to something or someone.

"Tariq."

Liora pushed the name with all of her remaining strength. She didn't know how far she could reach, or if he was even open enough to hear her. In the haze that filled her mind, she couldn't even say why it was his name that she called, but that was the name that stayed center in her thoughts when everything else fell away in the darkness.

"Liora?" his voice crackled over the headset near her stomach.

She pulled the helmet close with curled fingers, but couldn't make her mouth open.

"Liora, where are you?" Desperation touched Tariq's voice.

Liora couldn't keep her eyes open. She pushed toward him wordlessly, calling to him with anything she had left.

"Liora, I can feel you." He sounded confused, but determined. "I'm going to find you. Don't give up."

Liora did everything she could to keep her focus centered on him. The pain throbbed through her body in debilitating waves.

She heard salvagers closing in. After what she did to the last group, they would kill her for sure.

Hands grabbed her shoulders and forced her roughly to her back.

"She's the one from Mattin's camera."

"She killed them all."

"Is she dead?"

"She looks dead."

"There's one way to know for sure."

Liora forced her eyes open just enough to see the gun pointed at her forehead. A finger was tightening on the trigger. Liora couldn't move. The need to fight back tightened her muscles, sending more of the scorching poison through her locked limbs.

The slight mechanical clicks of the bullet preparing to fire sounded like cannon explosions to her ears. She wanted to scream, to fight, to defend herself, but she was trapped in a cage worse than any she had ever experienced. She was going to die without the ability to fight back.

A gunshot tore through the air. Liora closed her eyes, sure she would feel the impact.

Instead, a body hit the ground near her head. Shouts echoed up and down the hallway. More gunfire sounded. The impact of bodies falling shook Liora. Every sound was heightened, every shout painful. In her mind, Tariq had been shot and killed. There were so many scavengers, Coalition officers, and rebels. There was no way one man could get through so many. She shouldn't have asked him to come. He would die trying to save her.

A hand touched Liora's face.

"Open your eyes." Tariq's voice was soft and pleading. "Come on, Liora. You can survive anything. You've got to."

Liora wished she could tell him she was fine, but she couldn't even muster the strength to do something as simple as look at him.

Tariq's hands ran quickly over her body. "What happened to you?" he said, his voice quiet as though he spoke only to himself. "What could possibly take you down after all this?"

His hands paused at the knife wound in her shoulder. He moved on, checking the wound where the borrowed armor showed blood, but underneath there was nothing.

He opened her left hand and his actions stopped entirely. "No."

It was the only word he said. He slid his hands beneath her knees and back and lifted her as though she weighed nothing. Her knife fell out of her weak grip and clattered to the ground. Tariq turned, about to leave it. He muttered something in a language Liora didn't recognize and lowered her carefully to the ground once more. She heard him scoop up her knife and felt him slide it into the sheath on her thigh before he picked her up again.

"Let's go," Tariq said to someone else.

Liora's head lolled against his shoulder. She fought against the cloud of pain and fire, but it stole her breath and consumed her thoughts. His footsteps were the last thing she knew before the darkness won.

Chapter 17

Liora drifted in and out of consciousness. There were times she was aware of being on the bed in the Kratos' medical wing, and others where she had no idea of where she was or what had happened. In all cases, she couldn't move, speak, or give any indication she was conscious. Her mind floated, numb and muted in the cloud of medicine Tariq had put into her IV to chase away the worst of the pain.

"How is she?" Liora heard Devren's voice break through the haze.

"The same," came Tariq's short response. He sounded

sullen and angry. "We shouldn't have let her distract them alone."

"She doesn't exactly take orders," Devren replied.

"Why are you smiling?" Tariq snapped.

"Because she's still alive. You said yourself that a human would have died by now. It's her Damaclan blood that's keeping her alive."

"Is that supposed to be ironic?"

Devren let out a sigh. "Perhaps. Fate is fickle. Who really says what allows someone to live and others to die?"

"My hands." Tariq's words were said without inflection.

"What's that supposed to mean? You'd let her die?" Devren asked, his tone disbelieving. "Didn't you take an oath or something when you become a doctor?"

"Yes," Tariq answered, "And no, I wouldn't let her die. Even if I didn't take an oath. There's something…" His voice faded away.

"What is it?" Devren pressed.

Tariq was quiet for a few minutes.

Devren waited as if he knew better than to push his friend too far.

Tariq finally let out a breath. "She's covered in scars, Dev."

"She's a Damaclan," Devren replied with a hint of confusion in his voice as if he didn't understand what Tariq was getting at.

"They aren't normal scars," Tariq finally said. "I've seen Damaclan bodies before. They haven't been abused like she has. My equipment picked up several broken bones that were never properly treated. She has stab wounds, blunt injuries, and compression fractures all over her body."

"Was that a part of the training?" Devren asked, his voice quieter.

"I don't think so. Someone has been cruel far past the

point of discipline. Injuries like that are intentional, meant to hurt." His voice lowered. "Meant to break someone."

It was Devren's turn for silence. When he spoke, his tone was sure. "If she pulls through, she'll always have a place here on the Kratos. No matter what your differences, I'm not sending her out to fend for herself after all she's done for us."

Tariq's reply was muffled as the sharpness of Liora's thoughts faded away. She felt warm and cold at the same time, a feeling she remembered from a time long in her past.

Liora was young again and held another blade in her hand. This one was cold and curved, serrated at the tip to cause the most damage.

She stood in a ring she knew all too well. Members of the clan sat in silence around the two circles. Rain poured on the reflective metal roof, creating a dull roar in the background.

Liora watched the boy across the ring. She knew Vogun. He liked to inflict pain and watch weaker opponents squirm. She hated him. The golden child of the clan, Vogun was already being groomed by Obruo to inherit the title of chieftain despite the fact that the right should be Liora's. Her mother held the strongest blood next to Obruo, and even as a mongrel child, Liora should have been next in line to take the title of chief.

Vogun knew it was true, and he hated her for it. He never passed up the chance to remind her in little ways of his clever cruelty. She often found venomous snakes in her bed and had learned to never slide her feet beneath the covers without checking first. There were needles embedded in her breakfast chair, and poisonous bugs in her shoes. She never picked up her training gloves without checking them first for shards of glass.

Obruo had pitted them against each other for the past twelve years of her life. It was fitting that they should fight each other in the final battle.

For a Damaclan, receiving the clan tattoo was the highest honor a warrior could earn. Only four children would win the honor. Eight were of the age to compete. In order to earn the tattoo, a Damaclan child of twelve years must take his or her first life in the ring. Whoever lost in the battle for the clan marks would also lose his or her life at the hand of the stronger combatant.

Vogun twirled the double swords he had chosen for his weapon. As an honor to half of her bloodline, Liora had been given the choice of weapons first. She chose the knife for which her ancestors were known. Her mother had nodded proudly from the sidelines, approving of her decision.

Usually, a rival picked the same weapon as a matter of integrity, but when Vogun reached for the swords, Obruo had nodded his acceptance. Liora stood facing her rival armed with only a knife and her skills from years of training and discipline far harsher than any the other Damaclan child had experienced.

Vogun stood a head taller. Born under the first moon, the sign of strength, he had been given choice food and schooling his entire life. Liora had been born at the end of the season under the moon of the nomad, a bad omen for Damaclan because the harsh singe weather and the poor diet due to the lack of plant life from the strangling sunrays often killed a child before the year's end.

The clan had ignored her because they thought she would die from the elements, but Liora had survived despite the odds. Eventually even Obruo had to accept that she was around to stay until he could come up with a plan to get rid of her without it appearing as though he was attempting to kill his mongrel daughter outright. The blood of her queen mother was worth more than the half-lineage she had missed out on from his line.

Vogun grinned, revealing the tooth he had broken jumping into the river on a dare. He gave his proud, taunting smile often to display the symbol of his courage. Liora thought it represented his stupidity instead. Who jumped into a river everyone knew was lined with rocks when the deep space below the falls was shallow during the singe?

"Time to prove I'm better than you once and for all," Vogun said.

Liora kept silent. Vogun liked to boast. She knew her silence unnerved him.

"Come on, then, mongrel," he taunted. "Show me what you can do with your little knife."

Liora had never killed anything. Vogun and many of the other boys and girls often shot the small bats and feathered swimmers because they said it strengthened their souls. Liora couldn't see how death brought power to another. She felt like it showed weakness instead. Obruo said it was because her human side was too soft. It made her frail and pathetic like the headless creatures the children lined up proudly in front of their houses. Her refusal to add to their collections was another slight the chief took personally.

Vogun attacked first as she knew he would. While he beat her more often than not, Vogun had no patience. His swiftness was counterbalanced by his rashness, and the grace of his strike often showed the twitch of a too-eager hand.

Liora blocked the first sword and spun to the right to avoid the second. She lunged with the knife, but Vogun was too fast. He dodged and his longer arms allowed him to lay her arm open before she could pull back.

"First blood," Obruo noted.

Out of the corner of her eye, Liora saw the nods of approval from the clan. The boy Obruo had chosen to be their chieftain was proving worthy of the honor.

Liora blocked another blow. Vogun's attack was so strong the block rattled Liora to the bone. Her hand went numb and she almost dropped the knife. Vogun took advantage of her weakness to slice her leg up to the knee before he danced out of range.

"I'll cut you to ribbons," he taunted. "I'll fillet you piece by piece, the death of prey for the daughter of a human."

Liora breathed in through her nose and out through her mouth, reminding herself not to react to the boy's words.

Vogun charged again. He leaped into the air and spun, bringing both swords down at her in succession.

Liora blocked the first blade, but knew she wouldn't be able to avoid the second. Instead, before the blade could reach her, she dropped to the ground and spun, kicking his leg out from under him the instant it met the ground.

Vogun fell backwards with a surprised huff. He raised a sword the moment he hit the floor, but Liora knocked it aside with her knife. She put the weapon to his throat. It took a moment for her to realize that she had her opponent pinned, defenseless.

The clan was silent as they awaited the final blow. Liora could feel their shock. Up to that point, Vogun had been unbloodied. The fact that he now lay beneath Liora's knife was hard for her to accept; the speed with which it had happened left everyone stunned.

Yet the laws were as strict as they were merciless. Any child bested in the battle for clanship was to be slain by the warrior who defeated him or her. If Liora let Vogun live despite the laws, he would be cast out. He would die in the singe weather if he didn't end his own life out of shame.

Liora glanced at Obruo. The chief's face was tight, his lips a severe line in his tattooed face. It was obvious he hadn't anticipated the outcome. Suspicions had lingered in the back of Liora's mind that Obruo forced the decision for her to fight Vogun, the strongest child in the clanship battle. The suspicions were answered in the way he gripped the railing that ran around the circle, his knuckles white as though he wanted to tear it away and strangle her.

Liora turned her gaze to her mom. Tenieva gave a small nod. There was a light of pride in her gaze that didn't fade even when Obruo followed Liora's gaze to his wife. Tenieva had fought for her when she was young, and now Liora proved that her battle against Obruo had been worth it. Liora knew what she had to do to claim her blood right and receive the clan markings.

Vogun's eyes watered when Liora drew her knife through his skin. Dark red blood spilled over her hand. She would never forget the warm gush, nor the way his breath gurgled in his throat. He tried to fight even with his neck slit, but she held him down. His struggles became weaker; eventually, his eyes closed and his head tipped to one side.

A sob from Vogun's mother echoed through the building before she could stifle it. Though she had a right to her sorrow, it was the duty of the clan to be proud of the child who had survived the last trial. His mother would be punished for her outward display.

Tears fell down Liora's cheeks. When she met Obruo's gaze, his eyes narrowed at the show of weakness. His mongrel daughter may have killed the clan's strongest warrior, but she still showed the emotions of a human. She couldn't help herself. As much as she hated Vogun, and as hard as he had made her life, killing him was something she never had imagined she would have to do. Training to kill was completely different than taking an actual life.

Obruo then did something no chief had ever done. Instead

of applauding Liora's victory and leading his clan in celebrating her status as their newest member, he rose and walked away. The cement and metal aisle swallowed him into the shadows; his disapproval remained heavy in his wake.

Tenieva was the first to clap. It didn't take long for the clan to join her. As much as Liora's victory was a surprise, they applauded their newest warrior as tradition dictated. A few of the more accepting Damaclans shouted her name. Liora heard it through the hum of shock in her mind.

Liora's hands shook. She gripped the knife harder to keep from dropping it. The blade, her hands, and Vogun's chest were covered in dark, sticky liquid. She realized she was still sitting on him, pinning him down even though he could no longer move. Through sheer strength of will, Liora rose to her feet and moved away from Vogun's body.

As soon as she reached the outer ring, the clan descended on her, congratulating her and patting her shoulders. She was led by her mother to the white room where the clan grandmother kept the tattoo equipment. She was vaguely aware of the burn of the needle behind her ear as she received her first tattoo, the symbol of her clan. The symbols continued down her throat to her chest.

She didn't flinch. The burn felt good. It chased away the vision of Vogun's lifeless eyes and the way his pulse had faded beneath her fingertips. She breathed in the pain and relished the way it cut directly to her core where her soul ached.

When she was done, Liora looked at herself in the mirror. The clan grandmother had tattooed her warrior marks down her arms, the spiked curls like Gaul horns below her collarbones, the black and red marks down to her wrists from completing the training, and the red band on her right arm that said she was her mother's daughter and announced the

206

royal blood in her veins.

Liora felt like herself, and yet as if she stared at a stranger at the same time. She didn't know where the old Liora ended and the new one began. She had reached her goal. She had proven to Obruo that she was worthy to be a member of his clan. Yet he had been absent at the tattooing even though his presence was also a tradition, and she would never forget the disappointment on his face when she drove her knife through Vogun's neck instead of letting him do the same to her.

Liora left the room with her tattoos wrapped in the traditional white cloth. The blood that showed through was a sign of her new life. Her wounds were tended and she received smiles and praises from clan members who had never so much as acknowledged her existence before that day. It all felt surreal and fake.

"Why did I do it if it doesn't matter?" she had asked her mother that night.

"Of course it matters," Tenieva had replied. "You're a member of the clan now. I'm so proud of you."

Liora put a hand to her chest. The slight burn of the fresh tattoos answered. "But I'm not a part of the clan in here. I'm still the same."

Her mother had smiled at her. It was the image Liora would keep with her for the rest of her life. The nomad moon shone through the window, lighting her mother's dark hair and brushing her face with gentle fingers. The pride in her mother's eyes said more than a thousand words. What Obruo or anyone else thought didn't matter. Liora had done what her mother had said she would since she was born. She deserved to be a member of the clan, and now she had proven it.

"Wear those tattoos with pride, my daughter," Tenieva said. She tucked Liora's dark hair behind her ear so she could get a better look at the tattoos down her neck. "You deserve each and every one of these. Live your life knowing that."

"I will," Liora promised.

Tenieva hugged her gently. "You're a part of the clan now, Liora. You can choose a new name if you would like."

Liora knew what her answer would be as soon as her mother asked. "I'd like to be known as Liora Day."

"After your father?" Tenieva's eyebrows were raised in surprise. "Are you sure?"

Liora nodded.

"It'll separate you from the clan," her mother warned.

Liora lifted a shoulder. "It doesn't bother me."

"It makes you stronger," Tenieva replied, saying the words she had repeated for as far back as Liora could remember.

It was the chant Liora recited in her head whenever Vogun or the others picked on her. It was what drove her on when Obruo's cruelty got out of hand.

"I'm stronger than they are," Liora said.

She went to sleep that night with the knife in her hand and a small smile on her face.

Two days later, her entire clan was killed by the nameless ones.

***

The next time Liora awoke, she could see a form out of the corner of her eye.

Tariq was hunched over the bed, his elbows on his knees and his face in his hands. It looked as though he had waited there so long he had fallen to sleep.

Liora couldn't force her voice to work, so she merely watched him.

Asleep, the creases of worry in Tariq's forehead had faded. It made him look younger, less filled with the cares of life and loss. His black hair swept across part of his face, clinging to the scruff of the shadowed stubble he hadn't shaved. The backs of his hands were scarred with the nicks and gouges of a fighter. As he slept, his eyebrows pulled together slightly in a way that made Liora want to smooth the creases between them.

He looked so handsome in that moment that Liora wanted to raise a hand to his cheek to see if he was real.

The thought surprised her. Tariq may have saved her life, but her clan was responsible for the death of his wife and child. He would never forgive her, and her presence was no doubt a reminder of the never-ending pain in his life.

So why, then, had he saved her? As he had said in his conversation with Devren, his hands were the key to her life or death. He could have left her to die, yet he had carried her despite the danger to himself. He had rescued a Damaclan when he could have walked away without regrets.

Liora closed her eyes and let the darkness return to chase the confusing questions from her mind.

Chapter 18

When Liora next awoke, someone had turned down the lights in the medical ward. The quiet beeps of the heart monitor was the only sound in the room. She opened and closed her hands. Relief flooded her when her fingers responded. Her toes moved at her command, and she found that she could lift her arms without pain.

Liora pushed up carefully. It felt strange to do so without the accompanying fiery agony. She could breathe and swallow again. Even the pain from where the thorn had pierced her neck had faded.

She thought of Devren's words. The human side of her would have died from the poison; her Damaclan blood had saved her life. Yet again, the strength of being a Damaclan refused to let her go; and once more, despite everything, she was grateful for her mother's blood that pounded through her veins.

Someone had cleaned and folded the clothing she had received from the Zamarian woman on Gaulded Zero Twenty-one. The simple act touched Liora. She slipped out of the medical gown and set it on the bed. She reached for her clothes, and winced at the answering pain in her shoulder. A glance showed a tidy row of stitches where the knife had stabbed her just below the collarbone. Liora drew the clothes on and noticed that someone had stitched the matching tear in the cloth as well.

Liora walked up the hallway. By the lighting, it was nightfall. The ship's timers gave impressions of days and nights to help the crew stay on a regular circadian rhythm. Judging from the sounds of snoring from a few of the rooms she passed, they had been sleeping for some time.

Liora paused at one of O'Tule's paintings. It showed mountains lit by the orange and red rays of sunrise. The river below was green and animals Liora had never seen before grazed in the rising sunlight. The scene held peace and affirmation. She wanted to go there and view it with her own eyes. Her fingers trailed along the dried paint, feeling as much as seeing the beauty.

An angry voice caught Liora's attention. She left the painting and followed it to the bridge. When she put her palm on the reader, the door slid silently open.

Officer Duncan's eyes lit up and he gave her a wide smile. At his motion, she stood near him and watched the enraged face on the screen.

Colonel Lefkin's eyes sparked as he spoke. "Going dark isn't the best decision, Captain Metis. Timing is crucial. You need to deliver the Omne Occasus to Titus as soon as possible. If anyone intercepts your ship, you and the crew will be held in contempt for exposing the weapon to danger. Respond to this transmission as soon as you receive it. That is an order, Captain."

The screen went dark.

"There are five more where that came from," Hyrin informed Devren and Tariq who watched the screen with matching frustrated expressions. "Would you like to view them?"

"No," both men said at the same time.

"He called it a weapon," Devren said.

Tariq shook his head. "That's what I'm afraid of."

"I take it running away with the imploder hasn't exactly gone over well," Liora ventured.

Both men spun around. Devren's face broke into a wide smile while Tariq watched her as though searching for signs that she was still unwell.

"It's so good to see you up," Devren said, walking to her. "It sounds like it was touch and go there for a while."

It looked as though he wanted to hug her. Liora had received two hugs in her entire life; one from her mother after she had earned her tattoos, and the other had been from an Artidus woman with three arms from the circus because the woman said she could sense Liora's troubled past.

Liora didn't know how to accept the hug. It ended with her standing awkwardly while Devren gave her a cautious hug that concluded in a shoulder pat.

"Uh, thank you," she said, answering with an uneasy half-smile.

She glanced up to find Tariq watching them. She swore

there was the ghost of a smile on his lips at the awkward exchange.

As strange as the hug had been, it felt even more peculiar to be in the same room with the person who had saved her life. He had carried her from death. There was no doubt in her mind that she would be dead if he hadn't appeared. The bullet would have been fired. Her life, as little as it might be worth, meant a great deal to her, something she hadn't realized until it was about to be taken. The fact that without Tariq, she wouldn't have been standing there, was something she didn't know how to deal with.

A warning siren rang, saving Liora from the need to speak. Immediately, Hyrin's drowsy face appeared on the monitor.

"What's that?" he asked as he attempted to rub the sleep from his eyes.

"The monitor says 'Approaching Ship'," Devren told him.

Hyrin's tired expression vanished immediately. "I'll be right there."

"I'll head back to the med bay," Tariq said. "Let me know if you need anything." He paused on his way out the door and nodded at Liora. "I'm glad you're feeling better."

Liora watched him walk down the hallway until the door shut, blocking her view. She was grateful he spared her a hug. She didn't know how she would survive another one.

Devren glanced behind him. "Duncan, all hands on deck."

"Yes, Captain," Duncan replied.

He pushed a button on his console and a pulsing horn sounded down the hallways.

"All bridge members are required at their stations," he announced.

It wasn't hard to imagine snores changing to exclamations and crew members jumping out of beds. Within minutes, Shathryn, O'Tule, and Straham appeared at the door. The girls gave Liora hugs and exclaimed how good it was to see her. Liora took the hugs equally as awkwardly as she had Devren's. Straham looked as though he didn't know whether to hug her or shake her hand. He settled for a combination half-hug shoulder pat. She was glad the situation finally took their attention away so she could sit in her seat against the wall and pretend things were normal, or as normal as her unplanned position as an officer aboard a starship could be.

"There's two ships, Captain," Hyrin reported. His sideways eyelids blinked rapidly in his anxiety. "They just appeared through the Dakota transporter. One has Coalition markings."

"And the other?" Devren asked.

Hyrin brought the image up on the screen. It was Stone's ship from planet F One Zero Four of the Cetus Dwarf Galaxy.

"How'd they find us?" O'Tule asked.

"I'm not sure," Hyrin replied. "But Stone's trying to contact you."

"Put him through," Devren answered.

Stone's face appeared on the screen. "Captain Metis," he said with a respectful nod. "Yours is a hard ship to find."

"Yet it seems you found us," Devren replied. "Can I inquire as to why?"

Stone's amiable smile vanished. "Let's not play games, Captain. We both know what you carry aboard the Kratos. Frankly, I'm grateful you have it and the scavengers don't. I have to ask myself why Coalition ships are intent on combing the galaxy with pictures of your craft flashing on every mercenary's board." His gaze was intent when he said, "I can only assume you, like me, feel it's best to keep such a power away from all sides until you can deactivate it completely. Am I right?"

Devren hesitated as if he debated whether or not to trust the rebel. He glanced at his crew. His eyes rested on Duncan last. The older man gave an approving nod. The bands in his ears moved with the motion.

Devren turned his attention back to Stone. "Yes, you're correct."

"Captain, there are two more ships," Hyrin announced. "They're scavengers."

Before Devren could reply, Hyrin's face paled. "Three mercenary ships have just arrived through the transporter."

"You're in trouble," Stone stated. "I can help."

"Why should I trust you?" Devren asked.

"Two more Coalition ships, Captain," Hyrin reported. "I don't know how they're energizing the Dakota transporter. It should need to recharge."

"They must have portable power cells," Straham replied. "Those aren't cheap."

The images of the ships crowded across the side screen. Cannons fired from one of the Coalition ships at a scavenger vessel. Several other ships opened fire.

"The ships are fighting," Hyrin announced even though they could all see it. "Should we join in?"

"No; hold back," Devren ordered. "The Kratos can't take many more hits."

"You don't have any allies," Stone replied. "You've got to trust someone."

Devren kept his eyes on the monitor. "We've got ourselves in a bit of a bind."

"What if I told you I have a carrier not too far from here?" Stone asked.

"A carrier?" Devren repeated. He and Hyrin exchanged surprised glances.

Stone's smile returned. "I don't suppose you remember the

story of the Albatross."

"There's no way," Hyrin breathed.

Liora leaned over to Duncan. "What's the Albatross?" she asked the officer quietly.

"The Diamond Albatross is the biggest ship the Coalition ever made," Duncan whispered back. "It was named the SS Atlas. Years ago, on its virgin voyage, the Atlas disappeared, vanished, poof." He opened his worn hands. "Personnel, officers, and basic crew gone without a trace. The Coalition couldn't explain it, so they tried to cover it up. It's considered the biggest blunder they ever made."

"You're saying you know where it is?" Devren asked.

Stone nodded.

"Why would we go to a Coalition ship when we're running from them in the first place?" Shathryn asked as though she couldn't keep silent any longer.

"It's empty."

Stone's words made everyone pause.

"What about the crew?" Devren asked.

Stone shook his head. "I have no idea. When we found it, there was no crew, no message, and no sign on monitors or logs that they'd ever been there."

His words sent a shiver down Liora's spine. By the looks on the other crew members' faces, the news shocked them all.

"And you think we should hide there?" Devren pressed.

Hyrin let out a low whistle.

"Captain, that's a bad idea," Shathryn protested. "There's no way I'm setting foot on some empty ghost ship. Let the Coalition do what they want with us. It won't be worse than whatever haunts the Atlas."

"It will be worse."

All gazes shifted to Stone again. The older man's

expression was serious.

"It will be worse," he repeated. "Trust me on that. You're on the run from your alliance. You're a traitor." He paused, then said, "Face it. Finding the Omne Occasus has made you a rebel to your precious Coalition."

"You take that back!" Shathryn yelled.

O'Tule and Hyrin fought to keep her away from the screen. She struggled in their arms.

"We'll never be Revolutionaries," she shouted. "We're Coalition through and through!"

"No, we're not."

Straham's quiet words stole Shathryn's protest in a way Hyrin and O'Tule's attempts to calm her couldn't.

"Take it back," she pleaded, but her voice was heartbroken and her purple hair frazzled.

Straham shook his head. "Captain, if I can be so bold." At Devren's nod, he continued with his eyes on the screen of battling ships, "The Coalition wants that imploder for their own reasons. It sounds like they've gone so far as to send mercenaries after us."

At Shathryn's sounds of protest, Straham raised a hand. "Hear me out. Captain Metis," he swallowed, then said as if it was painful, "the *late* Captain Metis, often said he would rather take the right way over the easy way. In this instance, turning the imploder over to the Coalition is the easy way. We can let them take the machine, pretend we don't know it exists, and go on our merry path. Then, someday, somewhere in the Macrocosm, a galaxy disappears. It vanishes like the Atlas, but instead of a single Albatross, it's a network of planets, stars, and lives." His voice quieted. "And you will know at that moment that you could have stopped it from happening."

His words were met with thick silence.

Straham ran a hand through his short gray hair. "I, for one, would like to choose the right way over the easy way and make sure the Omne Occasus is destroyed forever. Let the pieces fall where they may."

"I agree," Officer O'Tule said after a moment.

"Me, too," Hyrin agreed.

Duncan stood. "Count me in."

Liora rose as well. She didn't speak, but she knew she didn't have to.

All eyes focused on Shathryn. Stone watched quietly, his expression pensive as he waited for the crew of the Kratos to make their decision.

Shathryn blew out a breath and threw up her hands. "Fine. Count me in. Captain Metis said he would haunt me from his grave if he ever died, and now I guess he is." She raised her voice, "You win, Captain. We're going to be rebels. You happy?"

Devren nodded at her. "I think he is." He turned his attention to Stone. "Alright. We're in. We'll hide at the Albatross."

"Your ship's in need of repairs; it's quite the journey. Can you make it to a Gaulded?"

Devren nodded. "We'll make it. We'll have to disguise the Kratos with so many mercs out looking for her. We'll sneak in and out. Where should we meet you?"

Hyrin jotted down the coordinates.

"I suppose you have a plan to get out of here?" Stone asked.

"My thought was to make a run for the transporter and close it from the other side," Devren replied.

Stone tipped his head in approval. "Trap them in battle. Smart. That'll give you time to run." His eyebrows pulled together slightly. "But your ship's been through too much to handle any of the potential blowback."

"Do you have a better idea?" Devren asked.

Stone nodded. "I'll distract them. Wait for my signal, then make a run for it."

"If we disable the transporter, you'll be stuck here, too," Hyrin pointed out.

Stone smiled. "I have a few tricks left up my sleeve."

The screen went dark. The silence that returned to the room felt different; it was charged with expectancy. Though they were on the run from everyone, including their supposed alliance, they had a purpose and a destination. It changed the desperate flight into something solid and possible.

Hyrin moved the image of the ships to the main screen.

"What do you think his signal's going to be?" Straham asked.

"I have a feeling we'll know," Devren replied. "Officer Hyrin, ready the thrusters and send full power to the shields. If anything goes wrong, we don't want the Kratos to blow up."

O'Tule looked at the captain with wide eyes. "Why did you have to say that?"

"It was a joke," he told her.

She rolled her eyes and gave an exasperated shake of her head. "Who jokes about a ship blowing up in the middle of some cursed galaxy in the center of some infuriating fight with an inconceivable plan to destroy a stupid machine nobody had any right to make in the first place?" she muttered loudly to herself. "We actually deserve to blow up at this point."

Apparently used to her rants, Devren kept focused on the screen.

"Officer Duncan, warn the crew that we are about to transport."

219

"Yes, Captain," the officer replied.

The ships were locked in a fierce battle. Missiles impacted; pieces floated away. Nobody seemed to notice the rebel ship drifting closer.

Hyrin sat up. He pointed wordlessly at something along the side of the Star Chaser.

"Is that what I think it is?" Devren asked.

Hyrin shook his head in amazement. "Where in the Macrocosm did he find a curvator?"

As they watched, the missile left the Star Chaser and arched high above the ships where it wouldn't be detected. At the top of the arc, small thrusters opened, tipping the nose of the missile down to aim at the middle of the cluster of ships.

"This is going to be big," Hyrin said.

A burst of flame propelled the missile forward. It hit the mercenary ship in the center of the battle. The ship exploded on impact. The other ships closest to it were impacted with debris. Surrounding crafts caught fire that was quickly snuffed out by the vacuum of space. The explosions ran through them in a domino effect.

Liora realized she, like the others, was staring at the chain reaction caused by Stone's attack.

"That's the sign!" she called.

Devren tore his gaze away from the screen. "Head for the transporter."

Hyrin hit the thrusters. The Kratos sped past the ships reeling from the explosions and reached the transporter before any of them had a chance to react.

Hyrin maneuvered the arm of the Kratos to the link on the transporter. As soon as it touched, he pressed the button and the toggle came out, locking them into place.

"Prepare for transport," Duncan called over the ship's speakers.

Liora felt the rushing sensation that came when the Dakota transporter contracted the space in front of the ship and expanded the space behind it faster than the speed of light.

She blinked and the feeling stopped. They had arrived at the opposite end of the transporter's coordinates. As soon as Hyrin unhooked the toggle, massive solar sails unfurled from the transporter in order for it to collect energy from the starlight to recharge for its return.

"Good luck, Stone," Hyrin breathed.

The officer fired one of the Kratos' Gatling guns, shredding the sails and disabling the transporter's ability to restore its energy.

"Stone's crazy," Straham said.

"He's kind-of hot," Shathryn replied.

Chapter 19

Liora wandered down the hallway. The damage to the ship would make their journey to the closest Gaulded a slow one. Apparently, while she had been fighting for her life against the poison, the crew of the Kratos had also fought for survival against the Coalition and scavenger ships that battled to take possession of the Omne Occasus. Hull damage and the loss of one of the thrusters made the journey slow but necessary. They didn't dare risk a trip to the Albatross with the chance that someone would come upon them unable to defend themselves.

Liora's goal was to go to her room and rest, but her feet took her past it to the medical wing. She peeked inside and found Tariq sitting on the floor with his back against the far wall. He held a book that looked as though it had been thumbed through so many times its pages barely held to the spine.

"Surely on a ship like this you can find a more comfortable place to sit," Liora said.

Tariq looked up. His forehead creased slightly at the sight of her. "Sometimes chairs are too soft."

Liora debated whether to enter the room or leave. She turned away, but Tariq's voice stopped her.

"Did you need something?"

She took a calming breath and looked back at him. "I don't want to interrupt you."

He closed the book and glanced at the cover. His fingers ran across the title as though it was an old friend. "I've read this one a thousand times, but for some reason, it still calls me back. Has that ever happened to you?"

Liora shook her head. "I've never read a book."

Tariq's eyebrows rose. "Can you read?"

She nodded. "Yes." She hesitated, then said, "Damaclans feel that reading for pleasure is a waste of time."

He gave a noncommittal sound. "And what do you think?"

"I'm not sure," she answered. "I've never tried it."

Tariq tossed the book to her. Liora caught it with the same care she would use to intercept a tarlon egg. "What are you doing?" she asked, shocked that he would treat the book like that.

"Giving it to you to read," he replied with a hint of amusement in his voice. "Try it."

"But this is yours," she protested. She crossed the room with the book out, afraid she would damage it by holding it.

Real paperback books were rare in the Macrocosm. Most of mortalkind read on loaded cards. She felt as though her hands were unworthy to hold the book that rested in them.

Tariq waved away her attempt to give it back. "If you're going to read a book, you could do worse than starting with that one." He paused and a thoughtful half-smile crossed his face. "You might relate to it."

The title 'The Count of Monte Cristo' showed on the cover. Liora ran her fingers across it as Tariq had. The letters were raised and worn. She could smell the faint ink scent of the pages. She lifted it to her nose.

"What are you doing?" Tariq asked, watching her.

The old paper smell was better than she could have imagined. An unconscious smile spread across her face. "It's wonderful."

Tariq gave a little snort. "You know that's not how you read, right?"

Liora rolled her eyes. "I know." She couldn't help the slight warmth that filled her at his gift. "I've just never held anything like this before."

Tariq studied her for a moment. She felt suddenly self-conscious, a feeling she wasn't used to.

He motioned to the floor a few feet away. "Liora, will you sit down? We need to talk."

Liora did as he asked. She cradled the book carefully in her lap. Her fingers smoothed the sides, enjoying the way the pages felt when she moved the pads of her fingers across them.

"Liora." Tariq paused as though unsure how to proceed. He cleared his throat and gave her an uncomfortable look. "How did you call me?"

It was the one question she had hoped he would never ask. She was sure her fears that Tariq would never trust a telepath, especially one with Damaclan blood, were about to be realized.

She lowered her gaze from his. "I don't want to tell you."

Tariq's hand caught her fingers where they ran along the pages. He squeezed them gently, beckoning for her to look at him.

"Liora," he said, his voice soft.

The way he said her name sent a shiver through her skin. It was a sensation she had never felt before. She wasn't sure she liked that he had such an effect on her.

"Please look at me," he implored.

Liora closed her eyes.

Tariq let out a quiet breath. "Liora, whatever you did..." He paused, took another breath, and tried again. "Whatever that was, when I saw you, your pain was so real I felt it. That image will haunt me for the rest of my life."

His words ate at her. She shook her head. "I shouldn't have asked you to come back for me. It wasn't safe. You could have been killed."

"And if I didn't, you would have."

"It wouldn't have mattered." The whisper escaped Liora's lips before she could stop it.

Tariq put his fingers under her chin and lifted so that she looked him in the eyes.

"It would have," he replied.

Tension filled the air with an energy Liora had never felt before. She wanted to press her lips to his and kiss him, something she had never done to anyone in her life. The urge to caress his jaw and run her fingers through his mussed hair was so strong she had lifted her hand before she realized what she was doing.

Emotions crossed Tariq's eyes, clouding the reflection of her searching gaze. He closed his eyes and shook his head.

His hand lowered.

"I'm sorry," he said quietly.

Liora was about to stand when his fingers touched her neck. Fire trailed where his skin met hers.

"I was hoping this would fade before you awoke."

Liora glanced down, but she couldn't see what he was talking about. "What?" she asked.

"Where the thorn pierced your skin. I thought it would go away, but it looks like you might be wearing it for life." At her confused expression, a look of sympathy brushed his face. "You don't know."

Liora shook her head. "I'm really not sure what you're talking about."

Tariq rose and held out his hand. Liora took it, touched by his consideration. He let her fingers go and crossed to the washroom. He held the door open and motioned for her to enter.

Liora did so wordlessly. Her Damaclan instincts told her not to turn her back on him, but she shoved them away. If he wanted to kill her, he would have left her to die on the red planet.

Her thoughts were swept away by the image in the mirror.

Liora's short hair was a mess and her face pale, but that wasn't what caught her attention. In the mirror, the dark marks along the right side of her neck were visible. She stepped closer, pulling the collar of her shirt to the side so she could see.

The place where the thorn had pierced her skin just above the point where her neck met her shoulder was black as though dyed by the darkest ink. Branches trailed way from it, streaking up her neck and down past her collarbone. Some were thicker, and others were barely a hairline.

"It looks like a tree," she said.

A breath escaped Tariq as though he had been holding it. "It's your Damaclan blood," he told her. "It fought back. I've never seen anything like it."

His fingers brushed her neck. The sensation was slight, but sent tingles across her skin. She met his gaze in the mirror.

Tariq's light blue eyes were troubled as he watched her.

"Why do you look at me like that?" she asked.

He lowered his gaze. "Because I can't look at you any other way."

"I know." Her words came out soft. The understanding in them brought Tariq's gaze back up to her. Liora knew she had to be honest with him. "When you were unconscious in the cave, I tried to help you with the pain." The admission was hard. She swallowed. "Instead of covering it, I was drawn into the memory you were having. I-I saw your wife and daughter, and I saw the man who killed them."

Tariq stiffened slightly. He searched her face in the mirror as she spoke. She knew she couldn't stop. He had to know the truth.

She lifted her gaze to meet his. "Tariq, it was Obruo, the chief of my clan and the man who raised me since I was born."

Tariq shook his head.

"He's supposed to be dead," she continued. "Everyone was killed." She shook her head, still unable to comprehend why Obruo was in Tariq's memories years after her clan had been slaughtered by the nameless ones. It didn't make any sense.

"But you're human, too," he said as if he needed something to hold onto.

Liora nodded. "My mother loved my human father, but he had to run because my mother was already married to the clan chieftain. Obruo sent ships to kill him when he found out what my mother had done, but they never located him." Her voice quieted. "I was raised Damaclan under Obruo's roof."

Tariq lifted a hand as if to touch her cheek, but he pulled it away before he reached her.

He shook his head. "I'm sorry, Liora."

Cold washed through her cheek where his touch should have been and she realized how much she had wanted it.

"Me, too," she replied, her voice just above a whisper.

She left him in the medical wing with a lost expression on his face. She had never felt such heartbreak before. She didn't know why she cared about Tariq, but his look of hurt stayed in her mind when she pulled her blanket and pillow to the floor. The fact that he was probably sitting against the wall again without a book in his hand to distract him filled her with guilt.

She held the book to her chest and closed her eyes with its weight keeping her from falling apart.

Chapter 20

Lieutenant Argyle's crew had worked through the night re-facing the sides so that the Iron Falcon looked like scraps; luckily, thanks to the beating the ship had received when they fled planet F One Zero Four, the work hadn't been too hard.

The crew had changed out of their regular uniforms into what O'Tule called, 'Questionable attire so bad, hopefully it'll scare away any inquiries.' Their faded, rag-tag clothes that were a mismatch of outfits Shathryn and O'Tule had found in a closet somewhere looked almost comical. Liora was the only one who had been able to wear her regular attire because it didn't bear the Coalition emblems.

Shathryn wore a sequined purple shirt that matched the exact shade of her hair. The gray work overalls O'Tule had on made her green skin stand out even more. Tariq looked especially humorous in the brown and yellow checkered shirt and torn blue pants while Devren was at least able to pull off the patched black and pink striped shirt Shathryn had found. Hyrin shocked everyone when he came out of his room wearing an orange dress with a matching wig.

"Did you already have those?" Devren asked, keeping his voice level.

Hyrin laughed. "Shathryn dared me. I think it looks great with my eyes."

Tariq shook his head. "We all look ridiculous." His eyes flickered to Liora before he turned away.

"Speak for yourself," Shathryn replied, smoothing the front of her shirt. "I might have to wear this color more often."

"At least you're not stuck in crappy coveralls," O'Tule complained.

"You were too short for the slacks. We'd have to roll them up by at least half," Shathryn reminded her.

The speakers beeped and Duncan's voice announced, "Captain, we've reached the Gaulded."

Everyone waited on the bridge with anxious expressions. The SS Kratos pulled slowly up to the loading dock of Gaulded Seven Zero Eighty-nine. Their worst fear was realized when the head officer Belanite of the Gaulded approached their ship as soon as they landed. A Gaul paced on either side, obvious security with their blade-tipped horns and the semi-automatics strapped across their chests. The Belanite's moon crest on his uniform reflected in the Kratos' lights.

"What's going on?" Hyrin asked, his eyes on the security camera's screen.

"I'm not sure," Devren replied. "But I'd better go find out."

He made his way to the loading ramp; everyone crammed as close behind him as they could get. He glanced back at his crew before he hit the button to open the door.

"Could you give me a little space?" he asked. "Perhaps we should try looking a bit less suspicious."

The crew backed off quickly so that only Devren and Tariq stood in the entryway. Devren pushed the button.

"Good morning, Officer," he said as soon as the ramp touched the ground. "It's a pleasant surprise to be greeted by your fine company."

The Belanite's gaze swept over the crew behind Devren. He looked at the captain.

"Do you have any Damaclans on your ship?" he asked without preamble.

Ice rushed through Liora's veins at the direct question. Nobody lied to a Belanite. They had expected him to ask if they were with the Coalition or if they had been anywhere near the Cetus Dwarf Galaxy. Devren had been prepared to give indirect answers that weren't lies; however, nobody had expected the Belanite's question.

Devren and Tariq looked back at Liora. She stood near the rear of the crew. The other crew members shifted, attempting to hide her from sight.

Devren finally nodded. "Yes, Officer. We have a Damaclan aboard our ship. She is a part of the crew and—"

"Bring her forward."

The Belanite's command left no room to argue. The crew flattened to the sides of the hallway. Liora took a steeling breath and walked down the path they formed.

"Be careful," O'Tule breathed, her fingers tightly linked in Shathryn's.

Liora nodded. Instead of stopping at the top of the ramp like she wanted, she continued past Devren and Tariq to the bottom.

The Gauls were larger even than those she had fought on the last Gaulded. She hoped they weren't related. The sound of their breathing was like bellows inside their massive chests. She almost expected steam to come from their noses.

"Are you the only Damaclan aboard your ship?" the Belanite asked.

The orange-scaled Belanite looked her over as one might inspect a zanderbin hide before purchase. He took in the tattoos on the side of her neck and visible at her wrists. His gaze paused on the marks from the poison. Its curved lines and random structure were so different from the severe Damaclan tattoos that the contrast seemed to surprise him. When his eyes met hers, they were questioning.

She held his gaze. "I'm the only one."

The Belanite nodded. "Let her pass. She's not the one we're looking for."

Relief flooded through Liora. She heard Hyrin's echoing sigh up in the ship.

"If I may, what Damaclan are you looking for?" she asked.

The Belanite gave her a small smile that surprised her. Belanites weren't known for their cordiality. "Someone far different from you. He's a big brute, ugly for a Damaclan. He has the same tattoos as those on your neck, and he seems to have taken a vendetta against the Gaulded."

"Why?" Devren asked, coming up behind her.

"We're not sure," the Belanite replied. "The investigation has been ongoing since the explosion."

"Someone attacked a Gaulded?" Tariq asked with disbelief

232

in his voice.

Since the Gaulded were neutral, they were considered untouchable by nearly all races regardless of their political standing. While disputes often happened aboard the pressurized chunks of debris that had been welded to form the mismatched trade structures, they were settled quickly by either the individuals or the Belanites' ruthless security. An attack on a Gaulded itself was unheard of.

"Gaulded Zero Twenty-one was destroyed after the aforementioned Damaclan left a bomb upon departure," the Belanite said, his voice level. "When we catch up to him, he'll understand the full meaning of cruel and unusual punishment."

The way the Belanite said the last phrase without any inflection in his voice made it sound even worse. He turned silently with his Gaul security guards and left. The crew of the SS Kratos watched him go.

"Another Damaclan?" Devren said quietly. "You don't think…"

"It's Chief Obruo." Saying the words aloud hit Liora hard. "It has to be. He's looking for me."

The fact that an entire Gaulded with merchants, tradesmen, mechanics, and families dependent upon the vocations within the post had been destroyed because of her left Liora feeling empty. The kind woman who had given her the Ventican clothing was gone. She had vowed to return and pay for the Zamarian's generosity to a stranger. Now, because of her, the woman and her son had lost their lives. Zran had been right to fear her.

"Liora?" Devren said, his voice gentle.

She looked up to find the crew watching her. By the looks on their faces, they knew whatever Devren had felt necessary to tell them of her past. It was his duty as captain to ensure that his crew felt comfortable with each member aboard. Their safety and ability to work as a team demanded at least that.

Yet the looks of pity on Shathryn and O'Tule's faces ate at her. Hyrin gave her what she thought was supposed to be an encouraging smile, but came out faltering. Devren's gaze held hers.

"I know that look on your face," he said. "I know you want to run. You think you'll be protecting us."

"Everyone I care about dies," she said. Her voice wavered slightly despite her fight to keep it level.

"We have a lot more against us than a single Damaclan," Devren reminded her.

"You don't know Obruo."

He lifted a shoulder. "I don't know him, but I know you. You're stubborn, angry, and the fiercest fighter I've ever seen." He tipped his head slightly to the side. "The way I see it, you have two choices. You can run by yourself and do the best you can against Obruo alone. If you choose that option, we'll do the same and fight our fight with guns and fists the way we know how."

He gestured at the Kratos. "Or you can stay aboard this ship and we run together. We use our brains and our skills to outwit both the Damaclan chief and the scavengers, mercenaries, and Coalition ships intent on claiming the death machine for themselves. We need to buy ourselves time to get rid of the Omne Occasus, and we're going to need all the help we can get in order to do that."

Shathryn gave Liora a pleading look. "We need you, Liora! We've seen you fight."

O'Tule nodded. "You're an integral part of our crew now. You can't just leave. We have to band together. It's the best chance any of us have to survive this. You're our sister, remember? Sisters don't walk away."

"Come on," Straham said. "You belong with us."

It was Tariq's gaze that completed her resolve. The hatred in his eyes matched her need for vengeance. They might not be able to make it as friends given their past, but they could be allies against the enemy who had destroyed both their lives.

Tariq nodded as though he guessed her thoughts. "Let's fight him together."

Liora's answering nod was met with a cheer.

"Great!" O'Tule exclaimed, hugging Liora in her enthusiasm. "Now we're getting somewhere!"

Liora lifted a hand. "I'll stay on one condition."

"Anything," Shathryn promised.

"No more hugs."

Liora's words were met with laughter. Straham patted her shoulder on his way past.

"Time to pay the crew," he said. "Come get your share."

"Pay your crew elsewhere," a Calypsan snapped from the dock, shattering the moment. The hooved man glared at them. "You've docked in my spot."

"Nobody owns a spot," Hyrin replied with a touch of discomfort. "It's a Gaulded."

"Just the same, I always dock here. Move your ship," the Calypsan demanded.

Devren and Tariq crossed quietly down the ramp to the rest of the crew. Liora waited with her hand near her knife in case she was needed.

"I think we can settle this like gentlemen," Devren said.

The Calypsan's eyes narrowed. "Who says I want to?"

Tariq took a silver bar from Straham's satchel and tossed it to the Calypsan. "There. That should cover your expenses for hauling your supplies further down the dock. Will that settle it?"

The Calypsan looked from the bar to Tariq as though contemplating whether he could get more from the human. Tariq's glare said not to press his luck.

"Fine," the Calypsan huffed. He stormed away.

"Take that from my share," Tariq told Straham. He glanced at Hyrin. "Let's get a drink."

The others filed out after them.

Lieutenant Argyle paused next to Devren with a list in his hand. "It's going to take a pretty copper to repair the Kratos."

"Do whatever it takes," Devren told him. He paused and smiled. "Put it on the Coalition's tab just before we leave."

An answering smile spread across Argyle's face, raising his bushy mustache. "Yes, Captain. It'll be my pleasure."

A young repairman with bandages in the place of a pinky finger hurried beside him.

"Come along, Bonway. We have a few things to add to our list," Liora heard Lieutenant Argyle say as they made their way through the ships.

Liora trailed after the other crew members. She had more money in her pocket than she had ever owned in her life. It felt strange to wander the shops knowing that she could buy what she wanted. She couldn't make herself spend it; however. The thought of the Zamarian woman she would have given it to ate at her, burning holes into the joy she saw on the other crew members' faces.

The women pulled her into the closest clothing stall.

"Try this on, Liora," O'Tule pleaded. "It'll look great with your eyes." She flourished an armored vest with black and silver charms fastened across the front.

"No, try this one," Shathryn said. She held up a purple and black jacket of worked zanderbin hide.

236

Liora shook her head. "Thank you, but I don't need anything."

She left the shop before they could protest.

Liora wandered the twisted paths and jagged walkways of the pieced-together Gaulded. Parts of ships and even the side of what looked like a building from Earth made up a crazy collaboration so random it would be easy to get lost.

Liora was about to turn around and head back to the Gaulded when a sign caught her eye. The poster had been plastered over an assortment of others. The familiarity of the script and the pictures below made Liora's stomach tighten. She tore it from the wall and glanced at the date. Her heart began to race.

"What is that?"

Before she could react, Tariq took the poster from her hands. He smoothed it out and studied it. As soon as he realized what it was, he shook his head.

"No. There's no way."

"I'm going, Tariq. There's nothing you can do about it."

The human motioned toward several Kratos' crew members who stood at a nearby merchant's spicy grub shop challenging each other to try the wares. It seemed by Jarston's watering eyes that he was unable to pass up a good dare. The merchant was thrilled at the chance to make a few coppers and held out the next item to be sampled.

"And what about them? You just promised them you'd stick around. They don't take that lightly. You can't just up and leave whenever the whim catches you."

"This isn't a whim," Liora shot back. She snatched the poster out of his grasp. "This is a chance. Don't you see?"

Tariq folded his arms across his chest. "It's irrational."

Liora glared at him. "Don't you get it? This is the next place Malivian's circus is going to be, and it's in two days. It's only a galaxy from here."

"So you want to ditch your crew and go confront Malivian. I get it. I just don't think it's a good idea."

Liora fought back the urge to punch him. "Chief Obruo just destroyed the Gaulded Zero Twenty-one, the last place I was at. Now we know where he's going to go next."

Tariq's eyes narrowed. "He's going after Malivian."

Liora nodded. "Eliminate everything I know. Make your prey run. Eventually, when they have nowhere else to go, they'll make mistakes. It's the Damaclan way."

Tariq's gaze was dark when he asked, "Don't you guys ever stop?"

Liora shook her head. "Never. He won't stop until everyone I care about is dead. I've finally found somewhere I want to be, and I'm not going to let that happen to them, too."

Tariq's expression softened a bit. He looked at the poster again. "Are you sure about this?"

"Sure enough to steal a ship." A plan formed in her mind as she spoke. She made her way toward the loading dock. "I'll meet you at the Albatross."

"Do you know how to get there?" he asked quizzically.

Liora nodded. "I memorized the coordinates when Hyrin wasn't looking." She lifted a shoulder and tried not to sound guilty when she said, "I thought I might need them sometime."

Liora paced along the ships looking for what she needed.

"You're just going to steal one?" Tariq asked. "I'm not sure that's a good idea."

She found exactly what she wanted. "Yes. I'm taking that one."

Tariq looked from the ship to the hulking figure loading the last of his supplies into the holding bay. The Calypsan that had tried to cause a fight with the Kratos crew hit the button to close the door and huffed away muttering about needing a drink.

"That's the first thing you've said that makes sense." Tariq headed for the ship.

"Where are you going?" Liora asked in surprise.

Tariq glanced at her over his shoulder. "You really think I'd let you go after Obruo alone? I owe him payback as much as you do. Besides," he said, pausing near the door. "I'm not sure letting you face off with your two worst enemies alone is a good idea."

"Who says they're my worst enemies?" Liora shot back.

Tariq opened his mouth to argue, then shut it again and hit the button for the door. It slid open.

"It wasn't even locked?" Liora asked in surprise as she followed him inside.

"I guess nobody's stupid enough to steal from a Calypsan."

"Except us," she reminded him.

A slight smile touched his lips when he slid into the pilot's chair. "Except us."

"Isn't Devren going to worry about you?"

Tariq glanced at her out of the corner of his eye as he flipped switches and checked the gauges. "He'd worry even more if I let you take off alone. Sit down and tell me what the fuel levels say."

Liora put her hands on her hips. "Who says you're flying?"

"I do," Tariq replied. "Now sit before you hurt yourself."

He revved the engine and backed the ship carefully from the dock. The last thing they saw was the Calypsan shaking a meaty fist before Tariq hit the thrusters.

Chapter 21

They took the Vermont transporter to planet Luptos in the Maffei One Galaxy. Liora's heart sped up as they drew near. Ships from all over the Macrocosm waited in rows for access to the better docks near land. Shuttles ran back and forth across Luptos' murky surface, carrying every member of mortalkind imaginable to the promise of entertainment.

"Wow. Everyone shows up to these things," Tariq said after they landed.

"Have you been to the circus before?" Liora asked him, careful to keep her voice level so she wouldn't give away how just being near a circus again set her on edge.

"I haven't," Tariq admitted. "I've always wondered." He glanced at her and said, "But I don't suppose it's worth the hype."

She shook her head. "A bunch of people and creatures staring at other people and creatures. I've never understood it."

"Yet you were a part of it." Tariq held out his hand to help her onto the shuttle.

"Unwillingly."

The gesture caught Liora off-guard. She wasn't used to someone watching out for her. She felt self-conscious when she slipped her hand into Tariq's and stepped onto the rocky shuttle.

Tiny creatures ran along the top of the water with the wooden planks across their backs. A man with six spindly arms dangled pieces of fresh meat at the front of the shuttle to entice the creatures onward. As soon as they reached the shore, he moved the meat to the other side. The creatures turned and ran back out.

Tariq and Liora stepped off the shuttle into a sea of chaos. It seemed every race of mortalkind wandered through cages, tents, and displays. Acrobatic acts performed by the eight-legged Arachnians competed with Calypsans executing feats of great strength. Gauls fought using only their horns while crowds lined up to view warriors throwing Zamarian stars and battle axes at each other. Members of the Weryn race disappeared and reappeared to music played on boula drums.

The sticky-sweet, cloying scent of sugared confections competed against the tangy, sharp odor of boiled ganthum. Slices of fried banarang seasoned in multi-galactic spices drew the attention of the carnivores while flat-toothed herbivores browsed racks of dried gungum leaf from the planet Tanus.

The scents were too familiar; they made Liora's stomach clench.

"Do you have a plan?" Tariq asked.

Liora touched the knife at her thigh.

"That's not much of a plan," Tariq noted. "It's quite poor, in fact. I'd say you're being a bit hasty."

"Let's see if Malivian's here. Once we know that, it'll give me a better idea of how to proceed," she answered.

Malivian would never turn down a circus opportunity like the one she walked through. Thousands upon thousands would be drawn to the entertainment. Even if Malivian had lost his prized Damaclan mind pusher, his pride alone would never let him back away from a show when he had so many anxious to see it.

The biggest tent caught Liora's attention. It had been set up in the center of the madness where the black and yellow furls would catch the eye of every circus-goer. The colors were enough to make Liora's stomach tighten even further. She hadn't considered how it would feel to walk back inside the environment she had hated so badly. Now that she was close, doubt and fear pushed at the edges of her mind. She focused on placing one foot in front of the other so she wouldn't be tempted to turn back to their stolen ship.

"Are you alright?" Tariq asked.

The concern in his tone made her look up at him. She realized how protectively he walked beside her, his shoulder turned to shield the majority of the raucous crowd from reaching her. It felt for a brief moment like he cared. She told herself it was easier to get through the aisles that way and he was just as anxious to be done with the planet as she was. She pushed down any emotions that argued otherwise and nodded.

"I'm fine. That's the tent."

Before he could say anything else, Liora strode ahead. She ducked beneath giants and spun around spindly Banthans who could definitely use more spatial awareness. She heard Tariq call her name, but didn't slow down. She felt as though if another person bumped her shoulder or kicked the back of her boot, she was going to have a meltdown and go Damaclan on everyone within reach.

Liora reached the tent and ducked inside. It took a moment for her eyes to adjust to the sudden darkness. For some reason, Malivian's tent was lacking the rows of caged and chained creatures that usually drew his crowds. Instead, the tent was completely empty, a huge, hulking waste of space except for someone who sat on a lone chair in the middle.

"Hello, Liora."

Memories swarmed Liora at the sound of his voice. She reached for her knife. The reassuring touch of the blade handle centered her chaotic thoughts.

"Did you miss me?" Malivian asked, his words slurred. He gave a laugh. "I'll bet that's why you came back. You missed me, didn't you? Well, I missed you, my little pet."

Liora grimaced. "I was never your pet."

Malivian smiled. "Of course you were. You begged, sat, and spoke in their minds when I ordered it. You obeyed all my commands just like a good little creature should. You were so well trained." He paused and his face twisted. "Until that little Coalition brat came along and screwed everything up."

Liora was almost to the circus master when her eyes focused completely in the darkness. He held a gun on his lap and it was aimed in her direction, only it wasn't just any gun. He held the biggest shotgun she had ever seen. If she ran, she was dead.

She pretended she didn't notice it and paused casually.

"What if I did come back?" she asked.

Malivian watched her with an unusual smile on his lizard face. His yellow eyes reflected the faint light in the tent.

"Did you come back to join me or kill me?" he asked.

"Join you," she said, grateful he wasn't a Belanite. "I've missed the circus."

Malivian's mouth twisted into a triumphant smile. "You liked being the center of the show."

Liora nodded. "Who wouldn't?" She swallowed past the tightness in her throat. "The crowds, the cheering. I missed hearing my name called by so many."

Malivian rose unsteadily to his feet. "You ruined me. We'd have to start completely over."

"We can do that," Liora said with an encouraging nod. "They would come just to see me. You know that."

"It's your beauty," Malivian replied. "It draws them all. My Damaclan beauty." His eyes darkened. "But behind the beauty lies a traitor. You left me. I can't ever forgive that."

"You can," Liora coaxed.

She pushed her thoughts at him. *Together, we can rebuild.*

Malivian paused with his head tipped to one side. There was a hint of craziness she felt when she pushed at him that sent a tremor of fear through Liora. It tangled his thoughts and pulsed back at her with an energy she had never felt before. As much as she hoped he would believe her, she realized Malivian was beyond reason.

"I loved you, Liora," he said. He lifted his gun.

A giant crack sounded and the entire tent leaned toward one side. A flap tore away. Liora saw Tariq on a massive moondu beast. He held one of the main cables that attached to the top of the tent's mast. Tariq cracked a whip. The center beam snapped and the human disappeared from sight.

"Not my tent!" Malivian yelled.

"Liora, run," Tariq called.

Liora dodged the falling canvas intent on reaching Malivian instead of running away. The black and yellow cloth fell in waves, folding and flattening.

Liora darted past the empty chair and into the collapsing sides. She could hear Malivian ahead, but couldn't see him in the darkness. The canvas pressed down. She wasn't able to go any further.

Liora drew her knife and sliced through the side. Hazy light filtered past the dark clouds that created a permanent cover for the swampland. She scanned the staring crowds hoping to see Malivian's too familiar checkered cloak. Liora's heart raced. She had to find him. She took a step forward.

Tariq grabbed her arm. "Liora, what are you doing? You walked right into a trap."

"I meant to," she said. "The only way to find Obruo is through Malivian. I needed him to trust me."

"And by trust you, you mean shoot you?" Tariq demanded.

"That may have been an oversight," she admitted. "I expected the tent to be full of his collection. He wouldn't have risked them. It would've given me leverage."

Tariq scanned the crowd with her. "Now what?"

Liora took off running for the docks.

"We have to find the ship," she called over her shoulder.

She heard Tariq's footsteps behind her.

"How are we going to find it?" he asked when they neared the shore.

An explosion from the middle of the shipyard stopped them in their tracks. Liora's heart slowed at the sight of the Kirkos on fire. Flames and chunks of debris flew to other ships, catching them on fire as well. Shouts rang out and crews from the circus charged into the swampland.

Tariq's hand grabbed Liora's shoulder. "Obruo's here, and he probably knows you're here as well. Come on."

They faded back into the crowd.

"The circus isn't safe. They'll start checking tents and ships for bombs. Maybe we should join them." He pointed toward a group of workers hurrying into of a tent marked 'Staff'.

Liora and Tariq waited for a surge in the crowd. She cut the side of the tent with her knife and they slipped inside. Rows of uniforms, rakes, garbage containers, staffs with hooks on the ends, and a vast array of clubs, rods, chains, and rings lined the shelves and tables. Several workers pulled on the yellow and red uniforms of bomb detectors.

Tariq strode to the hangers and withdrew two uniforms as if he belonged there. He handed a uniform to Liora and pulled his on quickly. She did the same and drew the hood over her head to hide her tattoos.

"Let's go," he said.

They searched through the tents with the bomb detectors, but instead of looking for weapons, Liora and Tariq were busy eyeing circus owners and the assortment of creatures in case Malivian hid among them. Giant snuffling adaroks with sweeping tentacles were led through each tent. The time it took made Liora's nerves tingle. She was afraid Malivian would escape, and had to keep reminding herself that his ship had gone up in flames.

Liora had just stepped outside of another tent when a body slammed into hers. It knocked her into the canvas and her hood fell back. She shoved her fighting instincts down when she realized the man who had run into her not only wore a Coalition uniform, but was surrounded by an entire squad.

"I'm sorry," the man said. He held out a hand to help her, then squinted. "Hey, I know you! This is the girl from F One Zero Four. She's part of the priority target!"

Tariq grabbed Liora's arm and pulled her back into the tent. They darted through men, women, and children of all races. Liora over-ended garbage cans and vendor carts in an attempt to slow the persistent Coalition. They twisted and turned through the maze of tents and displays until the Coalition was left behind.

Liora led the way down a side aisle and slowed to a walk to draw less attention. She glanced back to check their pursuit. A hand grabbed her arm. Another pressed a gun firmly to her head. If she struggled, she had no doubt what would happen.

"Take it easy," Tariq said, his hands raised. He followed Liora and her captors into a side tent. "We don't want any trouble." His eyes widened. "I know you," he growled. "Obruo."

The name sent cold rushing through Liora's body. She tensed, ready to fight.

"Don't move if you know what's good for you," Obruo said in her ear. "Remember, I know all your moves."

"Let her go," Tariq demanded.

Obruo lifted the gun away from Liora and fired. Tariq let out a cry of pain and fell to the ground clutching his leg.

Liora tried to keep calm. Her heart thundered in her throat that was being restricted by Obruo's tight hold. Malivian stood nearby with an angry glare on his reptilian face.

"You ruined my life," the Hennonite shouted, his yellow eyes bright with rage. "When you weren't at the last show, the Caredite family withdrew their funding. I lost everything." He turned his gaze to Obruo. "You owe me."

"You were supposed to control her," Obruo replied in a voice of deadly calm Liora knew all too well.

"She's impossible to control," Malivian argued. "She takes after her father."

Obruo turned the gun on Malivian.

247

The circus master held up his hands. "I didn't mean any disrespect, Chief. Honest. I just mean she's been difficult to work with, and calling the Coalition officers in has made my life more than difficult." His eyes remained on the gun. "I've been a faithful servant. You can't argue that."

When the gun didn't move, Malivian dropped to his knees. "Please. I'll do anything. I've lost everything I have trying to keep Liora prisoner. She ruined me."

"Welcome to my life," Obruo said. He shot Malivian in the forehead before his last word faded. The crack of the gunshot echoed in Liora's head as the circus master fell lifelessly to the ground.

Liora stared at the still body of the man who had controlled her life for so long. Blood ran from the hole in his forehead and dripped from the corner of his lizard mouth. A twitch jerked one side of his face into the semblance of an eerie smile.

Liora had to look away. Tremors ran up her arms. She wanted to fight, to run, to do anything but wait for Obruo to act again. The situation was spiraling so quickly out of control she couldn't figure out how to fix it. The best thing she could do was keep Obruo's attention away from Tariq.

She swallowed and said, "I thought you would never stoop to using a gun."

"The old ways are gone," Obruo replied. "You should know that by now." His arm constricted around her throat. "I'm looking forward to the next segment of your training."

"I finished my training," Liora said tightly.

"You think you did," Obruo replied with a humorless laugh as he pushed her toward the door. He glanced back at Tariq. "What should I do about the human?"

Liora lifted her shoulders in a shrug. It was the only way to protect him. "Shoot him again for all I care. He means nothing to me."

She couldn't meet the look of betrayal in Tariq's pain-filled eyes.

Obruo snorted near her ear. "It's too bad you're such a terrible liar. It's another one of those human traits I could never quite beat out of you no matter how hard I tried."

Obruo pointed the gun at Tariq.

Liora slid the knife from her sheath and spun. Obruo caught her wrist. She slammed a fist against the side of his head and his arm when he raised it to block the blow. The gun went flying. Obruo slapped her across the face. She tried to stab him in the eye. He tore the knife out of her grip, reversed it, and shoved the blade through her palm.

Liora gasped in pain as he forced the knife toward her throat with the blade still lodged in her hand.

"You forgot your training," he said with disapproval heavy in his voice.

"You forgot your gun," she replied.

Obruo's eyes widened. He shoved her backwards into Tariq before the human could fire the weapon. Tariq caught Liora and lifted the gun again. The Damaclan disappeared through the back of the tent.

"Go after him," Tariq said.

Liora shook her head. "I'm not leaving you like this."

"I'll be fine," he told her. "I know you need to stop him."

"The Coalition could come and—"

Voices they both recognized spoke on the other side of the tent door. Liora ducked under Tariq's arm and helped him to his feet. He limped beside her to the back of the tent. They fled the same way Obruo had gone.

Liora and Tariq reached a crowd that wandered through the pathways between the tents. They joined the group in an attempt to hide from the Coalition officers. A few members of the crowd shot them curious glances. Liora hoped they would pass as part of a circus act. She plastered a smile on her face to cover her pain.

"You know we look ridiculous, right?" Tariq pointed out a few minutes later; his voice was tight. "We're bleeding all over the place and you have a knife through your hand."

Liora laughed because it was all she could do. The pain in her right palm made her whole arm numb. She knew she should wrap Tariq's leg to stop the bleeding, but she didn't know how to do it until the knife was gone. Tariq didn't dare remove the knife until he had bandages to wrap the wound. They were caught in an absurdly painful impasse until they reached the ship.

As soon as the crowd neared the murky shore, Tariq and Liora branched away. Fortunately, the six-armed man who guided their shuttle didn't look twice at the pair past holding up one of his many hands for the payment Tariq pressed into his palm. They reached the Calypsan's Tin Sparrow and collapsed as soon as they made it inside.

"I'll get the med kit," Tariq offered.

"Don't even think about it," Liora replied. "I've got it. You've moved far too much already."

"I think my knee's okay. The bullet went higher than he meant it to. It's embedded somewhere in my thigh."

"You know that's not very reassuring," Liora pointed out as she lugged the medical kit one-handed to his side.

Tariq gave her a pained smile. "I'm a positive person."

"Since when?"

He gave an actual laugh, the first she remembered hearing. "Since this moment. I figure it can only go uphill from here."

"Hang around with me long enough and we'll prove that wrong," Liora shot back, winning another laugh from him. Her poor attempts at wrapping a bandage around his wound so he could work on her was a pathetic fail with the blade through her hand.

Tariq sat up gingerly and caught her fingers.

"Easy," he said at her wince of pain. "Let's take care of this first. Do you want an injection? I could numb it."

She shook her head. "I won't be able to get the bullet out if you do. I need to be able to move my fingers. I just don't think it should hurt as bad as it does." She tried to distract herself from what was going to happen.

"You mean getting a knife shoved through your hand should be easy?"

"Easier," she answered. Her voice tightened when he carefully grabbed the blade.

"Maybe we should tell Obruo not to stab his daughter."

Liora glared at Tariq. At that moment, he eased the blade from the wound. She held back a cry of pain and instead bit her lip so hard she tasted blood.

"It's alright," he said, his voice gentle. He concentrated on cleaning and bandaging the wound. "The hard part's over. I won't be able to check for damage until we reach the Kratos, but your fingers still work. That's a good sign."

Liora blinked quickly to hold back tears of pain. "I'm glad you think that's good," she said, her voice wavering.

Tariq looked at her closely. "Liora, I can numb this."

She shook her head. "I need to be able to use it. I'll be fine."

He finished wrapping the bandage around it and tied the gauze off. He was careful to tuck the ends of the bandage beneath the other layers so they wouldn't snag on anything.

"You've done this before," Liora said.

Tariq gave her a half-smile. "A few times."

She sat up, careful not to put weight on her injured hand. "Alright, it's your turn."

"Is this payback?" he asked. "I tried to be gentle."

"Don't expect the same from me."

He settled on the floor with a worried expression. "I'm not sure I like the sound of that."

"Trust me," Liora told him. "I've removed bullets before. This is going to be easy."

Chapter 22

Liora let Tariq sleep for as long as he could during the trip back to the Diamond Albatross' coordinates. As she flew, the reality of what had happened circled over and over again in her mind. Malivian was dead. Obruo was trying to kill her.

She knew better than to think the chief would give up. He had a vendetta, and he wouldn't rest until he made her pay. With him on her trail, nobody would be out of his reach. The Kratos crew might be safer sticking together, but Liora knew she was the one bringing them the most danger. She wasn't sure how to come to terms with that.

She heard Tariq limp forward from the passage.

"Are you alright?" he asked.

She nodded. "Are you?"

He eased into the copilot chair and stuck his leg out at an angle. "Sure. I don't know when I fell asleep."

"It hasn't been too long," Liora told him. "We're almost to the Oregon transporter."

"Thank goodness," Tariq replied. "I'm not sure how much longer we can stay on this Sparrow. Calypsans pack way too much grass for my stomach."

"I've never acquired the taste," she said honestly.

Tariq watched out the huge glass windows for a moment before he said, "So what have you been contemplating? Do I want to know?"

She glanced at him, debating how much to tell. "I'm not sure." She was silent a moment. Nobody had ever asked her what she thought about. The memories and images in her mind probably made that a good thing; however, thinking about the most recent events troubled her far greater. She took a chance.

"Obruo's the reason I was caged."

"I heard that." Tariq's voice was gentle with empathy. "I didn't realize it."

"I didn't either until he told Malivian he was supposed to keep me under control." She shook her head. "Obruo's been controlling me this whole time."

Tariq settled back in his seat. "Liora, if I know you at all, nobody controls you."

"Not anymore," she said firmly.

He nodded as if he appreciated the words. "Good. I'm glad to hear it."

A silver object drew near on the screen.

"There's the Oregon transporter."

"Thank goodness. I can't wait to get back to a real medical bay."

At Liora's surprised look, Tariq shrugged with a hint of embarrassment. "Do you know how pathetic those tools are back there? Mine would walk miles around the Calypsan's. You might even have stitches right now."

He raised his eyebrows invitingly.

Liora fought back the urge to smile. "As fun as that sounds, I think I'll stick with bandages."

She guided the toggle toward the transporter. As soon as it coupled, she hit the button to jump.

Liora sat back in the pilot's seat. The pulling sensation felt like cold water spilling over her from head to toe. Before she could decide if it was unpleasant, the sensation was gone.

"That's not the Atlas." Tariq sat up straight.

Liora's heart skipped a beat. In the exact coordinates where they were supposed to find the Coalition's lost Diamond Albatross, a different Coalition starship waited.

"Incoming," Tariq said. He pushed the receiver.

Colonel Lefkin's face came on the screen.

"Hello, Officer Tariq. What a pleasant surprise." The colonel gave a humorless smile. "I invite you both to come aboard my ship."

Liora and Tariq exchanged a glance. The invitation was a thinly-cloaked order. Malivian was gone for good. Obruo had vanished, and the Kratos was nowhere to be found. Colonel Lefkin knew exactly what Devren carried aboard his Iron Falcon. Given the number of Coalition ships and mercenaries the colonel had put on their trail, he would do whatever he could to ensure the Omne Occasus became his.

"This is what I get for being positive," Tariq said as he pushed cautiously to his feet.

Liora turned her head so the colonel couldn't see her

speak. "We could always run for it," Liora whispered.

"You're insane," Tariq replied.

"I'm part Damaclan," Liora reminded him.

He watched her for a moment. The slightest hint of a smile twitched at the corner of his mouth. He glanced at the screen, then back at her.

"I'm putting my money on the Damaclan."

DAYBREAK

About the Author

Cheree Alsop is an award-winning, best-selling author who has published over 55 books. She is the mother of a beautiful, talented daughter and amazing twin sons who fill every day with joy and laughter. She is married to her best friend, Michael, the light of her life and her soulmate who shares her dreams and inspires her every day. Cheree enjoys reading, traveling to tropical beaches, riding motorcycles, playing the bass for the band Alien Landslide, spending time with her wonderful children, and going on family adventures. Cheree and Michael live in Utah where they rock out, enjoy the outdoors, plan great quests, and never stop dreaming.

She loves hearing from her readers! Feel free to email her at chereelalsop@hotmail.com

REVIEWS

The Girl from the Stars Series

This is my favorite Cheree Alsop book now! Her best yet! I loved it. So many twists and turns, great characters, excitement and hints of romance. I can't wait for the next one in the series.
—Voca Matisse, Reviewer

Fantastic book! Cheree's ability to write an amazing character that you not only sympathize with but also grow to care for, is one of the fabulous writing abilities that she lends to every story. This story line was full of epic twists and wry humor that had me engaged the entire way through. All in all a fun enjoyable read.
—akgodwin, Amazon Reviewer

This was one of the best books I have read in a while. Sci-fi, adventure, thriller... could not put the book away. I already bought the second book in the series, and hope the third will come out soon.
—Kindle Customer

The main character, Liora, is a very mixed up but emerging person who is a genetic mutt! Half of her DNA is totally violence oriented whilst the other half is straight human, which is to say violent when necessary but basically well rounded. In the beginning she was a slave in a circus and had never known anyone she could trust or care for, and even when she is rescued from that hell she has a hard time adjusting to the idea that she can fit in anywhere. The action is frequent and well written and over time she keeps trying to both find reasons to fit in and reasons to strike out on her own. This is not resolved in the first book, and makes you want to read more. I like the series a lot and hope the writer keeps them coming.

—Sam, Amazon Reviewer

Dr Wolf, the Fae Rift Series

Dr. Wolf, the Fae Rift Series Book 1- Shockwave by Cheree Alsop is a movie transcript ready and suspensefully alluring tale that weaves the mind of the reader around the world of wild dreams.

— Rachel Anderson, Amazon Reviewer

Wow! Was not expecting enjoying this book as much as I did. Ms. Alsop had me drawn in front the get go. The writing was fantastic, the story just flowed so easily and I could not put the book down. I enjoyed all the characters and love her imagination. The banter with the characters had me laughing out loud (I love the fairy and the vampire). I really enjoyed the storyline and the whole what if of falling into a rift. I would highly recommend this book to anyone looking for a nice fresh look on paranormal.

— Amazon Verified Reviewer

Demon Spiral picks up right where Shockwave left off...Once again, I could not put this book down. The flow of the story is amazing and the banter that the author was able to put into the book just made for a very enjoyable read. I highly recommend Cheree Alsop and look forward to reading the next in this series as well.

—Crystal's Review, GoodReads Reviewer

I had to download the sample for this because I was sure I wanted it. I bought the book after the first page. It's almost like Dr. Who with Fae.
—Chris Hughes, Amazon Reviewer

The Silver Series

"Cheree Alsop has written *Silver* for the YA reader who enjoys both werewolves and coming-of-age tales. Although I don't fall into this demographic, I still found it an entertaining read on a long plane trip! The author has put a great deal of thought into balancing a tale that could apply to any teen (death of a parent, new school, trying to find one's place in the world) with the added spice of a youngster dealing with being exceptionally different from those around him, and knowing that puts him in danger."
—Robin Hobb, author of the Farseer Trilogy

"I honestly am amazed this isn't absolutely EVERYWHERE! Amazing book. Could NOT put it down! After reading this book, I purchased the entire series!"
—Josephine, Amazon Reviewer

"A page-turner that kept me wide awake and wanting more. Great characters, well written, tenderly developed, and thrilling. I loved this book, and you will too."
—Valerie McGilvrey

"Super glad that I found this series! I am crushed that it is at its end. I am sure we will see some of the characters in the next series, but it just won't be the same. I am 41 years old, and am only a little embarrassed to say I was crying at 3 a.m. this morning while finishing the last book. Although this is a

YA series, all ages will enjoy the Silver Series. Great job by Cheree Alsop. I am excited to see what she comes up with next."
—Jennc, Amazon Reviewer

The Werewolf Academy Series

If you love werewolves, paranormal, and looking for a book like House of Night or Vampire Academy this is it! YA for sure.
—Reviewer for Sweets Books

I got this book from a giveaway, and it's one of the coolest books I have ever read. If you love Hogwarts, and Vampire Academy, or basically anything that has got to do with supernatural people studying, this is the book for you.
—Maryam Dinzly

This series is truly a work of art, sucked in immediately and permanently. The first line and you are in the book. Cheree Alsop is a gifted writer, all of her books are my complete favorites!! This series has to be my absolute favorite, Alex is truly a wonderful character who I so wish was real so I can meet him and thank him. Once you pick this book up you won't put it down till it's finished. A must read!!!!!
—BookWolf Brianna

Listed with Silver Moon as the top most emotional of Cheree's books, I loved Instinct for its raw truth about the pain, the heartbreak, and the guilt that Alex fights.
—Loren Weaver

Great story. Loaded with adventure at every turn. Can't wait till the next book. Very enjoyable, light reading. I would recommend to all young and old readers.
—Sharon Klein

The Galdoni Series

"This is absolutely one of the best books I have ever read in my life! I loved the characters and their personalities, the storyline and the way it was written. The bravery, courage and sacrifice that Kale showed was amazing and had me scolding myself to get a grip and stop crying! This book had adventure, romance and comedy all rolled into one terrific book I LOVED the lesson in this book, the struggles that the characters had to go through (especially the forbidden love)...I couldn't help wondering what it would be like to live among such strangely beautiful creatures that acted, at times, more caring and compassionate than the humans. Overall, I loved this book...I recommend it to ANYONE who fancies great books."
—iBook Reviewer

"I was not expecting a free novel to beat anything that I have ever laid eyes upon. This book was touching and made me want more after each sentence."
—Sears1994, iBook Reviewer

"This book was simply heart wrenching. It was an amazing book with a great plot. I almost cried several times. All of the scenes were so real it felt like I was there witnessing everything."

—Jeanine Drake, iBook Reveiwer

"Galdoni is an amazing book; it is the first to actually make me cry! It is a book that really touches your heart, a romance novel that might change the way you look at someone. It did that to me."
—Coralee2, Reviewer

"Wow. I simply have no words for this. I highly recommend it to anyone who stumbled across this masterpiece. In other words, READ IT!"
—Troublecat101, iBook Reviewer

The Monster Asylum Series

What a rollercoaster, wow!! I never ever cried when reading a vampire book, but I did this time. I must say it's the best vampire book I've read since ever. One of the best books ever read so far.
—Conny, Goodreads Reviewer

I downloaded this book because of Cheree, I love her imagination. This one is so much fun to read; once I started I couldn't put it down. And now I believe not all Monsters are bad!! Looking forward to the next book in the series. Thanks Cheree
—Doughgirl61, Amazon Reviewer

Keeper of the Wolves

"This is without a doubt the VERY BEST paranormal romance/adventure I have ever read and I've been reading these types of books for over 45 years. Excellent plot, wonderful protagonists—even the evil villains were great. I read this in one sitting on a Saturday morning when there were so many other things I should have been doing. I COULD NOT put it down! I also appreciated the author's research and insights into the behavior of wolf packs. I will CERTAINLY read more by this author and put her on my 'favorites' list."
—N. Darisse

"This is a novel that will emotionally cripple you. Be sure to keep a box of tissues by your side. You will laugh, you will cry, and you will fall in love with Keeper. If you loved *Black Beauty* as a child, then you will truly love *Keeper of the Wolves* as an adult. Put this on your 'must read' list."
—Fortune Ringquist

"Cheree Alsop mastered the mind of a wolf and wrote the most amazing story I've read this year. Once I started, I couldn't stop reading. Personal needs no longer existed. I turned the last page with tears streaming down my face."
—Rachel Andersen, Amazon Reviewer

"I just finished this book. Oh my goodness, did I get emotional in some spots. It was so good. The courage and love portrayed is amazing. I do recommend this book. Thought provoking."
—Candy, Amazon Reviewer

Thief Prince

"I absolutely loved this book! I could not put it down. . . The Thief Prince will whisk you away into a new world that you will not want to leave! I hope that Ms. Alsop has more about this story to write, because I would love more Kit and Andric! This is one of my favorite books so far this year! Five Stars!"
—Crystal, Book Blogger at Books are Sanity

". . . Once I started I couldn't put it down. The story is amazing. The plot is new and the action never stops. The characters are believable and the emotions presented are beautiful and real. If anyone wants a good, clean, fun, romantic read, look no further. I hope there will be more books set in Debria, or better yet, Antor."
—SH Writer, Amazon Reviewer

"This book was a roller coaster of emotions: tears, laughter, anger, and happiness. I absolutely fell in love with all of the characters placed throughout this story. This author knows how to paint a picture with words."
—Kathleen Vales

"Awesome book! It was so action packed, I could not put it down, and it left me wanting more! It was very well written, leaving me feeling like I had a connection with the characters."
—M. A., Amazon Reviewer

The Shadows Series

"This was a heart-warming tale of rags to riches. It was also wonderfully described and the characters were vivid and vibrant; a story that teaches of love defying boundaries and of people finding acceptance."
—Sara Phillip, Book Reviewer

"This is the best book I have ever had the pleasure of reading. . . It literally has everything, drama, action, fighting, romance, adventure, & suspense. . . Nexa is one of the most incredible female protagonists ever written. . .It literally had me on pins & needles the ENTIRE time. . . I cannot recommend this book highly enough. Please give yourself a wonderful treat & read this book... you will NOT be disappointed!!!"
—Jess- Goodreads Reviewer

"Took my breath away; excitement, adventure and suspense. . . This author has extracted a tender subject and created a supernatural fantasy about seeing beyond the surface of an individual. . . Also the romantic scenes would make a girl swoon. . . The fights between allies and foes and blood lust would attract the male readers. . .The conclusion was so powerful and scary this reader was sitting on the edge of her seat."
—Susan Mahoney, Book Blogger

"Adventure, incredible amounts of imagination and description go into this world! It is a buy now, don't leave the couch until the last chapter has reached an end kind of read!"
—Malcay- Amazon Reviewer

"The high action tale with the underlying love story that unfolds makes you want to keep reading and not put it down.

I can't wait until the next book in the Shadows Series comes out."
—Karen- Amazon Reviewer

". . . It's refreshing to see a female character portrayed without the girly clichés most writers fall into. She is someone I would like to meet in real life, and it is nice to read the first person POV of a character who is so well-round that she is brave, but still has the softer feminine side that defines her character. A definite must read."
—S. Teppen- Goodreads Reviewer

The Small Town Superhero Series

"A very human superhero- Cheree Alsop has written a great book for youth and adults alike. Kelson, the superhero, is battling his own demons plus bullies in this action packed narrative. Small Town Superhero had me from the first sentence through the end. I felt every sorrow, every pain and the delight of rushing through the dark on a motorcycle. Descriptions in Small Town Superhero are so well written the reader is immersed in the town and lives of its inhabitants."
—Rachel Andersen, Book Reviewer

"Anyone who grew up in a small town or around motorcycles will love this! It has great characters and flows well with martial arts fighting and conflicts involved."
—Karen, Amazon Reviewer

"Fantastic story...and I love motorcycles and heroes who don't like the limelight. Excellent character development. You'll like this series!"

—Michael, Amazon Reviewer

"Another great read; couldn't put it down. Would definitely recommend this book to friends and family. She has put out another great read. Looking forward to reading more!"
—Benton Garrison, Amazon Reviewer

"I enjoyed this book a lot. Good teen reading. Most books I read are adult contemporary; I needed a change and this was a good change. I do recommend reading this book! I will be looking out for more books from this author. Thank you!"
—Cass, Amazon Reviewer

Stolen

"This book will take your heart, make it a little bit bigger, and then fill it with love. I would recommend this book to anyone from 10-100. To put this book in words is like trying to describe love. I had just gotten it and I finished it the next day because I couldn't put it down. If you like action, thrilling fights, and/or romance, then this is the perfect book for you."
—Steven L. Jagerhorn

"Couldn't put this one down! Love Cheree's ability to create totally relatable characters and a story told so fluidly you actually believe it's real."
—Sue McMillin, Amazon Reviewer

"I enjoyed this book it was exciting and kept you interested. The characters were believable. And the teen romance was cute."
—Book Haven- Amazon Reviewer

"I really liked this book . . . I was pleasantly surprised to discover this well-written book. . .I'm looking forward to reading more from this author."
—Julie M. Peterson- Amazon Reviewer

"Great book! I enjoyed this book very much it keeps you wanting to know more! I couldn't put it down! Great read!"
—Meghan- Amazon Reviewer

"A great read with believable characters that hook you instantly. . . I was left wanting to read more when the book was finished."
—Katie- Goodreads Reviewer

Heart of the Wolf

"Absolutely breathtaking! This book is a roller coaster of emotions that will leave you exhausted!!! A beautiful fantasy filled with action and love. I recommend this book to all fantasy lovers and those who enjoy a heartbreaking love story that rivals that of Romeo and Juliet. I couldn't put this book down!"
—Amy May

"What an awesome book! A continual adventure, with surprises on every page. What a gifted author she is. You just can't put the book down. I read it in two days. Cheree has a way of developing relationships and pulling at your heart. You find yourself identifying with the characters in her book...True life situations make this book come alive for you and gives you increased understanding of your own situation in life. Magnificent story and characters. I've read all of Cheree's books and recommend them all to you...especially if you love adventures."

—Michael, Amazon Reviewer

"You'll like this one and want to start part two as soon as you can! If you are in the mood for an adventure book in a faraway kingdom where there are rival kingdoms plotting and scheming to gain more power, you'll enjoy this novel. The characters are well developed, and of course with Cheree there is always a unique supernatural twist thrown into the story as well as romantic interests to make the pages fly by."

Karen, Amazon Reviewer

When Death Loved an Angel

"This style of book is quite a change for this author so I wasn't expecting this, but I found an interesting story of two very different souls who stepped outside of their "accepted roles" to find love and forgiveness, and what is truly of value in life and death."

—Karen, Amazon Reviewer

"When Death Loved an Angel by Cheree Alsop is a touching paranormal romance that cranks the readers' thinking mode into high gear."

—Rachel Andersen, Book Reviewer

"Loved this book. I would recommend this book to everyone. And be sure to check out the rest of her books, too!"

—Malcay, Book Reviewer

The Million Dollar Gift

...This was a very beautiful, heart warming story about a young man who finds love, and family again on Christmas. I really enjoyed this short story. It truly inspires the meaning of Christmas in my eyes. It was utterly beautiful, and I highly recommend it. The plot is very interesting, and the characters catch your heart and lead on this very sad and happy story.

—Whitney@Shooting Stars Review

I recommend The Million Dollar Gift as a way to remember what Christmas is about: Love. Family. Friendship. Because a life without love isn't really worth living anyway.

—Loren Weaver

When Chase risks his life to save a brother and sister just before Christmas, his life becomes entwined with theirs more intricately than he could have imagined. Emotional and moving, this is a story of a young man whose troubled heart is tested by the one thing he is unprepared to face, love. MY TAKE- This is a fast, fun, emotional Christmas read. Made me cry.

—Donna Weaver

DAYBREAK

Never stop dreaming!

Made in the USA
Monee, IL
10 August 2021